The Sunken Road

Garry Disher grew up in rural South Australia and now lives near the Victorian coast. In 1978 he was awarded a creative writing fellowship to Stanford University, California, where he wrote his first short-story collection. A full-time writer for many years, he is the author of novels, short story collections and books for children.

The Sunken Road

Garry Disher

FOURTH ESTATE • *London*

Preliminary work on this novel was undertaken in 1978 and 1987 when I was in receipt of grants from the Literature Board of the Australia Council, the Commonwealth Government's arts funding and advisory body.

First published in Great Britain in 1996 by
Fourth Estate Limited
6 Salem Road
London, W2 4BU

2 4 6 8 10 9 7 5 3 1

A catalogue record for this book is available from the British Library.

ISBN 1–85702–485–0

Printed in Great Britain by
Clays Ltd, St Ives plc

for
Hannah and Lucinda

Loss

ONE SWELTERING MORNING in the worst year of the Great Depression, when kerosene-tin shanty towns were starving along the city's creeks and the farmers of the northern highlands were walking off the land, a cruising shark snatched a young wife from the shallows at Henley Beach, compelling the stricken husband to flee inland with his baby son, to the main street of Pandowie, where dangers lurked above the ground. He never remarried but the son flourished, joining Stock & Station and marrying an Ison, an old name in the district, settling with her in the big house on Isonville and beginning a family of his own: Anna Antonia Ison Tolley, born in 1949; Hugo Walter Ison Tolley, born two years later. When Anna started at the primary school, it pleased her to come into Pandowie and see her surname above her grandfather's shop: Tolley's Four Square Store. Perhaps Anna resembled her lost grandmother—leggy, wilful, auburn-haired, always talking back—or perhaps Grandfather Tolley was reminded of how tenuous life could be, for when she sliced her knee open on the coils of barbed wire displayed in his shop window one afternoon after school, he panicked, staunching the blood with his vast khaki handkerchief, shaking her until her teeth rattled: You're a wicked girl, Anna, unmanageable. The children's other grandfather warned them to watch out for flash floods, which had been known to barrel down the washaways on Isonville in the blink of an eye. Bucketing rains, Grandfather Ison explained, indicating the pink-smudge Pandowie Hills, then he bent his well-fed back and slash-cleared the star thistles that collared the gravestone of the shepherd boy lost in Ison's Creek. *James Son of Geo. Taken by the Flood 5 April 1875 Aged Six Years and the Angel Sayeth Unto*, the rest indecipherable, every carven *S* tilted forward as if straining against the waters. Anna and Hugo squatted nearby, their chins cupped in the palms of their hands. Anna was forever asking why: Why did the shepherd carve his S's that way? Because, Grandfather Ison replied. When Grandfather Ison died of asthma, leaving Isonville solely to Kitchener, his son, the Tolleys found themselves living on borrowed time in the big house. Anna's mother inherited nothing but a dusty sideboard from the will, and suffered a loss of faith in one of life's certainties—the regard of a father for his daughter. The little family moved out of Isonville to a struggling farm farther along the sunken road. The schoolbus from Bitter Wash passed by the front gate, and it pleased Anna to sit where Lockie Kelly could peer along her slanting thighs. Anna was away at the university when the boys she'd known at school began to fall in a foreign war. Matt Heinrich was the first, and Anna heard the news on the day she skipped lectures to march down Frome Street to a subsidiary of the Raintree Corporation, a napalm manufacturer. She sat in the road, refused to move on, and when she got back to her room at Women's College, paint-streaked and hysterical, there was a note under the door: Call home. Matt Heinrich, shot by a sniper at Nui Dat. Little Matt. Terrible, but still, a week later Anna found herself being jostled outside the US consulate, and a month after that some of her acquaintances were arrested on a loitering statute that dated from the 1700s. Oh, they were puerile. Then a second boy was shot dead, a third torn apart when he stepped on a Bouncing Betty. In Anna's mind, those dead boys were transmuted into friends, not simply kids from Pandowie High who'd tried to touch her up in the scungy back seat of a car. All those beautiful boys. Of the eleven in Anna's Leaving Honours class, the ballot had selected eight for service in the army. When a fourth drowned in a rice paddy and a fifth died of wounds, Anna began to tremble. She was trembling for Lockie. He'd been her one true love, a wild, laughing, beautiful boy, but she'd hurt him and now she trembled for fear that he'd be taken from her forever. Her luck was turning bad. She could not breathe. She stopped studying. She would not sing 'Military Madness' on the steps of Parliament House again. She had been little Miss Smart-arse, the first from Pandowie to go to university, turning her back on boys who were content to be farm fodder, girls content with kids and a wedding ring. Well, Anna would not be thinking offhand unkindnesses like that again. She came back to Pandowie, where she belonged. Of Anna's own children, Michael slept through the night and Rebecca struggled against her from the very start. Yet sweet, peaceful Michael it was who died, lost in a car wreck on the sunken road, and Rebecca developed the conviction that Anna might, through inattention, kill her, too. Whenever Anna negotiated the devil's elbows, headlights burning in the roiling dust, she felt her daughter's gaze settle upon her from the passenger seat, eyes like coals and ice in the little face. There's been another foreclosure in the district, another farm lost to the banks, and the Showalter Park artificial breeding scheme has collapsed, owing the banks, taxpayers and local investors sixteen million dollars. The strain is showing: jobless sons are apt to shoot themselves, loved ones to aim their speeding cars at SEC powerline pylons, and last week a young mother ran exhaust gases into the family station wagon at the Showalter Hill lookout above the sunken road, asphyxiating herself and her baby daughter. Pandowie is suffering a loss of spirit, and Anna has argued so in her column in the *Chronicle*, arousing a string of bitter letters to the editor: Surely we deserve better than this from the very person who has been commissioned to write a book celebrating our 150th Jubilee? Anna is taking a thematic approach for the Jubilee history. Scratch notes: Death on the frontier. A hundred and fifty years ago we lost our loved ones to diptheria, dysentery, scarlet fever, pneumonia, jaundice and typhoid. Snake bite. Spears. Even tar—according to the old records, a shearer on the Showalter Park headstation tossed a Ngadjuri suffering from smallpox into a tub of boiling tar. Rebecca has announced that she and her lover intend to have a baby. Anna will watch her granddaughter grow. She'll make a point of not hovering with nervy fingers. When her great-grandchildren come to visit, Anna will be pleased, and pleased to see the backs of them. She won't offer advice. She'll have none to give. A loved one may be lost to you in an eyeblink but Anna will not be the kind of old woman who says things like that.

Settlement

ABSORBED BY ANNA from the cradle: The first Showalter had come from India, the first Ison from Natal, and both from the Home Counties before that, and so their occupation of the redsoil country at the edge of the rain shadow was driven by notions of rural England and the hazardous frontier. They placed their sheep in the care of shepherds, marked their boundaries with stonewall fences, employed blacksmiths and scullery maids, drew water from boarded-over wells, fired carbines from the saddle, warned off the wretched Ngadjuri who camped on the banks of the dividing creek, and at the day's end sat erect in cane chairs on their cavernous verandahs, watching the sun settle upon their pastoral runs. The hard ground was not entirely flat. The Razorback sat like a chiselled city on the grassy plain, small, pink, wind-humped hills marked the horizon, and the dusty roads dipped unexpectedly through sandy creekbeds. In 1869 the Strangways' Act opened up the land to yeomanry, and among the farmers who sowed their six-forty acres with wheat and barley were the Jaegers, the Hartwigs, the Heinrichs and other Silesian Germans. Shopkeepers and publicans followed the farmers, staging tiny dazed towns every twenty miles or so across the newly cleared grazing land. They measured the breadth of their streets by the turning circle of a bullock-drawn wagon, and erected a pub, a general store, a bank and a post-and-telegraph office at the four corners of the crossroads. Houses straggled behind these hubs of commerce. In winter the streets were churned mud, in summer iron-hard, deeply rutted under a layer of dust. There had been huts along the Pandowie Creek as early as 1843, when Colonel Frome was surveying the northern reaches of the colony, but no town until 1850, the year that George Catford spotted traces of copper oxide in the local stone. South Australia might have foundered if not for Pandowie and its mine. Twenty years later the shafts were depthless blue pools of water that defeated the pumps, and the Cornish Jacks migrated to other towns, other mines, but not before the hillsides and flatlands had been denuded of trees, the timber consumed by the boilers or stacked against the pressing earth deep within the mineshafts. Great Aunt Beulah Ison had learned some of these things at her grandfather's knee. She waved her papery hand over the treeless plains: Anna, dear, this used to be scrub for as far as the eye could see. The shepherd boy had drowned ten years before Beulah was born, but she knew for a fact that the father was the last man transported to the colonies and the mother was a riverbank gin. The etymology of the *owie* suffix in Pandowie, Terowie and other placenames was quickly forgotten if ever it was known, the children of the mid-north—including Grandfather Ison and his five sisters—meeting their first blacks in the pages of their school primers. Grain and high-grade merino wool poured into the whistlestop railway towns in heaving, top-heavy wagons until the 1920s, when spoke-wheeled Ford lorries replaced the bullocks and horses and the whip-lashing, cursing men who drove them. By now Pandowie was a pastoral town in the shade of the stony Razorback. The main line pushed northward through spinifex, bluebush and saltbush country, where a hillock might be named Mount Misery or Mount Remarkable and the topsoil conceal rock-bound traces of silver, lead, zinc and radium. In a few days you were in Darwin. The traffic was all one way in 1942, all guns and soldiers. General MacArthur stood on the Terowie platform and growled: I have come out of Bataan and I shall return. Grandfather Tolley's shop prospered with the town, and the wool boom meant plenty of work for stock agents like Peter, his son. The Showalters and the Isons did well out of the Korean War: all that soldiering in icy winds and snow, all those woollen coats and scarves and gloves. It was said that old Leonard Showalter carted clover hay for his stud rams in the boot of his Bentley at the time; certainly he did not bother to deny it. It was generally known in the district that he'd played polo with governors, colonels and visiting earls, and that the Princess Royal had stayed at Showalter Park when Showalter was a baby. But he was a bony, chin-damp wreck and close to death when Anna assembled with the other kids to hear him address the school on Empire Day: Mr Showalter is a link to our past, children, and Anna watched the old man hawk and spit and shuffle his feet, his mind beginning to cloud, a look of panic settling over his stretched white features. I remember, he said, and abruptly stopped, his gummy mouth snapping closed, mute and defiant in the gathering silence, while the children breathed, sulphur-crested cockatoos screeched in the nude dead gums behind the *Chronicle* office, and a car passed through on its way somewhere east or west. Old farming couples too old for heavy work retired to Californian bungalows in the town, where they grew roses and sweetcorn in soil nourished with sheep droppings raked from beneath the slatted floors of woolsheds and soaked with river water pumped overland from the Murray. They raised money and built a clubhouse, and rolled and seeded and mowed a couple of bowling links between the almond trees on an unused block behind the Copper Lode Tearoom. But still they felt half-useless. They longed for the merino-stud field days in April; they took the *Women's Weekly* tour to London; they meddled in the affairs of their married sons. Their bones ached. They wore wrist bands of beaten copper that had been mined last century from the ground beneath their feet. On Saturday afternoons, when the last wobbling ball had been bowled, they wandered off to the Bon Accord Hotel in Market Square. Anna liked to drink there with Lockie and Chester whenever she came home between semesters, the three of them seated in the tiny lounge, close to the open fire. The sticky walls were dark with photographs of Showalter Park stud rams, the biggest and most valuable in the world, ribbon-draped at the Royal Show, the studmaster's hand inches deep in the wool upon the heavy back of the latest champion, Pandowie Showalter Lustre 4, which had sold for $30,000 in 1969. Anna said: You could refuse to register for the call-up, you know. Go underground. There are people who would hide you. Lockie and Chester looked at her humorously, searching for the joke. I mean it, she said, ignoring their mates, who were calling off-colour jibes at her through the serving hatch, ignoring the angular, eruptive high school boys, who were slamming billiard balls off the tiny corner table and across the cracked floor. You been listening to too many stirrers, Anna. For her *Chronicle* column this week, Anna writes: The old ways are disappearing, turning upside down. A Saudi Arabian conglomerate has bought Showalter Park, there are no jobs for the young ones, and there's more money in angora goats than in merino sheep, in legumes than in wheat. Anna will settle in a house by the sea after her husband dies. Whenever she returns to Pandowie to mark the changes, a voice, a gait, a peppercorn tree, a sun-warmed verandah post will take her back, pleasure and pain in complicated doses.

Beach

THREE HOURS FROM Isonville to the Delmonte Hotel, where inland families holidayed for the summer. On Boxing Day every year, the Tolleys powdered along the sunken road, braked at the Main North Road intersection, and emerged nose-up on the bitumen for Adelaide, a corner flap of tarpaulin sounding their progress, snapping in the wind above a roofrack top-heavy with suitcases, a beach umbrella, beach toys in a string bag. They rode high through a land of silos, sidings, sharefarmers and country towns, the railway children staring after them, and two and a half hours later were slowing for the Gepps Cross stoplights. They jerked and crawled through the baking tiled suburbs, Anna's father tapping the temperature gauge from time to time, his ear cocked to the muttering radiator. Anna saw a seagull on a bus shelter. That was the first sign. Suddenly they were in a tunnelling street, advancing upon a sea flash at the end of it. Anna remembered the little square: clock tower, palm trees, kiosk, milkbars where proprietors whisked away the tracked-in beach sand, sparse buffalo grass, the jetty poking like a stubby finger into the sea. The breakwater, the boat basin, the winking shallows, the pale sand, the kerb outside the Delmonte, where her father angled the Stock & Station Holden, the chrome bumper resting against a salt-scummed verandah post. An airliner banked above the water. The engine ticked. Anna's father said: Here we are again. He said it every year. Every year he said: There were no trips to the sea when I was growing up, and until she put two and two together—the shark in the shallows, Grandfather Tolley's retreat to the dry country—Anna assumed that her father and his father had been too poor for a holiday at the beach. She looked up, shading her eyes, then grinned and waved. Two men and their wives were shouting from deckchairs, waving glasses of beer and shandy. Anna's father saw them and he flourished an arm and bowed deeply. Her father was loved and remembered from the previous summer and all the summers before it. He was an eye-glint charmer, a man who joked and raised the stakes, whose laughter ringed the hotel for three weeks every January. Women looked at him covetously and were compelled to rest their fingers on his forearm, occasionally on his chest. And Anna saw that her mother was desired. She saw a man parade by on the baking sand later in the week, his stomach tucked painfully in, while her mother lay utterly still, her eyes possibly open behind her black lenses. When Anna felt her body begin to change, when acute cramps crippled her every thirty-one days and the doctor prescribed the Pill to control it, she became secretive and elusive, infected by a drowsy kind of appetite for the flat brown planes of the boys on the beach or in the Delmonte's corridors. You could never find her. She missed meals. Her mother examined her lips for stubble rash and her neck for lovebites. She was on the spot when the authorities drained the boat basin and sent a line of police cadets shoulder to shoulder through the car tyres and mud. The people crowding the rail were avid for bodies—small, abducted, anus-torn—and failed to notice that the boy clasping Anna around her middle, his chin on her dreamy shoulder, had slipped three fingers inside the elastic at her waist, deep enough to brush her groin and unlock her. The Kellys had never taken their children to the coast. Lockie's parents were too narrow, too embedded, too poor. Lockie had to wait until Anna lived at Women's College before he saw the sea for the first time. They'd make love in her room, then head for the beach. Lockie would say: Take away these houses, give me a clifftop, and I could live here, looking out at the water. They lay face to face on broad blue towels, watching the minute workings in one another's eyes. They were so close that Anna's cocked hip concealed her hand inside his bathing suit. He felt hot and alive in there, still crusted from their lovemaking. Two years after Lockie was killed, Anna met Sam Jaeger. She liked him for unexpected reasons: his comforting bulk, his shyness, the way he sent up his parents' church. The Ascensionists, he said. I wish they'd rise up and disappear. Anna didn't love him when she married him, but she wanted to belong to the community again, she'd put her wild past behind her, and he was companionable, so surely a kind of loving would develop over the years. But love needs a generous climate. Poor Anna, poor Sam. It was quickly made plain to them that they should value frugality. Mr Jaeger told Anna: Shearers don't need icecream. A holiday? The missus and I haven't had a holiday in twenty-eight years and it never did us no harm. Anna put her mind to work. She talked long into the night to Sam, low and hard and coaxing, occasionally placing her cool, dry palms on his anxious cheeks: We'll tell your parents we're going to a friend's wedding, somewhere at the back of beyond, we'll be away five or six days. They'll never know. Sam looked anxiously over his shoulder at the shadows in their bedroom. She turned his face back to hers: Sam, don't chicken out on me now. And so they told a lie and took themselves off to the Grand in Victor Harbor and let the waters wash away the cares of their penny-pinching marriage. Anna was certain that she felt Sam's climax one morning when the sun beat against their curtained window, and sensed that there would be a baby. When Michael was up on two legs she loved to see his tiny spine and wing-bud shoulderblades crouched absorbedly over an upended bucket in his moated, turreted sandpit. It has been many years since she saw the sea, not since the *Chronicle* sent her to cover the Isolated Children's Federal Conference in Port Lincoln in 1985. But the sea is there in her head—and Lockie, sun- and water-splashed, warm, smiling and fine-boned. If he had not been taken from her, would they be together in a house on a clifftop, looking out to sea? Anna is obsessed with the notion of a house beside the sea, a flat or a unit in her declining years. She will live alone, calm and contemplative, having put many ghosts to rest inside her. She will babysit her granddaughter from time to time, turning the child's small plump feet in the water from her garden tap to wash away the sand. She will walk twice a day, before lunch and before sundown, no matter the weather, just to remember, and wait for the end, and smell the seaweedy air, just like any old leathery retiree with a replacement hip.

Farmer

IN 1853 WALTER Ison noted in his journal:

> There are persons hereabouts that wold take your life for an ounze of gold if you was not well upon your gard. One such blackgard goses by the name, Sydney Dan. I have nuggets to the weight of twenty pound strapt around my waist, over which I wear a blue serge shirt and a leather jerkin. I was fortnate in meeting with a compny of Adelaide men, who, like myself, are returning from Ballaarat to spend the Christmas. We have abundance of firearms at the ready, and watches by turn during the night. By day we march to a song, in militry fashion, at intervals firing a voley into the sky. I have a mind to lease another run in the Mid North but Hugo is desirous to increase our flock. I daresay that we soon at logerheads shall be upon this matter.

Lives of desperate loneliness and hardship, wrote Mr Wheelwright, in a copperplate hand, line after line filling the blackboard. Heads bobbed up and down like a sea-chop in the classroom. Pens crawled across the pages of exercise books. At least copying was better than dictation, for Anna liked to dream, and when she dreamed she lost whole sentences, whole facts. In 1875 a shepherd lost his son in

Ison's Creek. Anna, no one knows for sure who he was. Some say he was a ticket-of-leave pickpocket from New South Wales. Others will tell you he was a free man, born in Somerset, a shepherd all of his life. It's also been said that he was from Maryland, a veteran of the American Civil War, or that he'd run with Joseph Storey and the Blackfaced Robbers, stealing cattle and raiding homesteads near Adelaide before it got too hot for him. Some of the squatters lived on the land; others were absentee landlords with grand houses in Adelaide. The term 'squatter' has been replaced by 'grazier' or 'pastoralist'. The Strangways' Act of 1869 alienated the large leases and so a pattern of closer settlement evolved in the mid-north, resulting in the small to medium-scale agriculture and grazing that we find today. Pens down when you're finished. Anna's father took to farming when the little family was forced out of Isonville. Peter Tolley had grown up in the town, where all he knew about farming was that farmers bought barbed wire, wool-clipping shears and raddle from his father's shop. He joined Stock & Station when he was sixteen, sweeping, running errands, helping in the stockyards at auction time. He was taught to memorise the local brands and ear-tags; to part the rubbery lips of merino ewes and judge their ages by their teeth; to run his eyes over their haunches and his hands into their fleeces. By the time he was twenty he was doing the rounds with the older stock agents, assessing flocks, buying and selling skins, arranging clearing sales. That's how your dad and I met, Anna's mother said. He came around one day to look over some hoggets that your grandpa and your Uncle Kitch were selling, stayed for a cup of tea, and it was love at first sight. When Anna was seventeen her father seemed suddenly to clarify in her mind: A town kid, a newcomer to the district, mother taken by a shark, father gloomy, being ordered around the countryside by all those farmers. Did he envy the

Isons? He didn't look like a farmer, even when he bought the six-forty acres and dressed and worked like one. The legions of farmers. If not tall, scarecrowy dustbowl survivors, they were gnomish, glum little grey-gaberdined portly men belted high at the waist, with over-large greasy hats upon their skulls and tens of thousands in the bank. You couldn't get a laugh out of many of them. Not like her father, tall, sinuous and graceful, always ready with a grin, always ready to pull over for a yarn on a back road. Then there were men like Lockie Kelly's father, who ran a handful of question-mark sheep on a handful of mortgaged acres, drove the council grader and were married to wheezing large women given to braying, phlegm-laden laughter around wooden kitchen tables. Anna married into the Jaegers, farmers on the Terowie Road. On the day that Sam first drove her home to meet his parents, they climbed in low gear along a dirt track from the front gate and came to the lip of a gully. Anna looked down, upon feed sheds, tractor sheds, a stone house, a battery-hen shed as long as an ocean liner; upon gleaming metal roofs and squared-off garden beds and orderly fences; upon bulk fuel tanks standing on galvanised legs like machines for traversing the wastes of the moon. You'll be working with the eggs, her father-in-law told her, shortly after her honeymoon. Collecting, grading, packing. There's quite an art to it. In bed that night, Anna leaned on her elbow: Nothing was said about my working in the chook shed after I married you, Samuel dear. Sam winced; winced was the only word to describe his contortions: It's kind of expected of us to all pitch in. I see. And how much do I get paid? He winced again. When Grandfather Tolley died in a room behind the Four Square Store in Pandowie, Anna's father called a family conference: I'm quitting the farm. I have to confess, my heart has never really been in it. He looked at Hugo, at Anna: Your mother and I have decided to move into town and run Dad's shop. Anna love, Hugo will take over the farm, but I want you both to realise you get equal shares of it, and of the shop, when your mother and I finally kick the bucket. But Anna was the last daughter on earth to get into a fight over inheritance: That's fine, Dad, I understand. Hugo: I can't pay you anything. Anna: I don't want you to. In the kitchen afterwards, Anna's mother whispered: It's been wearing him down for years. Plus he and your brother are always arguing. Do it this way. No, do it that way. Spend money on this. No, spend it on that. Your dad's a bit too slapdash, really, whereas Hugo's too careful—though I suppose that could mean he'll make a go of it. Anna can't leave the Showalters alone, a year after the collapse of their sperm-bank scheme and the loss of investors' money. She snipes at them in her *Chronicle* column: Grazier. Doesn't that have a nice solid ring to it? Once you're a grazier you may paint your surname in broad strokes upon your rooftop and be seen from the air by buyers flying in for the field days. If you're especially grazier-ish you can afford to renovate with Carrera marble and Laura Ashley drapes. I don't know, Anna, Carl Hartwig says, shaking his head over her copy before press day. You'll get me sued if I publish this. The bank will foreclose on Sam and Anna. Sam will elect to stay on as manager, a deal brokered by the bank and the new owner. Sam will say: What else can I do at my time of life? Where else can we go, Anna? He'll argue with the new owner, a man keen to try angora goats, legumes and peas. He'll say to Anna, late at night, perplexity and disappointment permanently knotted together on his brow: I mean, this is wheat and wool country. Anna will stick it out, and when Sam dies she will move south to the coast, where her sun-narrowed eyes in a nest of wrinkles will mark her out as a farmer's widow.

Space

THE HOUSES, SHEDS and outbuildings of Isonville homestead sprawled along both sides of Ison's Creek, but only heat shimmers were visible from the sunken road, heat caught in the soil itself, in the walls of local stone, in the baking rooftops. The roofing iron, steeply raked, and the verandah iron, low and capped, caught the sun as though water rippled there among the stands of blue gum, peppermint gum and sheoak. A palm tree loomed at the side of the main house, home to a hundred starlings. Ancient, knotted quince and mulberry trees screened the main house from the overseer's house, a square, blockish, unloved cottage on the opposite bank of the creek. But Isonville was no Showalter Park. There hadn't been an overseer on Isonville since the end of the First World War. When Peter Tolley, son of the widower shopkeeper in Pandowie, courted Eleanor Ison in 1949, he found two households living in the big house on Isonville, sharing fourteen cool, deep, shadowy rooms, with ceilings of pressed tin, the pressed tin extending right along the broad central corridor that linked both halves of the house. Eleanor lived with her parents and her brother, Kitch, at the eastern end of the house; her Aunt Beulah lived in the western end. Then Peter married Eleanor, precipitating a further divide: Anna, dear, we couldn't afford to buy a house. No, we didn't want to live with his dad behind the shop. It made more sense for him to come and live with me here. It was a bit cramped. We didn't have much privacy until Kitch decided to do up the overseer's cottage for himself and Mum and Dad retired to Adelaide. My poor mother was worn to the bone from looking after Auntie Beulah. We should have hired a housekeeper long before we did. Anna and Hugo stopped listening for a moment. Great Aunt Beulah was shuffling past their kitchen window, la, la, la. They waited. Sure enough, there was Mrs Mac, hurrying to fetch her back. One day the children's Uncle Kitch went to a stud breeders' conference over in the west and came back with a fiancée: This is Lorna. Hand shakes, edgy laughs, then Lorna's head swung down upon the children. Anna and Hugo froze. Lipsticked, glistening teeth, powdered pores, desperate eyes, hair stiff as wheat, assembled inches from their faces: What adorable kids. Kitchener and Lorna had twin daughters. They spilled out of the overseer's cottage on the opposite bank of Ison's Creek, and Anna heard her mother say uneasily: It's as if they're waiting, Pete. Don't you feel it? Waiting to get rid of us? They did not wait for long. Grandfather Ison died, Beulah died, and Mrs Mac moved on, all in the space of a year. At once Uncle Kitch moved his family across the creek and into Beulah's half of the house. The Tolleys seemed to shrink back from the stained-glass dividing door at the dead centre of the long corridor: Pete, they make me feel temporary in my own home, the home I grew up in. For six months the Tolleys searched for another house to live in. Finally: I've had enough of this, Anna's father said, and he quit his high-mileage job with Stock & Station, scratched up a loan, and bought a tractor, a header, a little Austin truck and six hundred and forty acres plus house. Their new home was small, overgrown with oleanders, subject to northerlies and rising damp, but it was all theirs. Some long-ago builder had scored fine, white, dead straight lines in the cement that bound the russet creek stones together. The outside walls were warm to the eye and warm in the angling sun. The Bitter Wash schoolbus passed by the ramp at the end of the potholed drive. Pandowie, nineteen miles. Their party-line signal was one long ring, one short, one long, but, anxious to know that they were wanted and loved, Anna and Hugo snatched up the phone every time it rang, to be told by an irritated neighbour: Do you mind? The first house of Anna's marriage to Sam Jaeger was a transportable kit house, a present from Mr and Mrs Jaeger. It resembled a log cabin, and the truck hauling it north from Adelaide took a wrong turn at Pandowie and arrived three hours late. Sam and Mr Jaeger raged uselessly at the driver, who shrugged, caught Anna's eye, winked obliquely as if to say: What have you let yourself in for, love? Anna spent the next two years landscaping the garden. She set deckchairs on the splintery verandah and enjoyed drinking sundowners there, where Mr and Mrs Jaeger were bound to see her through the lace curtains in their stone house in the gully below. She found it impossible to call them anything but Mr and Mrs Jaeger. Mr Jaeger, stabbing his finger at an item in the monthly ledger: I see you've been buying icecream for the shearers again. Michael and Rebecca, toiling up the hill from the stone house, red-faced and elated: Mum, we've been clapping hands for Jesus. The Jaegers had also given them little books to read. Anna would not clap hands for Jesus: Mum, are you the anti-Christ? That's what Grandpa Jaeger says. After five years of being crowded by his parents, Sam said: We're moving out. It was Grandfather Tolley who told Anna about an advertisement on his noticeboard: 'House to Let. Restored schoolmaster's residence near Showalter Park. Late-nineteenth-century charm, adjacent to picturesque ruin.' Good God, Anna's mother said. My old school. Are you sure you'll have enough room? There's never been a family in it, as I recall, just a string of batchelor schoolmasters. Sam sat Michael on one knee, Rebecca on the other: Just temporary, kids, till we fall on our feet. Anna lost count of the roofs Sam painted, the post holes he dug, the truckloads of wheat he carted for the locals. Hugo and her father brought him in to help sow and reap the six-forty acres. The Showalters hired him to work with the stud manager. He was paid a hundred dollars to appear in a film as a Boer farmer galloping down the skyline, footage that was never shown. Anna herself found two days a week at the *Chronicle*, helping Carl Hartwig with his hatch, match and dispatch stories. Just temporary, but Sam and Anna lived in the schoolhouse for fifteen years, until old man Jaeger died and the Mrs retired to a house in Pandowie. Back to what's mine, Sam said. Back again to the transportable house at the lip of the gully. Anna had no intention of moving into the stone house where Sam's parents had lived: Your father's spirit still moves there. The transportable house badly needed a new coat of paint, new carpets, a slow-combustion stove for winter: I don't remember it being such a chilly place, Sam, do you? I guess we were young then. Sam put his hands on his hips: Anna, the kids got colds every winter. Becky developed asthma. How could you forget that? There was another reason why Anna wanted to install a slow-combustion stove in their old house. She wanted to drive out the sourpuss residue of all the crackpots who'd stayed in it temporarily over the years, clap-hands-for-Jesus guests of the Jaegers in the gully below. These days Sam is learning to grant his daughter some space—as Rebecca would call it. This evening he stands musing on the verandah long after Meg and Becky have waved goodbye and bumped down the track to the Adelaide road, and now he's rasping a worn hand along his jawline: Anna, if those two are planning on having a kid, I guess it can't be temporary? Drily: No, Sam. He blushes: Umm, how do you reckon, you know, they'll go about it? Without a man, I mean? When Sam is gone, Anna will move to the coast. One day she'll get a call from Hugo: Mum died in her sleep last night. Anna will drive back to Pandowie for the funeral, step into the little stone church for the first time in years, and be struck by how small it is, no more than a boxy room with dusty roofbeams, and yet it had seemed such a vast, booming chamber when she was a kid.

Invest

WITH THE HELP of a loan from Grandfather Tolley, Anna's father bought a small farm in difficult country out near the Razorback. The investment didn't end there. He bought a red Austin truck, a Massey Ferguson tractor, and implements to plough, sow and reap, all second-hand from the dealer in Canowie Belt. Throwing in a good job with Stock & Station, changing careers, going into debt—he called these things an investment or a gamble, depending upon how the season was going. Either way, investment or gamble, he hoped for a pay-off somewhere down the track. One dry year he said, very patiently, edged with impatience: Eleanor, love of my life, I can't help feeling you're being unrealistic about this—we could go under. Now, it's good that you're not a worrier, a good example for the kids, but I think being an Ison has cushioned you a bit, made you not anticipate things enough. The high school offered an academic stream and a commercial stream. Anna was disappointed when her best friend chose bookkeeping over Latin. Like her, Maxine had always been disruptive, slangy and free, her head fixed unfirmly upon her shoulders, so where had it come from, this sudden investment in her future? No one had taught Anna to be sensible in quite that way. Within the space of a summer, the two girls had little to say to one another. Within a year, Anna scarcely knew Maxine, didn't recognise the person who nimble-fingered typewriters, columns of figures, sewing machines and cutting boards. All Anna owned was a brain that poked uselessly in all directions. The careers counsellor glanced over her list of subjects and said: Latin. Teaching Latin, that's all Latin's good for. Maxine was working at the Inquiries counter when Anna went in to arrange the transfer of her savings from the Pandowie branch to the University branch. The bank had fitted Maxine in a pale pink uniform that strained at her breasts and hips and filled her waist with air, so that she looked briskly stern and mature, her body unflattered and irrelevant. Her motions, so quick with her pen and her date stamp, intimidated Anna, who badly wanted to slang off at someone or something with Maxine but was reluctant suddenly to assume that a common ground still existed between them. Anna saw Maxine at the fortnightly dance whenever she came home between semesters, but they rarely spoke now. Eventually Anna came to believe that Maxine was better than her in unnameable ways. When she prepared to fly off to London, no return date planned, she knew—even though distracted by her grief for Lockie—not to apply to Maxine for travellers' cheques, for that would underline the difference between them. She felt undeserving, and imagined the reproach, the contempt, in Maxine's face. When Anna married Sam Jaeger, her mother-in-law's refrigerator seemed to admonish her: You young wives, so slapdash! Mrs Jaeger's hands whirled about the kitchen, filling it with sound: of cutlery riding loose in a drawer, of air seals breaking, of greaseproof paper whispering, of bread, tomato and mutton falling away in slices, of Tupperware lids snapping down over peaches in syrup, of tea the colour of dark-tan boot polish splashing into a vacuum flask destined to end its days flattened by a tractor tyre. Mrs Jaeger seemed to be telling Anna, as she packed the smoko buns and lunches and cold-water containers into a cane basket: It's an investment of love in the menfolk. The menfolk came back at nightfall and dumped the dusty basket on the shoe-cleaning cupboard on the back porch: Corker lunch, you two. Anna thought: I spent hours sorting and packing eggs today. Where was *my* lunch? Chilled water in summer, that was Mrs Jaeger's most loving investment. She kept the freezer stocked with metal beakers of frozen rainwater, and before the sun was up she had the beakers thawing on a bench, a few minutes' thawing until a frosting of condensation on the metal sides told her that she had blocks of ice ready to tip into the menfolk's drinking water. I'll say one thing, Mother—you sure do look after us. The twenty thousand that Anna's father left her in his will was not enough for a deposit and yet it was too much to spend, so Anna went to Pandowie Accounting Services in the main street, where Chester Flood drew up an investment portfolio: It's best if we diversify it a little—stocks and shares, bonds, property, some of it high risk, some of it low. But the market's healthy at the moment, so I don't anticipate any problems. Chester was still angular and vivid to look at, and Anna watched his hands, one bracing the prospectus upon his desk blotter, the other cuff-scraping a cross with a scratchy pen at the dotted line: Sign here, here and here. Such beautiful hands. Those hands had once invested love and passion in her, one warm April day, the day Michael was killed. This afternoon Anna is helping her brother water trees on the six-forty acres. Hugo's been planting them up and down creeks and gullies and washaways, inside tiny chicken-wire fences to keep the sheep and rabbits out. A hundred trees, and I haven't had to pay a cent. Anna pours a bucket of bore water around the base of a golden cypress, a good windbreak tree—slowly, slowly, for the stone-flecked red dirt is in a repelling mood. Hugo has left a little plastic flag on this one: 'Invest in Australia's Rural Viability. Plant a Tree and Help Stop Soil Degradation.' Anna would urge Sam to plant a few trees, but Sam has lost a bundle investing in the Showalter Park sperm-bank scheme, and he'll only say: What's the point, when we're going to lose the place anyhow? He's harder to live with now, more like his father every day, but Anna will stay with him, she owes him that. When he's gone there will be her granddaughter to invest in. And Becky. Anna will never stop investing something in her daughter, even though Rebecca had never been an easy person to love.

Rooms

THERE WAS NEVER quite enough space on Isonville. It was unspoken, but Anna's mother looked forward to the day when she could add Aunt Beulah's seven rooms to her own. The children squabbled over everything and nothing, hot and unreasoning, leading with jutted lower jaws and windmilling arms, until she would be there among them, clasping their thin wrists with fingers as tight as steel bands: I've just about had it with you two. The only answer was to move Hugo's bed, wardrobe and chest of drawers along the corridor to the room set aside for Grandfather Ison's visits. Anna sighed. She entered a period of rainbow-chasing and peace. Hugo left a hole in her room but she quickly filled it with girls' annuals and an old club chair fetched from Great Aunt Beulah's end of the house. She pressed fat cushions into the horsehairy corners and adjusted the limbs of the rag and celluloid dolls who sat there through the days, watching as she window-gazed and read. She talked to herself and sang. She clipped horses, dogs and disdainful cats from magazines, and Grandfather Tolley gave her a framed set of mail-order prints for her walls. Then one day she told Uncle Kitch, Aunt Lorna and the twins about her new room. Aunt Lorna sniffed: All right for some. Anna felt instantly tactless and small. Of course—Uncle Kitch and Aunt Lorna hated living in the overseer's cottage. They stared through their narrow kitchen window at the big house across the creek, waiting for Aunt Beulah to die. Anna sensed this, seated with them at their linoleum-topped wooden table in their muttony kitchen. The dark corners and rotting holland blinds trapped the fumes of chops and cabbagy soups. There were dents and chips in the canisters above the sink. Their dog slept in the house and its yellow claws and muzzle grease were there on both sides of the back door. They had uncomfortable habits, their packet biscuits harboured dampness, they were full of glittering envy. I must go now, Anna said. Anna won a bursary to pay her Women's College fees. She loved her room in the new wing, set redbrick and square where the land at the rear of the Children's Hospital climbed up to the hedged and tiled North Adelaide mansions. It was like a nun's retreat, squared-off, low and functional, with cement bricks painted white, hoary brown industrial carpet, a single divan with a bed-head shelf and bed-base drawers, a tiny desk, a two-shelf bookcase. She pinned Che Guevara to her wardrobe door and Ho Chi Minh above her desk. A buzzer connected her to the front desk, a buzz to let her know that she had a visitor waiting, a buzz at ten minutes to ten, all visitors out. Much better in a room than in a cramped car seat on a back road behind the Razorback. The patchwork quilt upon her bed had been passed on to her when Great Aunt Beulah died, and she made love on it on sultry afternoons when Lockie drove down from the bush to be with her. They had never made love in a room before. Lockie didn't feel so guilty on a proper bed, even if it was narrow. We could get married, he said, you know, before I go in the army. Anna lived in that room for three years, until she was unhinged by grief and fled. She wandered dazedly around England; her money ran out; she stuck her thumb in the air on a sleet-lashed junction near Leeds. Two New Zealanders in a

Transit van, and by the time they were on the North Circular, Anna had somewhere to live. Bringing home hitchhikers was a tradition of that Hammersmith house. Dear Folks: From my room I can see mile upon mile of London's damp rooftops and chimneys. Whenever trains pass on the suspended line just feet from my window, the whole house shakes. Feeling much better—return ticket in more ways than one! It was Sam Jaeger she married, and they lived in a weatherboard and plaster transportable home at the lip of a gully, its four small rooms looking out upon the hills, the valley, and the grim stone Jaeger homestead below. The laundry clarified that house for Anna, leaving her ragged and miserable. The reconditioned washing machine was from Leo's Discounts in Terowie and it shook the house and shimmered unstoppably far across the tilting floor. Paint blistered in the humid air and her father-in-law told her that she could not have a dryer and don't waste water. He said, the deep grooves deepening on either side of his fleshless mouth: Icecream, phone bills, and now you want a dryer? Come now, Missy. Her mother-in-law put in: Let's have a bit of elbow grease on those oil spots in Sam's khakis. Sometimes Anna stared at the little separated mountains—reeking nappies, greasy overalls, blue singlets, sodden towels, her own greyish whites, over every inch of the floor—and felt helpless, paralysed. At the end of the day Anna shut the laundry door and sat with a sundowner in her chapped hands and thought about Lockie Kelly, his loving hands. Then Sam fell out with his father and they moved to the empty schoolmaster's house on the sunken road. A cheerier laundry this time, steeped in sunlight—but that room turned on Anna when Michael was killed. Sometimes, in the months following the accident, Anna would pick her way across the damp floor with Rebecca's little pants, blouses and skirts bundled in her arms and almost, just for a moment, believe that she still had Michael's things to launder too. Everyone agreed that Anna's father died a good death. He'd had his setbacks—a lost finger and years of struggle—but you cannot keep a wild man down, and he'd bloomed again when he inherited the Four Square Store from his father. He enjoyed chiacking with all the women, who liked his long, sly face and shopped more often than was necessary and drove home in a little foggy glow. The strokes laid him out in a sunny back room behind the shop. From his heaped pillows he could watch the dipping wagtails on the overgrown lawn outside. There were books from the lending library stacked beside the bed. He liked to turn the thick leaves of his father's only photograph album, lingering upon a shot of his mother, who was crinkling her eyes against the steep sun on Henley Beach as grey-pointer sharks lurked unseen in the shallows behind her. Anna wondered if he'd rescued her in his mind, been enjoying her embraces all these years. She saw him every day toward the end. When Rebecca skipped classes at the Conservatorium to be with him one last time, she came out blinking, sniffing: Grandpa still makes me laugh. Now that he is gone, the room has become a den: sewing machine, filing cabinet, desk, fraying club chair and divan bed. It's a room full of memories for Anna's mother, who runs the shop alone now. Rebecca and her lover have a house in North Adelaide. It was built when Isonville was built, but it has five rooms, not fourteen, and it was intended for a respectable working family, not a squatter's brood. It's in the renovated part of North Adelaide, and Anna likes to spend a night in the spare bedroom from time to time, even though she still has a sense that Rebecca continues to watch her warily, as though fearing that she might turn her life upside down again. A baby will come along and the spare room will become a nursery, but by then Anna will have a place of her own, somewhere in sight of the sea, where she may think of her lost son, her lost loves. The perfect distraction for a fractious grandchild will be her Pandowie Jubilee keyring, hung with keys and lives.

Obsession

SINCE GRANDFATHER TOLLEY had failed to save his wife, he became obsessed with preserving his son. Anna's father said: He used to watch me like a hawk. Anna's mother smiled and touched his arm: And you rebelled against it. He returned her smile; they were very close. Stung, and a little confused, Anna butted in with her tuppence worth: When we waited in the shop after school for someone to take us home, he watched us like a hawk, too. Don't do this, don't do that. Remember when I cut myself? He got really mad. Anna's other grandfather was obsessed with how great Isonville could have been. As great as the Park, he said, if it hadn't been split up. One day Great Aunt Beulah took Anna aside: The Isons are related to royalty, dear. Anna stared at her. If you go to Chancery in London, you'll find the Ison fortune just sitting there, waiting for a claimant. Beulah was obsessed with Chancery and red tape until the day she died. Anna had long since ceased her wanderings along the back roads to find her father, but became obsessed with his safe return: Please, God, don't let him have an accident, don't let him die, don't let my bad luck rub off on him. When Mr Wheelwright gave the kids a local history project, Anna became obsessed with the identity of the shepherd who had lost his son in Ison's Creek. For a brief, superheated time when they first became lovers, Lockie's penis consumed her thoughts and senses. She controlled and admired it, grasped it in her fist, peered at the ribbing of veins, measured in heartbeats the heavy tick of the stalk. She tasted the word 'engorged', a word of salty heat and shapely red-brownness. Lockie was gratified, of course he was, but sometimes a touching delicacy and self-consciousness seemed to leave him wide open for some rough-housing, and then he might twist away and she'd know that she'd gone too far. It was all tied up with sin and penance. She saw the change in his face—regret, and the ebbing of love—after he'd spurted inside her. It was as if he'd been wrung dry. But he was killed and she fled the country to recover. It helped if she counted things. She counted the wall tiles in the bathroom in the house in Hammersmith, counted her way through sit-ups and knee bends, counted the paces from the Sloane Square tube stop to her sales job in the bookshop in the Kings Road. She wondered if Grandfather Ison had been a counter too, when he was recovering from the lost weeks of his life. She wondered if these things ran in families. One day an aerogramme arrived from home: Bet you're surprised to be hearing from your Uncle Kitch! We were wondering if you'd have time for a little task on behalf of the family, now that you're in that part of the world. Remember old Auntie Beulah always going on about Ison money being tied up in Chancery? It's probably all pie in the sky, but why not give it a burl, I always say. Anna sought connections, and for a while could think of nothing else. Conspiracies obsessed her father-in-law. The Jews were in bed with the Reds and the secular humanists. They shared internationalist aims—a one-world government, controlling finance, thought patterns, our Christian way of life. The greatest trap inherent in this philosophy, he said, is that it's so devilishly clever. He told Anna that the Australian farmer was bearing the brunt of it—the international grain cartels, the international banking cartels. He tapped the cover of a crack-spined, well-thumbed book, his bible, and hissed the title conspiratorially: *None Dare Call it Conspiracy*, letting fly two filmy white specks of spit. He jerked back embarrassedly, drew a ragged forearm across his mouth, stepped forward again and made a clumsy wipe at Anna's jeans with one of the huge khaki handkerchiefs so carefully ironed by his wife. Mrs Jaeger's obsession was with crumbs, grains of salt and sugar, which she whisked away with a damp cloth. Her benches gleamed, and at a bench was where you'd find her. Dust was pouring into Anna's car. The car rolled and she and the children were thrown about inside it. When the car had settled there was still dust, choking clouds of it inside and out. Dust acted on Anna like a midnight footfall outside a window after that: creeping dread, paralysis, then flailing panic. She could not get it out of her mind, her mouth, her nostrils. Dust menaced her; she lived in a dusty country. One day, she told herself, I shall live beside the sea. The dust broke up before her eyes eventually, but did not fully disappear. Traces congregated on the surface of her hands, trapped by the moisturising cream she applied ten times a day to keep her hands from drying out as a result of her compulsive washing. For many, many years after the accident, Rebecca seemed to watch Anna obsessively from the passenger seat. Although she developed slender, fluid, dark and watchful good looks, she could not be convinced that she was beautiful. Rebecca examined herself obsessively: the mirror didn't lie. It told her that she was carrying too much weight. If she dropped her chin toward her chest, she felt a fold of unwelcome flesh. Her cheeks might look finely drawn from eyebrow to jaw but she had only to perform the pinch test to demonstrate that the skin there was, in truth, too slack. She sighted along the planes of her body and saw a faint swelling between breastbone and hips: surely she should be concave? She was certain that fat had accumulated on her upper arms. Even her stubby Tolley fingers spoke of fatness. Anna remonstrated: Becky, sweetie, you're wasting away. Rebecca might have progressed to starveling wretch if Meg had not chanced along and saved her. Now Anna and the two young women make it a point to order cheesecake, profiteroles or icecream whenever they meet for lunch or dinner. Rebecca blithely shovels it in, her thin, sculpted cheeks briefly mobile and overblown. These days Rebecca's fixation is with home security, for the little house in North Adelaide has been burgled twice. She has installed alarms and bars and better locks, and likes to make the house look occupied and lived-in whenever she goes out. Anna has bursts of house cleaning from time to time. She washes her hands a touch too often. These and other mild obsessions will accompany her to the grave. She will understand that obsessions are common and natural and mostly harmless, ideally a release valve for something, but now and then she will encounter in someone a preoccupation that is dark and corrosive, such as her granddaughter's conviction that the world will expire in a nuclear war. No six-year-old has any business fearing something like that and Anna would like to wring someone's neck.

Shades

THESE WERE ITS chief colours: gold, pink, khaki, black. By Christmas Day the mid-north was cast in gold: golden hills rolling away to the north, buttery gold stubble by the acre, dusty gold grain-spills at the paddock gates, dead gold grass on the uncultivated land, forearm hair bleached gold in the sun. Then wind, drought and time wore away the gold, and it was a pink country, the pinkness of dirt and dust and skin revealed to the open air. The sheep carried dusty pink fleeces upon their backs and tracked busy pink paths to water troughs, shade-trees, hand-scattered hay. Grandfather Ison went pink in the sun, his cheeks pink with roast dinners and white bread. Anna's father went brown in the sun, a sinewy, olive-hued man, except when he tipped back his hat. A startling band of naked pink forehead, creased a little in worry: Aren't you seeing a bit too much of that boy? One day Lockie led Anna along a stony path on the Razorback. Wild goats hoof-rattled in panic ahead of them. They came to a declivity hidden from the road and protected from the winds. Lockie took her onto a granite shelf, past a gnarled tree, to a crumbling hole in the side of the hill. She peered in, on her hands and knees, Lockie comfortably at her side: Can't you see it? Rock art. Anna concentrated. A stencilled ochre hand, ochre stick-men hunting a kangaroo, an ochre moon face. Overcome, she retreated with Lockie into the warm grass. Propped on one elbow, burrs caught in his hair, his hand on her breastbone: I love the way you go all pink here and here. By late May, the crops and wild grasses were shooting, young and green, trembling in the wind—except that the district was never entirely green, for the damp earth was too dark, the chlorophyll too deep, the licheny hillside rocks and tree clumps too shadowy on the distant hills. Khaki, Anna decided, musing aboard the bone-shaking Bitter Wash schoolbus. The driver dropped a gear to negotiate the switchback bends of the sunken road. Anna's face was inches from pink rockface; no sun penetrated; the gearbox howled. Then they were emerging onto the flatlands, where the Showalter Park lucerne sat as dark as camouflage, and the sun blazed into the dusty bus again, lighting the gold stripes on Anna's tunic. She looked at Lockie, seated opposite her, and caught him gazing at her gold-banded purple thighs. Lockie's eyes were green at certain times, in certain lights. Otherwise they were grey-green or greeny brown. Honey flecks danced in them. Anna rode the train to Pandowie before Easter in her third year away at the university, dreaming, attempting to re-create his face. She had not seen him for many months. He'd had his hair cropped close to his scalp and gone willingly away to war, but now she wanted him back again, and recalling him in her mind's eye was a start. But it was hopeless; he would not stay fixed. She looked out. Piebald hills behind the town, pale dead grass patched with ash from last summer's bushfire. The Razorback was in shadow, its black slope as wickedly jagged as sharks' teeth. The train slowed for the level crossing outside the town. First the silver grille, then the black snout, then the windshield and black roof of the Showalters' Bentley. The train rumbled past. Anna could not see if Wesley was at the wheel, or old Mrs Showalter herself. A black Bentley to match their black hearts, so Grandfather Tolley liked to say. And a Bentley, note, not a Rolls. A Rolls would be too flashy. Anna felt a sudden blessed release as Michael slid from her body. He looked stretched and squashed, clotted-red, slippery, spilling out of her with a rush of fluid onto a waterproof sheet. They said two things: It's a boy! He's a red head! Anna amended that. Auburn, she said. He gets it from me, and I got it from my Grandmother Tolley. Anna dressed Michael in shades of green and blue, matching and offsetting his blue eyes and auburn hair. His favourite colour was blue. Anna and Sam buried him in his best blue shirt, his head nestled on his tiny eggshell-blue pillow, the casket lined with royal blue silk. These were not decisions that Sam could make. Anna made them alone. For a time in her late teens, Rebecca wore black jeans, black tops, black capes. Black hair framed her small white face, and she emphasised all that she said with her white hands, hands cut off at the wrist by black cuffs. Sometimes she wore lipstick the colour of a blackening plum. Christ Almighty, sweetheart. You're going to be wearing black soon enough when you join an orchestra—why do you want to wear it now? Rebecca, dark and sly: Your basic separatist black, Dad. The Showalters got rid of the black Bentley and bought twin black Mercedes saloons. They gutted the big house and lined it with polished hardwood and Carrera marble, one massive black slab of it under the front door. They sank millions into the sperm-bank scheme, promising investors they'd be out of the red by the end of their second year of operation. Bless their black hearts, Anna says now. The collapse has turned Sam's hair grey. Only the prospect of the town's 150th Jubilee at the turn of the century is enough to keep him going, she sometimes thinks. Anna will stick it out with him. She will watch her history of the town spill from her printer, the black sentences accumulating, spidering across the page. She will help her mother choose a new lounge-suite fabric, a muted tartan pattern this time, mild reds and greens. Sniff: If your Dad were alive it would have been our silver wedding anniversary last Wednesday. Oh, Mum, I'm sorry, I forgot. Anna will ask herself: What, exactly, is the colour of the sea today? She'll stand still, intent, telling herself to identify what is there, not what custom tells her is there. As much silver and grey as blue and green, she'll decide. Her granddaughter will confound shoppers and kindergarten mothers. Hesitant fingers pinching her red overalls and green top: A boy or a girl? Auburn hair, though. No doubting that. Almost as if she were a Tolley.

Sunken

FOR MOST OF its length the Bitter Wash Road, like any road, scribbled across the landscape in plain view, but for a short distance—linking Showalter Park and Isonville—it wound along the bottom of a gorge. The best-preserved sections of stonewall fencing in the mid-north stood on this section of the road. The locals liked to say that the early Showalters, for whom the road was built, could not tolerate losing good grazing land and so the road was trained along the stony gorge, which was useless for anything else. In Anna's mind it was the *sunken* road, a name she'd absorbed from the cradle. Everyone on Isonville called it the sunken road. She saw that it sank from view and supposed that that was how it got its name. But when she took the sunken road into the wider world, she met snideness and incomprehension. Fiercely she defended the name, and cried in frustration: They laughed at me. Her mother swung her on to her knee: Ignore them, sweetheart. It's just a name Grandpa brought back from the war, after a trench he dug to fight the Germans. The road began at a T-junction on the Main North Road, between the Redruth Gaol ruins and a row of miners' cottages built for the Cornish Jacks in 1856. First it passed through a region of undersized farm blocks, ten and twenty-acre patches of erosion and helplessness, fenced tiredly with rusted wire and rotting posts, where clamorous quick families, the Kellys among them, spilled out of fibro houses and balding hens scrabbled among the car parts buried in the dead grass. Between Showalter Park and Isonville the road sank from view, appearing again through an area of small farms, alienated by the Strangways' Act into lots of up to six hundred and forty acres. It finished at Bitter Wash, a collection of stone ruins somewhere behind the Razorback. Muddy in winter, corrugated in summer: these were the two constants of the sunken road, no matter how often the district council ran a grader over it. Road signs warned of hairpin bends and rockfalls, but the untried, the careless and the trusting continued to scrape their cars against the stony edges or spin out on the gravelly corners. Everyone had a sunken road story—a cracked windscreen, a blown tyre, a lost hub cap, a near miss, a kangaroo skittled at sunset. The dust boiled thick as talc in the summer months; you'd drive with your headlights on for safety. Sometimes you could sit for an hour by the side of the road and not see another car. One day Mrs Mac made the school-run. She collected Anna and Hugo from the shop at four o'clock, passed the time of day with Grandfather Tolley, said: Home, James, and at four-fifteen felt the rear tyre blow and shred and throw Auntie Beulah's car from side to side in the gravel banked at the road's edge. Phew! That was exciting, she said. She got out, looked critically at the tyre, and rummaged in the boot. When was the last time anyone checked this car? she demanded. No wheel brace, and the jack was seized up with rust. Anna and Hugo said nothing, feeling obscurely ashamed. The minutes passed and Mrs Mac began to tap her fingers on the steering wheel. I could do with a drink. Half-past four, a quarter to five, five o'clock. Godforsaken country. I need my head read. She snorted: Her ladyship won't be pleased. She'll be wanting her tea in a minute. Anna's ears burned to hear Auntie Beulah talked about like that. She looked out. A rundown house stood a short distance back from the road. As she watched, children began to drift into the yard from the house. The Kellys. She knew Lockie from school. The Kellys were quick, funny and risky, but that day they stared and she stared back at them and there was no movement in the landscape until the stud manager from Showalter Park found them, thirty minutes later. Vegetation grew thickly on the broad verges of the sunken road—rye grass, wild oats, Salvation Jane, dandelions, soursops, lucerne, and wheat, barley and oats sowed by the grain-spills from passing trucks. It was understood that a man whose paddocks had been eaten to the bone may take his sheep on to the sunken road and so keep them alive for another day. A welling kind of love rose in Anna's breast as she read her father's letter: My darling first born. How are things at the varsity? Your old man's sitting in the ute again, pad propped on his knee, minding the sheep in glorious spring sunshine. We could do with a good soaking rain (where have I heard *that* before, I hear you ask). The feed at the side of the sunken road isn't going to last forever. Anna read through to the end and his voice was in her head, the smell of sunbaked earth and air in her nostrils. She went to the college payphone in the corridor outside her room: Mum, I'm coming home for the weekend. Can you pick me up at the station? She called another number: Mrs Kelly? Tell Lockie I'll be up for the weekend. When Anna's son was killed on the sunken road, Carl Hartwig wrote in the *Chronicle*: It's time the Council did something—sealed it, straightened the bends, put in guardrails, anything to stop these senseless deaths. But what were you doing on that part of the road anyway? Sam wanted to know. It's miles out of your way. It was a fair question. Anna supposed that she deserved it. Wariness in her daughter's eyes, reproach and suspicion in her husband's. The sunken road is to be sealed soon, a gift from the government in the lead-up to the town's 150th Jubilee celebration in the year 2000. Money talks, Anna says. Do you think funding would have been approved by junketing MPs if our application had gone in *after* the Park and all its millions had gone belly-up? But Sam is jubilant: This is a feather in our caps. We could time the opening ceremony to coincide with the Jubilee Parade. When Anna visits from the city in the years to come, she will drive along the sunken road and be struck by how broken-down it's become, the bitumen holed, buckled and unloved now that the Showalters are long gone and the Council is strapped for cash. She will be blasted off the road once or twice by tour buses heading back from photographing the wildflowers around the claypans on the dark side of the Razorback, and feel her heart leap into her mouth again, no fun for an old woman.

Split

ISONVILLE USED TO be five times the size it is now, sweetheart. Anna knew the story. Grandfather Ison returned from the Western Front in 1919 to find his parents dead of influenza and the broad acres parcelled up among his many married sisters. The homestead itself and five thousand acres had gone to Beulah, the unmarried sister. My poor dad, Anna's mother said. He felt betrayed. He had a young wife to provide for, then I was born, then your Uncle Kitch. One day he simply set off to carve out a new place in scrubland near Pinnaroo, intending to send for us later, but he lost his reason in all that solitude, and we had to go and find him and bring him back. I was only two at the time, Kitch was just a baby. Auntie Beulah took pity on us, bless her heart, and signed Isonville over to him, with the understanding that she could live here until the day she died. So we lived down this end of the house and she lived up the other end. Kitch and I used to go and say goodnight to her, just like you kids do. She'd say: Eleanor, Kitchener, a kiss if you please. Oh, she was hard to love sometimes. She wore my poor mother out. It's a good thing Mrs Mac doesn't take any nonsense. Now go and tell her goodnight. Anna and Hugo, in pyjamas and dressing-gowns, approached the stained-glass door at the mid-point of the house. In their minds a mad woman and a wrinkled crone lived on the other side. Every night they saw the old woman creep from one low-wattage patch of embroidered upholstery to another. Great Aunt Beulah jerked awake. Her lips moved. The children shut their senses down, brushed her cheek, sprang back from her chair. High, high where the air was close, dim and laden, Mrs Mac's teeth glistened down at them: Night, night, sleep tight, don't let the bedbugs bite. Grandfather Ison came up from Adelaide once a month, sleeping in the spare bed in Hugo's room. According to Hugo, Grandpa Ison's bottom was very round, very white. He stayed long enough to open and close a few gates, ride around the sheep with Uncle Kitch, give Mrs Mac her pay, check to see that she hadn't been hitting the bottle, then hurried in relief back to the city. Anna was twelve when the old ones died and Uncle Kitch inherited Isonville. Her mother inherited nothing but a dusty sideboard, and Anna came to understand that her mother heard an aggrieved justification beneath the dry tone of Grandfather Ison's will: When I came home in 1919 I found my sisters and their husbands sitting on land that should have gone to me. The Isons would have been as big as the Showalters if not for that. I will not let my own son suffer so. It's only fair that Isonville should go to Kitchener. After all, you have Peter to support you. Uncle Kitch stopped Anna on the broad verandah one day and said: How's the house-hunting coming along? Anna retorted: Why? Getting impatient? During her second year away at the university, Anna felt herself growing apart from Lockie. They argued about the war, the call-up, how a life should be led: No, Lockie, I don't want us to split up. What, then? I don't know, she said miserably. But Anna saw that he looked out of place, felt out of place, in the corridors of Women's College at ten minutes to ten—his hair, his outdoors skin, his beat-up utility in the street outside. Soon she was saying in her head the words: I have taken another lover. One night Lockie shadowed her to a house in Unley, and he waited outside for her until the bitter dawn: Are you two-timing me? Was I just an interlude for you? Later there was a postcard, just one, cheerfully describing the sun stretched like fire upon the South China Sea, and Anna thought that her heart might split open. She took comfort from the notion of a lucky wound. Grandfather Ison's journal:

> Pozières Heights, 15 August 1916. The fellow next to me has had the great good fortune to suffer a 'lucky wound' to the shoulder. It will remove him to England and then home by ship to his wife, lucky blighter.

So maybe Lockie would only be separated from her temporarily, and come home intact when his two years were up, or at worst be winged and come home sooner. It all came down to how her own luck was running. On the day that Anna married Sam Jaeger, she danced with her father-in-law. He grasped both of her shoulders, waggled his head from side to side: Well, well, well, Mrs Jaeger, I presume? Anna blinked, wondering wildly for a moment: A Jaeger? A Tolley? Who am I? Within five years Sam was saying: A pittance, that's all my old man pays me. Never gives me a say in running the place. Always looking over our shoulders, feeding garbage to the kids. Well, I've had enough. It's time we split. And so Anna and Sam found themselves snatching a morning here, an afternoon there, inspecting hovels to-let on forgotten back roads behind the Razorback, a land of nettles and heartbreak. It would have broken Anna's heart to live like that. Uncle Kitch and Aunt Lorna offered them the overseer's house on Isonville, and in their desperation they almost accepted. Anna has been with an archivist all day, collecting information for her history of Pandowie. She decides to call in on Meg and Rebecca. It's a three hour drive to Pandowie and she needs a coffee boost. A relaxing coffee, she says, when Meg opens the door. But it's not a relaxing coffee. Becky's in a faintly agitated, probing, questing mood today, inflecting her conversation in the form of questions, as though she's seeking to settle some ghosts:

Mum, I remember how gloomy it got after Michael was killed. It's a wonder you and Dad didn't separate. A lot of people would have. I remember I badly wanted you to have another kid. It's also amazing we stayed on in the schoolhouse, given that Wesley Showalter, our *bête noir*, lived just across the way from us. Anna can feel herself shutting down. She doesn't feel quite ready, quite able. She wants to say: Give me some time. She sidesteps, says goodbye, makes her way out to the car. When she retires, Anna will scratch about for a way of signing off from the *Chronicle*: I've trodden on a few toes, ruffled a few feathers, but only because I felt so passionate about the district and the people. It's my heartland, after all, and I intend to return as often as I can. Scratch that. Start again. In the end, Anna will not write a final column. Her name will simply disappear between one issue of the *Chronicle* and the next. At her place on the coast she will walk the shallows, attend to her memories, share banana splits with her granddaughter.

Friendship

ANNA'S MOTHER HAD been friendly with the Showalter boys, Wesley and Rex. There is a photograph of her with Kitchener and the Showalter boys sitting in a sulky, an old painted horse sniffing the dirt. One Showalter was stitched with cannon fire in the skies over Germany and the other grew into a glossy, twice-married ugly drinker and household name. She'd also assumed that her brother was her friend: So how could Kitch connive at driving me out of my home? Anna's first real friend was Maxine, from the town. But Maxine's father was the stationmaster, she lived in a simple railways cottage, and the big house at Isonville always seemed to deflate and subdue her. Desperately Anna entertained Maxine, but Maxine remained flat, small and precise at the table, incapable of conjuring the sheepyards, the sheds and Ison's creek into a place shimmering with promise—then at school on Mondays she'd behave as though the weekend had never happened. Maxine got her nerve back when the Tolleys were forced to move to the smaller, plainer, four-square farmhouse on the six-forty acres. That house reduced Anna to a manageable size, and the fretting salt-damp walls indicated a degree of poverty and strife. Maxine was also older now, with a steady head on her shoulders. So steady that Anna felt left behind. All Anna wanted was to muck around through the years, as though she—born of an Ison—should not be obliged to plan or calculate or think past tomorrow, but Maxine knew that her only hope lay in a skill learned, a job, a marriage and children. Maxine shrugged off Latin, mathematics, the sciences. Even her body changed. She grew calm, unhurried, somehow taller, always half-smiling pleasantly, the secret of life behind it. Anna responded by becoming ratty. Her intimates now were boys, and then only for as long as it took for her to milk them dry under the cover of darkness and a tartan rug. She still wrote to her penfriend in Leeds but she did not call that a friendship. There was nobody warm, flooding or unselfish in her life. Then Lockie came along. He stayed and he stayed and he stayed. He actually liked talking to her. Was it that he knew nothing about her past—and she could not believe that—or that he knew but did not care? He loosened her tongue. She sprawled in his utility, lazy-lidded, lips swollen, a flush on her breasts that she loved and rued and was helpless to control, her spine accommodating the worn springs and cracked upholstery as if she were a dozy cat, feeling more alive than she could remember. What came first, the tingling or the friendship? Did she tingle only because he was also her friend? She admired his uncomplicated friendship, an attraction of opposites, with Chester Flood, the orphan boy. To Lockie, everything was a huge joke. He was full of constant cheery exertions and would live forever. Chester was smarter, quieter, more subversive, laying the groundwork for his life. The three of them became friends. But then Anna went away to study and small serpents slipped into the garden. Anna began to change, going about with a frown of fury and concentration and a heart that threatened to burst. Soon Chester refused to drive down with Lockie to visit her at the college. Their arguing distressed him and he was not interested in the war. They'd become mismatched, Anna and the boys from home, their concerns were different. But, shortly after that, Anna befriended a woman in her dance class who also cared nothing about the war. Am I being inconsistent? Anna asked herself. Perhaps my attachment to Connie works because there is no history to trip us up and nothing at stake between us? What is right, and what is wrong? She burned with these questions. And Connie was unsound in fundamental ways. Connie took her to Hindley Street pubs after dance classes, advised her to dab rosewater or sugarwater on her nipples, made her laugh unsoundly. The next thing Anna knew, Connie was stripping for the R & R boys in a Kings Cross nightclub: *Don't* wish you were here, said her one cheery postcard. When Anna next saw Chester, seven years had passed, but she fell easily into an old, wisecracking affinity with him. Quick wits and risk-taking had bought him money and influence. Got any cash to invest? Me? Anna laughed. My husband has fallen out with his father, we're renting that old schoolhouse out near the Park, and I'm working two days a week for Carl Hartwig at the *Chronicle*. No chance. She looked at him, scarcely breathing. She needed some love, luck and whirling joy in her life. Surely Chester brimmed over with good luck—how else could he have escaped the call-up, escaped an untimely death, which Lockie's had been? She needed him inside her. As it happened, they made love only once, in April, when the roads were dust-choked and shuddery and Anna had gone straight to him from the Showalter Park field day, wearing a shapely, flawless summer dress that she wanted him to feast his eyes upon for a moment before he stripped it from her body. She saw him again after the accident, and even though nothing was said, it was clear that they would not be lovers again. But they were friends for life. Chester was her friend at a time when many people were wary of friendship with her. Anna could not forget that, not even when he took one risk too many with the twenty thousand she inherited when her father died. The Public Prosecutor, the judge and jury, the hungry press, all said that he was a crook. Anna makes no such judgment. She visits him at the prison once a month, kisses him on the lips, holds his hand. She has come to believe that sexual attraction is an element in all friendships. She feels it with Maxine sometimes. There has always been a passionate edge to their friendship. The period when they fell out had been like an inflexible stand-off between quarrelling lovers, solved by Anna's capitulation: Dear Maxine, I'm writing to ask if we could be friends again. There are times—when Maxine bubbles over with laughter or a secret, when her breasts are soft and her lips mobile, damp and blooming—that unsettle Anna. She can imagine being naked and unwithholding with Maxine. She knows that Maxine knows it. Maxine blushes, tosses back her head, oddly pleased. Most of the men whom Anna knows would say that their best friends are their wives. No wonder they are so often left high and dry. How must it be for Hugo, who has never married? Am I his best friend? Is our mother? In a community organised around the notion of couples, a single man is unlikely to be invited to dinner, no matter how many dinner parties he himself might hold. A man alone upsets the balance. There must be something wrong with him. If he has to be invited, then a single woman will have to be invited. Doubt, then suspicion, lodge in the orderly mind contemplating the unmarried man. Poor Hugo. Anna will be friends with Rebecca and Meg, attending concerts and often dining with them, but there will be things that the younger women won't share with her. Anna won't need many friends in her place beside the sea. Fewer friends but deeper friendships, old men and women looking out for one another.

Money

ANNA BANKED HER pennies, halfpennies and weighty scarce florins in a nude plastic pig. From time to time she hefted it in her hands but felt no satisfaction, only greed, spite and injustice. She settled that by upending Hugo's tin moneybox and shaking out a handful of his savings and transferring them to the pig. The guilty expect guilt in others, and so Anna told herself that she was simply stealing back what her brother had stolen from her. Probably stolen from her. They were Tolleys and the Tolleys were poor. They had come from nowhere with Grandfather Tolley and they had no money, not like the Isons, her mother's family, who had been around forever and had money to burn. Great Aunt Beulah Ison took Anna aside on her tenth birthday and said: There is an Ison fortune tied up in Chancery, dear. I've missed my chance. Your grandfather stopped in London on his way back from the first war but the blighters bamboozled him with red tape. Your mum's not interested and, frankly, your Uncle Kitch wouldn't have a clue, so it's up to you. That's Ison money, dear. See you get it back for the good of the family.

And so Anna was reminded that she was an Ison *and* a Tolley. Her birthday present from Uncle Kitch and Aunt Lorna was a cheque for five shillings, and in a Tolley counterstroke she altered the five to fifteen. Uncle Kitch could afford it. He had got Grandfather Ison's acres and Anna's mother had not. For seven years Anna waited for a hand to descend on her collar. She'd heard that a statute of limitations existed for certain crimes, that after seven years had elapsed she could not be prosecuted. Lockie visited Anna every weekend when she left to study in the city, and in the course of her first year away she noticed a shift in him, a gradual refinement in the configuration of his dress, hair, face and conduct. He'd been observing her friends. He didn't want to stand out, the country bumpkin. One day he said: The blokes back home, I told them you pay your half when we go out anywhere, and they looked at me like they thought it was a great idea but it would never reach further than the suburbs. A laugh bubbled up in Anna. She remembered the solemn ritual of a year, two years, ago: The man always pays. But as doubts and differences crept in to shape their hours together, Lockie began to practice small, irritating, unnecessary economies. Why can't we see a flick? Doesn't cost much. Because I'm saving, he explained at last, hot-faced, defiant. For what? Stubbornly: For when we get married. Anna's husband fell out with his father and money was at the root of it. I'm worth more, Sam insisted. I do all the hard work. I've got brains. I'm not a slave. But what will you do for money? Anna's mother asked, when she heard the news. Anna stuck her jaw out; she didn't want anyone to know her business: We'll manage. They rented the old schoolhouse on the sunken road, and in those times, marked by the seasons, when the locals had no odd jobs for Sam, the little family relied upon Anna's pay cheque, two days a week on the *Chronicle*. Sam didn't fully come to terms with that. One day

Rebecca asked him for a Star Wars toy, and got a dry crackle from his newspaper: Hadn't you better ask your mother? They drove to Isonville for the reunion of the Isons, and the first thing Anna saw, when she stepped into the hall, was a table piled high with Uncle Kitch's booklet, *The Ison Family: 1850–1975*. A money box, a small card: $5 please, to cover costs. Anna flicked through the pages and found 'The Wit and Wisdom of the Isons' at the back: If you spend two bob, the other fellow has it and you can't get it back again. Don't look at the sky, that won't make it rain—best look at the ground, where you might find a sixpence. Anna wandered through the big old rooms. There was wallpaper where there hadn't been wallpaper before, a textured Regency pattern that seemed to crowd her in. Here and there Uncle Kitch had taped reminders under switches: Turn Off After Use. With infinite patience, never raising her voice, making it a game, never letting her frustration show, Anna taught her daughter about paying her own way: No I won't buy that outfit for you, but I will help you make one like it, or you can buy it yourself when you earn enough pocket money. Because we're poor, that's why, and your cello lessons cost money. Sam said nothing when Anna's father died, leaving her twenty thousand in his will. One, it was her money; two, if Sam laid claim to it he'd feel that he was little better than his mean-spirited father. Anna took that twenty thousand to Chester Flood one day and asked him to put it to work for her. They rarely talked about Lockie, but Anna could picture Lockie whenever she saw Chester. Lockie and Chester had flashed their white teeth and crinkled their eyes at the world, one cheerily, the other knowingly. Men like that are apt to make you feel better. They can bring you luck. If they make a mistake it's not through obvious greed or spite or calculation—so Anna likes to think. The Department of Public Prosecutions had asked her to give evidence against Chester, but she could not, she would not. She was one of dozens who'd lost money—let someone else bring him down. Today, as Anna and Sam are driving through North Adelaide on their way home to the bush, a young suit—sharp as a blade, ear-ringed, mobile phone—darts through the traffic, forcing them to brake. Sam punches the horn and pounds the wheel. Anna has never seen Sam so teary, frustrated and vicious. Yet she knows it isn't the yuppie man as such, it's the loans manager saying no thirty minutes earlier, confiscating their chequebooks, suggesting that they stay on as managers until a new owner can be found. No wonder the Pandowie branch's recent offer to mount a float in the Jubilee Parade and finance the time capsule is more hypocrisy than Sam can bear. The Showalters have gone from Showalter Park. A receiver-manager lives in the big house now. Put all that together, Sam says, and what have you got? Hidden forces at work, serving the interests of international finance, that's what. The banks determine the availability of credit, placing us in unmanageable debt so they can take us over. Anna's mother tends to agree with him. Sales and turnover at the shop have dropped by fifty per cent in recent years, and she can no longer afford to employ the local kids. Australia is ageing and one day Anna will be one of the aged. She will depend on the government for a pension, for who in her position has superannuation? She will never have quite enough money, but she'll not let anxiety about the lack of it wear her down.

Luck

GRANDFATHER TOLLEY HAD the bad luck to lose his wife to a shark. Anna grew solemn when she heard that, impressed by the notion of a swift, random, soulless agency at work in the world. Why was Grandma taken and not someone else? And why to begin with? This led her by degrees to a contemplation of luck: good luck, bad luck, no luck at all. She decided that she was a person to whom good things happened. In this regard, she'd not been tainted by the blood of the Tolleys. She had a sly, nimble, distracting beauty and a good brain in her head, and she was an Ison—even if her name was not—growing up on Isonville, once home to a merino stud second only to Showalter Park's. And then she was undone by a string of frustrations, reversals and unfortunate reminders, all in the space of a year. She scored low in tests and exams, the other kids ganged up on her unaccountably in the playground, and she was a little ashamed of the public way in which her father was obliged to spend weeks racing around the countryside at the wheel of the Stock & Station Holden, usually at the beck and call of the Showalters. Anna referred to this run of misfortune as bad luck. It was a short step from that to overlooking all the good things in her life and seeing herself as a luckless person to whom more bad things would happen; and from there to comprehending that she *was* bad luck, full stop. She transmitted bad luck to others, merely by existing. What if she were to replay the past, erasing herself from the story, and her parents' meeting and marrying, and Grandfather Ison's many sisters? Why, her mother would not have been cheated of Isonville land when Grandfather Ison died, that's what. Anna was there the day her father lost the tip of his finger in the auger drive. It was a harvest-time of broken tailshafts, ruptured tyres and wheat fouled by star thistle seeds, and to top all that off he suffered cruel pain and fear, all Anna's fault. Something went out of him after that. No one fondly called him a wild man again, as if Anna had bled the wildness out of him. Oftentimes a whole year could be bad. Anna told herself one

December: This year Matt Heinrich broke my hymen with his finger, I lost Maxine's friendship, they began to call me names. Maybe next year will be better. Anna dared not hope for a good year, only a better one, by which she meant that no bad luck would come her way during the course of it. And so her teenage years went by. She was ready to believe that fortune smiled upon her when Lockie Kelly stole her heart. She dared to hope. A year went by, then a second and a third, and he continued to adore her. But badness crept in, finally, staining everything that Anna touched. Anxious, confused, she cast about for its cause—and remembered her bad luck. Funny how she'd forgotten. Bad luck had left her alone for three years, and she had bounced back so thoroughly that she had forgotten all about him. He had a human shape. He was a colourless chill shadow moulded to her back. He poisoned everything. He leapt across lighted spaces and brought down her loved ones. Lockie need not have died like that, Anna sobbed. A damn shame, but these things happen, the family replied, consoling her, but Anna knew better. Before she married Sam she warned: I should let you know, bad things happen around me. I think I'm jinxed. She watched his open face closely, trusting that he would laugh away her fears. She was not disappointed. Sam was so solid and dependable, so lacking in an inner life, that he could not see the figure on her back. Sam repelled everything that bad luck stood for. He might lack grace, agility and swiftness, but not simple strength. Bad luck would fail to find a handhold on Sam's broad back, would slide to the ground, wither and die. But oh, she should have been more vigilant. She should have known that bad luck was easily provoked. Her joy in her children provoked him, her joy in Chester Flood provoked him, and he undid all of her happiness in a moment's inattention. Another mother might have overcompensated after the accident, erecting safety barriers around her surviving child and smothering her with over-anxious love, but Anna took a fatalistic step or two back. Sam didn't. He hovered. And so Rebecca was the product of bipolar love. She's had to learn to be her own warden. It has been twenty years since she landed a smacking kiss on Anna's lips. But at least bad luck leaked away through that fractured side window, twenty years ago. Anna has maintained a wary watch over her loved ones since then and not seen him strike again. She cannot feel him on her back any more, and she's certain that he did not slither through the wreckage of the car on to Rebecca's back. Rebecca likes to read books about goddess medicine and goddess magic. There's simply no comprehending, she says, all that's carried in the head and heart of a woman. Meg, her lover, is apt to scoff. She's more down to earth. She might state that Friday the thirteenth is lucky for witches, lesbians and the left-handed, then throw back her head and laugh. Sam attributes the attitude of the bank to a conspiracy of the Jews; Anna attributes it to the times they live in. Neither mentions luck. Anna would like to have been able to reassure the suicidal woman on Showalter Hill: You were not the cause of anything. You did not bring bad luck upon yourself, or others. Anna will have no time or patience for worriers, crystal gazers or the lessons of history. Even if certain events can be prefigured, she won't waste time on searching for patterns in the bad memories or in depending for her happiness on the good. She knows that she is bound to die sometime but she'll not look ahead to the day.

Wool

GREAT AUNT BEULAH had an S.T. Gill lithograph on her wall: 'Labourers washing sheep, Isonville headstation, 1847'. The Isons, their habits of thought and action, were founded on wool. An entry in Anna's baby book: Funny Sayings. As I was watching Grandpa butcher a hoggett for the coolstore I said 'You can't cut my legs off and throw them away, I want to wear them.' One afternoon in late May, Grandfather Ison rattled back from the end paddock with a pair of three-day-old lambs in the tray of the Land Rover, the offspring of a first-time mother confounded by triplets. The children helped him to untie the twine that bound their spindly forefeet and carry them into the laundry. Where Grandfather Ison saw years of profit saved from foxes and icy winds, Anna saw painfully concave bellies, tiny bowed spines, ears like flaps of pink-tinged white velvet, mucousy nostrils, a viscous brown plug stopping each sorry anus. She named the lambs Cynthia and Bert. The children fed them heated milk from a bottle twice a day, panting, laughing, calling out involuntarily at the sensation of powerful small mouths tugging on the teats. The ropy little tails wiggled ecstatically; a milky froth gathered at each set of tiny jaws. Anna gave her middle finger to Cynthia. The tug was there, certainly enough, and it was powerful. Each lamb wore a ribbed nap of greasy white wool. Anna always washed her hands each time she fed the lambs. Cynthia and Bert were released into the yard a few days later and back with the ewes at the beginning of August. For about a year after that, the children were able to identify them in the mob, and Cynthia and Bert half approached or acknowledged them out of habit, but time, a new season and a coat grown and shorn and grown again soon made them forget. When Anna was twelve she woke up screaming from a dream of slathering, bloodied lips. Earlier in the week a knotted old bushman had come to help her father tail the first mob of lambs he'd produced on the six-forty acres, and Anna had seen the man draw the testicles from the lopped scrotum of the male lambs with his teeth. She'd watched, fascinated, as he neatly dipped his head, snapped his teeth on each pale nude bulb, jerked back, spat. Hugo and her father were in the pen, catching the lambs one by one, proffering the crotches on a stained wooden rail. Hugo was small, but he wanted to feel useful. He closed his eyes and turned his head as the blades trimmed and sliced the flesh, uttering a high, nervous hum and whistle that calmed no creature there in that gory corner of the sheepyards. The blood: gouts of it on the old bushman's shirtfront, flecked in his whiskers. It sprayed finely from every tail stump, masking Hugo's face. Anna stood far behind the old man's shoulder and when her father noticed her watching he gave a quick jerk-frown of his head as if to say: Lovey, you shouldn't be seeing this. Later he said: The last of the oldtime ways. For three years Anna and Lockie made love on a woollen blanket. It was tartan. They had nowhere else to go, only a sagging bench seat behind a worn steering wheel and a cluttered glove box that refused to stay shut. The blanket protected them from dust and erupting seat springs. Anna identified another odour in Lockie's composition of odours: he smelt of wool, of the lanolin in wool. He worked the sheds of the district and the wool kept his hands soft, even as bale hooks, blades, rough-weld holding pens and jute bales abraded the skin. One Sunday afternoon, returning flushed from their lovemaking on a back road behind the Razorback, Anna and Lockie ploughed into a poddy lamb that his brothers and sisters were rearing. Lockie wailed. He braked. The tyres skated in the red dirt. Anna saw him scramble for the door handle, and when she found him a moment later he was on his knees, sobbing wretchedly: I didn't mean it. Don't die, I didn't mean it. She knelt with him. The lamb bleated, struggling under their probing fingers. I've broken its back. No you haven't—only its leg. They severed the leg where the splintered bone had torn through the flesh beneath the centre joint, then sewed a flap over the wound with stiff black cotton. Lockie splashed antiseptic over the stump and lifted the lamb to its feet. They watched it totter away, clearly puzzled, shaking the shortened limb as though it were whole and somehow offensive, maybe mired in wire or mud. Behind them Lockie's dog bellied closer, snapped the amputated leg in its jaws, crept away. I wanted to bury that, Lockie said. Anna had noticed, but kept to herself, that the lamb carried the earmark of Showalter Park. So Lockie was a bandit in the night, not only a lover creeping to her window. She smiled to herself. The Kellys were entitled. They had shot and burnt and buried two hundred sheep during the drought and needed to build up their flock again. And here's another contradiction, Anna would say, in her arguments with her father. You're anti-communist yet you don't mind selling your wool to Russia or China. Your lot would sell it to North Vietnam if there was a buck in it. There were starved sheep grazing on the tussocky banks of the sunken road the day that Anna returned from seeing Chester Flood. She could feel him leaking out of her. Her breasts tingled with the memory of his hands; his sheepskin hearth rug still cushioned her undulating hips and spine. One by one the old family properties are being broken up or sold to agricultural companies. The decline and fall of the Showalters has been the most spectacular in the district. Wesley Showalter borrowed sixteen million dollars from the banks to develop his sperm-bank program, and now the only sheep on the property are the embryos and straws of semen sitting frozen in tanks of liquid nitrogen. Many of the locals had subscribed, all had lost their money, and if they were to meet the Showalters face to face now, some would spit on the ground. Notwithstanding that, the 150th Jubilee Committee has obtained a handspan of Pandowie Showalter Lustre 8's fleece for the time capsule. Anna jokes: Maybe they should include a foreclosure notice as well. There is not much money for Christmas presents this year, but Anna has scraped together the cash to buy Rebecca and Meg a wool underlay for their bed. The significance of this gift, and others like it in the years to come, will lie in Rebecca's realisation that her mother has let her lead her life without remark or interference—acceptance, indeed, and support. When she is old, a permanent chill in her bones, Anna will wear wool next to her skin, wool on top. But she'll shop for youthful styles, and the girls in the North Adelaide house will exclaim admiringly over her. Mutton dressed as lamb, according to Anna.

Soil

THE SHEPHERD BOY'S headstone squatted on the bank of Ison's Creek as if it were a natural stony eruption, not something planted there by a grieving father. Wind and rain had stripped the nearby soil away, leaving an impression of pebbles and coarse sand held together by a poor glue of red dirt and fibrous star thistle roots, so that Anna fully expected to see the boy's ribcage laid bare one day, or at least the box or the cloth he was buried in. Farther back from the creek a mat of grasses held the topsoil together, broken here and there by busy sheep tracks, meandering like the veins that map a drunkard's cheeks. A risky business, Mr Wheelwright said. He tapped the wall map with his cane. The map recoiled. The children went very still, watching the cane tip trace a winding course through the mid-north, past placenames they used in conversation every day: As you can see, Goyder's Line passes very close to Pandowie. Goyder advised that anyone who farmed east of the line did so at his peril. And he was right. You've all seen the stone ruins out there. It might look a picture in the spring, carpeted by wildflowers, it might look green after a fluke wet year, but it's not sheep country, it's not wheat country. It's a place where dust storms rise and minerals lie buried. Anna wanted to tell him about the gold diggings in a remote corner of Showalter Park, alluvial gold washed down the creek system over the centuries, but Mr Wheelwright was writing on the board again. Did you find any, Mum? Nuggets and things? The children's mother went faintly pink with pleasure: I remember Rex Showalter gave me a tiny glass vial of gold dust. I wish I still had it. That was the only gold I ever saw. It was a miserable place. Very little gold to begin with. The day Rex Showalter took me out there in the horse and buggy, only about a dozen men were left, trying their luck. They were living in dugouts in Noltenius Creek. Yes, holes in the creek. They'd dig a horizontal drive into the bank, leaving about four feet of soil over their heads for a roof. The more enterprising had fireplaces, with a small hole through to the surface to let the smoke out. Cool in summer, warm in winter, one man told us. He had no teeth, as I recall. They lived in faint hope, those men, but this was the Depression, no jobs around. She smiled: Your Uncle Kitch and I tried panning in Ison's Creek once, when we were kids. No luck. But one of the original Ison brothers joined the rush to the Victorian goldfields. Apparently he found gold there but was killed on the way home, poor fellow. Grandfather Tolley had twin storerooms at the rear of the shop, groceries for the house-wife, agricultural supplies for the farmer. He was an agent for superphosphate, malathion, fencing wire, sheep dip, sprays and ploughshares. It's putting goodness back into the ground, Anna's father said, his hands and trousers white, the air acrid, with superphosphate. The soil around here is low in nitrogen. It's been punished pretty hard over the years. Farmed to the bone, so to speak. Sixty-seven was a dry year. What little grass was left by Christmas was stripped away by hungry teeth or chopped about by frantic hooves. The price of hay quadrupled. It was a tired-red landscape they lived in. If you were a Kelly, there were no buyers for your wretched, starveling sheep, and you had nothing to fall back on. The council provided the grader and the bullets. Lockie did the rest, penning their two hundred ewes, then shooting them in the back of the head, while his father and the grader driver stood back and smoked and waited. First I felt squeamish and sorry, then I went on automatic pilot, now I just feel awful, a monster, a slaughterer with blood on my hands. Hush, Anna said, wrapping her arms around him. All you can see now is this mound of dirt, but to me it's a mass-grave. Lockie, hush. One of Anna's tutors had a low, goading voice and a face that expressed weary contempt, the face of a man who wanted you to know that he hurt inside. Poor Anna, out of her depth. The more he expressed his loathing, the more she wanted to make him feel better. The more he made Lockie seem like a raw youth, the more she wanted his misanthropy—which could so quickly soften into need. She saw him in his study above North Terrace and let him pinpoint her guilt. He put her on a horse and in a private school and from an exclusive set. No, she protested, my family is poor, but he brushed her denials aside. He talked about superphosphate bounties, and the myth of the soil, and graziers in parliament. If someone like you is against the war, then it's playacting, not heartfelt, he said. One day Anna saw how restless her father had become.

He was fifty-five years old, a man who loved to yarn and have people around him. He sighed: I must be the only cocky in Australia who knocks off in the middle of the day to pay social calls. Anna nudged the plate of scones toward him. She laughed: I saw you less often when I was a kid! His soil-engrained hands curling around her Liberty mug; his black nails; the black fissures where he'd torn the skin on fencing wire; the horny nail stub, all that was left of his shortened ring finger. Anna realised that her father craved company, not solitude on a tractor on a hillside. He stared morosely through the dusty window at the lucerne flats on Showalter Park, his attention caught by the sprinklers, shooting jewelled arcs of water over the green. Ahhh, farming's a mug's game. What do you think, love? Should I take over the shop when my dad dies? He leaned forward suddenly: Ah, the schoolbus. And there's my little Becky. Chester Flood has been convicted of misuse of clients' funds and incarcerated in a low-security prison on the Adelaide plain. I asked for the library, he tells Anna, so they put me in the garden. I wonder where they'd have put me if I asked for the garden? The laundry, probably. He stares at his hands: Lovely soil, black, rich—not like up home. He looks at her sadly: Think of me next time you buy flowers in the Rundle Mall. More than likely I grew them. Rebecca and Meg will drop their daughter at Anna's house for four hours every Friday afternoon. Come along, little one, Grandma's taking you to the beach. They will sit side by side and look out upon the water, the one cramming sand into her mouth, the other running it through her fingers, thinking, thinking.

Washing

THE LAUNDRY ON Isonville abutted a wall at the rear of the big house, probing into a corner of the shrubbery that was rarely ever warmed by the sun. Low-roofed, cramped, chilly all year round. No one thought to move or modernise it, or even to clear the shrubbery—it was the laundry. A dented copper, massive cement troughs, iron taps poised like complicated birds, a washing machine that yew-yawed through the hours. In a heatwave, that's where you found Dad, home from crisscrossing the countryside in the Stock & Station car, flat on his back on the glassy floor, Kippy in the crook of his arm, hat tipped over his face, maybe half a bottle of beer nearby. Anna and Hugo stretched out with him. All right for some, Aunt Lorna said, arriving to fetch her washing, to wheel it back through the dust to her house on the other side of the creek, sheets and trousers piled in a cane basket half the size of a bathtub, perched on a spindly, waggle-wheeled trolley. Silly cow, why doesn't she bring the car around? Because she wants to rub it in, that's why. She'd love to be living where we're living. When Mrs Mac had a puncture on the sunken road, Anna watched the Kelly children watching them stranded there. All those children, Mrs Mac said. All that washing. They watched Mrs Kelly advance massively upon a line of flapping sheets and then, in a quick, curious, delicate swoon, press the fabric to her nose and overheated cheek. Poor woman, dust always blowing in from the road. Anna finished primary school and went away to her mother's old school in the city, knowing how to rinse out her things by hand. But she saw at once that it would not do to be seen rinsing your things out by hand where everyone could see you—it admitted too much, it marked you out as somehow lower class, an unloved, furtive figure bent over a porcelain sink in a bathroom where rich girls thronged by the hundred. Anna lasted exactly one week and then she ran home. There was no washing machine in the Hammersmith house. Everyone in London uses the local laundromat, Anna wrote, in her first letter home. She was there to put Lockie's death, put time itself, behind her, but the present intruded: It's as if I've had to learn a set of new skills, a whole new routine, revolving around a tiny roomful of washers and dryers crammed between a corner pub and a fish and chip shop. There are seven of us living here and when a few loads have mounted up we scrounge for coins, head down the street, fill two or three machines to the brim and go next door for a pint, except I have halves. An Adelaide QC restored the old schoolmaster's residence on the sunken road, used it as a weekender for many years, then offered it for rent. It was a small, stone, coldish house, but better than anything else on offer in the district, and the rent was cheap. Anna, Sam and the children had only been there for a year when Michael was killed. He was gone from them, yet for a long time he seemed to linger nearby, always slipping away at the edge of sight. Everything Anna did reminded her that he'd been a part of her life. She might walk across the laundry floor with Rebecca's little bundle and think: There's not enough here for a load. Sam might plunge-snort his face and hands into a sink of water before coming to the table and she'd almost, almost, hear Michael's glee: Do it again, Daddy. Isonville and Showalter Park were both visible from the kitchen window. Anna's mother liked to visit, always choosing the chair that allowed her to look out upon those distant chimneys and treetops. It was an unfocussed gaze, all the focus in her mind, not her eyes: I never told you this, dear, but Kitch and Lorna had the gall to offer us the overseer's house when your grandpa died. They couldn't wait for us to move out. It was indecent. A clink of china, Anna pushing away her cup and saucer: You, too? Mum, when Sam fell out with his father they also offered it to *us*. Mother and daughter sipped their tea, elbows on the table, staring along the years. Mum, why didn't you challenge the will? Oh no, I couldn't do that, lawyers, a court hearing, couldn't air our dirty washing in public. Rebecca came in from the bus, dropped her homework on the table and walked on heavy legs to the bathroom. Anna read misery and discomfort in her daughter's stiff back: Has your period come, sweetheart? Give me your pants to wash. No, Mum, I want to do it, and Anna heard a tiny note of elation: At last. Anna whispered to her mother: Her first one. Rebecca is still small and reed-thin, a wisp in the orchestra's string section, a speck on the stage. Her lover, Meg, intends to get pregnant sometime in the next few years. Apparently Meg has a friend who will donate his sperm. Meg and Rebecca have announced this defiantly, expecting opposition, but really, they should know better. Besides, Anna is too distracted by the image of that man knocking on their door with a syringe in his hand to object: the Brunswick Green door closing swiftly in his face, Meg assuming the missionary position on the hallway carpet, Rebecca depressing the plunger, the claggy swiftness of the whole deal. The image grows large in Anna's imagination, and, just for a moment, until reason takes over, her skin crawls and she wants to wash her hands. She will visit the house in North Adelaide, edge past the Nappie Wash bin next to the change-table, bend to kiss her granddaughter's damp cheek: Lovely to see you, my poppet. Especially lovely given that the locals back home think Anna is washing her hands of them, those things she's been saying in the *Chronicle*.

Dogs

THE FIRST KIP was a border collie blessed with a sweet, alert face, a glossy black coat patched with white, and a huge boredom. He was underemployed, and he hated it. He wanted to live. His yawns were vast, prostrate, heavy with reproach. He cocked an eye from the verandah whenever Anna left the house, ready to bound if this were an adventure that she had embarked upon, not simply another egg or firewood run. But, once a month, Grandfather Ison would visit from the city and deliver him from boredom. *Wishty, wishty, wishty,* Grandfather Ison whispered, a kind of sibilant secret language that Kip strained to interpret, yipping a little, eyes intent in his cocked head, just like the man talking to him. Grandfather Ison worked Kippy to the bone on useless sheep musterings that made both of them feel useful, and they returned from the paddock lathered and panting and ate huge meals at bedtime. Kip liked to patrol the stock ramp at the front gate, where letters, bread and the daily paper were lodged in a milk can marked Isonville. The family knew that he was a chaser, but they couldn't catch him at it. One day Anna heard a horn, a thump, Kip's infernal howl, and ran from the house with streaming hair and eyes. She found the mail contractor's station wagon idling beside the ramp. The driver's door was open and the contractor, stricken by Anna's face, began a ceaseless dry-washing of his hands: No warning, love. He just ran right under the front wheels. Anna knew that her luck was running bad that day. The second Kip was a red kelpie. Rarely in his short and cranky life did he ask more of the family than food and shelter. He had a favourite spot in the slanting sun on their verandah, another on Great Aunt Beulah's, and even when Beulah was dead and gone and Uncle Kitch and family had claimed her rooms, he continued to pad around to her part of the house every afternoon, following the sunlight. Anna didn't know what that Ison mob had done to hurt him, but one afternoon after school she found Kippy stretched, blood-flecked and imploring, in his morning spot. She explored his coat for broomstick injuries, Aunt Lorna's style. Kippy never ventured around the corner again. When the family moved house he claimed new places in the sun. He wasn't interested in the six-forty acres, only in sleep, but Anna's father took him out to the paddock anyway, for his own good. One day he emerged from the stubble, whimpering softly, proffering his paw. There was a star-thistle spine in the pad behind his claws. Anna felt that it was a kind of loving for him to need her so, and she hugged his head, overwhelmed. But Kip had run out of love and warned her off, a snarl starting low and deep in his throat. At the bleakest hour of an all-night party, Anna and two friends took a taxi back to Women's College, smelling, at 3.00 a.m., of incense, Buddha sticks and beer. They sprawled over the seats of the taxi, dangerously bored, as ready to fall asleep as to bare exultant teeth and buck in heat if the right lover came along. You girls look like you enjoy a good time. It was a question, not a statement, and slowly they turned their heads to look at the taxi driver, a man wearing a twenty-four-hour smile crammed with gold fillings. He continued: I could take you to see something you would not believe. They watched him. There's this woman, he explained. She does it with a dog on her hands and knees. They shrugged. It was a way of saying, So what? to the man, as if it wouldn't mean anything for them, either, to shrug off two decades of good breeding and perform contemptuously in front of a nobody like him. The taxi driver went on: Before her husband went to Vietnam he gave her an Alsatian. He was killed over there. It's sad, like the dog's a substitute. But you gotta see it. I can arrange it. Ten bucks a head. Anna's first punch grazed his cheekbone. She landed another on his ear. Five boys dead in a foreign war, her own true love gone over the sea. If Lockie were taken from her, what would she do? How would she live? Hey, Jesus Christ, get her off me, fucking bitch. Get out the cab, go on, the lot of you. Little bitch. Anna could not be consoled in the chill dawn on that dismal street. The others wrapped her in their arms and said to one another above her head: What on earth's got into her? One day in the second year of Anna's marriage, an exclamation of pure delight drew her to the kitchen window. Bluff was dragging Michael along the verandah by the strap of his overalls. Dog and baby seemed to regard each other as siblings, so perhaps it was inevitable. Bluff had two black paws, two brown, and her wiry coat was black flecked with fawn lights. She could not walk in a straight line and her hindquarters never kept pace with her front. Mrs Jaeger would say to Sam: I hope you know what's going on in your house. When Bluff proved to be unmanageable around sheep, the Jaegers called in Anna's father and the latest Kip, hoping that a trained dog would settle her. As the men watched the two dogs channel a dozen headlong ewes in the sheepyards, Anna watched the men, particularly her father, as if for the first time. She recognised clearly that she loved and admired him, a feeling reinforced later when he took her aside and said: No offence, sweetheart, Sam's a nice bloke, but his old man's not too bright, is he? Suddenly Anna wondered what she had done with her life, marrying into the Jaegers. There is a new Kippy in Anna's life, Rebecca's dog, bought as a companion for Meg's dog. Young women and their dogs. When Anna visits and if the weather is fine they might spread blankets in the park. Rebecca likes to sit and talk but Meg likes to scoot over the grass with a dozen other women and a dozen dogs, in full cry after a soccer ball. There was another mother there recently. Anna nodded briefly, gravely, and the other woman returned the nod, communicating everything: Your daughter too? Today Meg's old flatmate has come along to the park, a young woman with a husband and new baby. The husband concentrates mutely on the baby's curls, aware that he is of no account here, today, in this company. The wife talks too brightly, too tolerantly, her eyes jumping in her head at every brushing sleeve, every footfall in the grass behind her. Anna thinks: You have a long way to go. Maybe I have a long way to go. But so do these women. Anna will retire to a unit where she may keep a dog, although she will choose to keep a cat. Its self-sufficiency will suit her. She will show her granddaughter the tiny scar, rather like a ragged fishhook on the back of her wrist, where one of the Kips had bitten her. She won't always be certain which one, or when.

Illness

YOU COULD FALL ill. Worse, you could die. In 1919 entire families were lost to influenza. You'd no sooner arrive home from burying your parents when you might have to turn around and see your brothers and sisters into the cold ground. Grandmother Ison died, worn to a shadow from caring for Great Aunt Beulah. Asthma killed Grandfather Ison: asthma and air-conditioned air and cigar smoke in the Adelaide Club. There were germs floating in the air or nudging invisibly on dogs, door handles and old bones, every one of them casting about for a human to latch onto. Anna washed her hands. She learned to freeze, inches from contamination, whenever anyone warned: Watch out for germs. She did not fall ill, unlike the pale, thin, starveling children of railway gangers and shearers, or suffer from Sandy

Blight, unlike the Aboriginal children who came in on the Dead Man's Corner bus. She queued to examine the chicken pox-spotted penis of the grocer's son. Anna did not run a temperature or break out in spots or rashes, yet it seemed to her only a matter of time before illness might strike her down. She tried to scrape the coating from her tongue. Whenever she walked through long grass she listened for tiger snakes, and afterwards inspected her legs, certain that she would find puncture wounds among the scratches and scabs. She turned all her senses inward, urging them to register the first signs of fever, nausea or the plague. Instead, it was Hugo who suffered. All through the spring and summer months he gasped and sneezed and his eyes itched and watered. He might wake at night clawing at his throat, desperate for air. God had done this to him and he sobbed at the unfairness of it. The children's parents said: We're at our wits' end, and took him to see allergists and quacks. Anna broke down and cried out: I've brought him bad luck, but everyone looked at her oddly and replied: Of course you haven't, don't be silly. When Anna was warned to expect her first period, the words everyone used were *the curse* and *your monthly*. Nothing had prepared her for so much discomfort and pain. Her blood flowed copiously; she felt ragged and vile. Every thirty-one days, for six days, it was like clockwork. She missed one day of school at the onset of each period, and she hated having to explain, hated having it known or surmised the next day. Her damned luck, that's what it was. She would lie curled in bed, a hot water bottle clutched to her stomach, and stare through the dim light at all the possible lives and worlds beyond her bedroom wall. Why me? she demanded, and her tears broke her mother's heart. Her mother came to her one day, pinkly embarrassed, avoiding her gaze: Dr Pirie says it can be controlled if we put you on birth control pills, and suddenly the question of license was there between them. A month later Anna said: I feel so much better. She was fifteen. She began to test the waters. She didn't tell the boys that she was protected but enjoyed their sidling anxiety at school on Monday mornings: What if I've put you up the duff? She was waiting for a true love. Telling him would be like bestowing a precious gift. But soon everyone knew; Anna had not counted on treachery from her best friend. I am sick at heart; I have a sickness of the soul: nothing else described so accurately Anna's emptiness when he died. She lost weight and colour and stared through the people who loved her or talked to her; fine, angular bones appeared beneath the surface of her skin; she breathed in microbes and had no resistance to them. Yet Anna was not aware of these manifestations, only that she was unutterably sad, and sadness cannot be weighed or poked at or treated with pills. Anna suffered from nausea, exhaustion and perverse twinges and pain when she was pregnant with Michael. Sam hovered about her, fiercely tender and protective, delivering weak tea and toast and hot water bottles to her bed and keeping the Mr and the Mrs at bay. Then Michael was born and she lost all memory of the long months. Instead, she recalled her pregnancy as an interval of patience and tranquillity, time measured in heartbeats. Michael slept, he put on weight, he rarely coughed or sneezed. But Rebecca did not want to enter the world and seemed to be wary about her tenure in it. She was small, dark, withholding, a child who believed that all surfaces were a lie. Rebecca grasped her asthma spray in both hands and would not let go. She sucked automatically, fatalistically, thinking her dark private thoughts. Unlike her Uncle Hugo, Rebecca did not blame God. She did not blame anybody for anything, but she did expect them to make mistakes. Anna watched her grow. Later the asthma regressed until only extraordinary circumstances might bring on an attack and before long, Rebecca had even cured herself of these. Anna's father lingered for several months in the sun-drenched room at the rear of Tolley's Four Square Store. He'd found happiness in his final years in the town. But his third stroke robbed him of speech, movement and recognition, so that Anna, wiping the damp, slack mouth in the skin-and-bone face, prayed for a swift death. He felt so light in her arms; the copper band rattled now on his bony wrist. There seemed to be nothing to him, yet one day she saw his penis and was startled by the loose youthfulness and size of it. Sam's mother is likely to die soon. She has found life unsupportable without her husband. And so Sam will have been spared the long death of ailing parents, but he does not draw much comfort from that. He is sick at heart because he has lost everything his father put together. You want to know what's really wrong with this country, Anna? he wants to know, winding himself up again: The New World Order, that's what. One world government, he says, counting on his fingers, one world bank, one world currency, all devoted to the interests of international finance and international Jewry—and the Australian farmer can go hang. So how come you write about the recession, drought, falling prices, increased costs, over-borrowing, ageing, the collapse of Showalter Park? How come you're waving our little tragedies in our faces, our suicides, divorces and bankruptcies? These are *symptoms*, Anna. Anna will be advised by her doctor to walk a few kilometres each day. She will visit her mother in the Clare hospital and be shocked by the length and purple rawness of the stitched incision in her mother's skinny flank; but her mother will grin like a maniac and flex her new steel and plastic hip: Good as new. Hugo will continue to smoke too much out on the six-forty acres. He'll ignore Anna's warnings and say: I'm not Grandpa Ison.

Drought

THE DROUGHT PAINTINGS. Grandfather Ison expected something recognisable, not fire distortions, wind-twisty bare cliffs, men and women as stripped and spindly as dead trees on the baked earth, sheep's jaws grinning in the drift sand, carcasses offering up ribcages like tented fingers, bony dogs resembling no dog he'd ever seen in all his years in the station country. He snapped his catalogue against a khaki sky. Have you kids ever seen anything like this in nature? Anna and Hugo shook their heads dumbly: those canvases were their first drought. They trailed behind him through the Gallery's exit doors and back along North Terrace. After a while, Grandfather Ison said: Pom, pom, pom, for want of anything to say to them. Their mother was waiting outside the Adelaide Club, barred by the doorman, shopping bags at her feet: Hello Dad, hello my darlings! By the year's end Anna had undergone another drought. Locusts darkened the sky, a dusty soup of them, smearing windscreens and ticking, engorged, from leaf to leaf. She stood paralysed in the schoolyard with Maxine, eyes closed, mouth closed, head pulled in, dress gathered tight at the knee, but still those creatures snapped on her arms and crept in her hair. Then the winds bore the topsoil away. Hugo wrote 'dust' on the sideboard, grit particles scratched among the filmy pages of the Methodist hymnal, and cars crept home from church with their headlights burning. For a brief time in 1967, Anna's father wrote her two or three letters a week. She imagined the pen barrel balanced awkwardly against the stub of his missing finger: My darling first born. I'm sitting in the ute, pad propped on my knee, in glorious spring sunshine. Kippy's asleep in his usual place behind the back wheel somewhere. The sheep are spread out between Dead Man's Corner and the railway cutting, but there's not much in the way of feed around here. Maybe some maniac will take the corner too fast and put a few out of their misery. Hugo will spell me for a while this afternoon before we take the mob back to the paddock. They're losing condition fast. It breaks my heart, it truly does, but you don't want to hear your old man's tale of woe in the middle of your exams. After the exams Anna answered a newspaper advertisement. So did thirty others, faces she recognised from lectures and the library stacks. A glittering American revealed his white teeth from behind a table-load of encyclopaedias and said: Why, one of our salesmen earned enough money in his first year to buy his own airplane. Now he flies from sheep ranch to sheep ranch in the outback, where they're hungry for knowledge. Bullshit, Anna snorted. She was contentious, easily excited, easily wounded, her auburn hair crackling around her head. She went home to Pandowie, to work for a handful of dollars and be with Lockie for the summer. Lockie's friend, Chester Flood, said wryly: We thought we might have lost you to the longhairs. Well, it had been a close thing a couple of times, but Anna would never tell them that. Besides, Lockie and Chester would not be turning twenty for another eighteen months, so the call-up was not yet an issue between them. She fell with relief against Lockie's flat, flawless chest, his skin stretched brown and hot over flexing bones. Lockie, wild and laughing, and they went on unchanged. When he was forced to shoot two hundred starving ewes, Anna whispered hush into his trembling neck. Two years later he was dead, and as Anna recovered from six weeks of blankness, a gap in time lost to her forever, sensations of home and childhood flared in her so vividly that she saw quartz reefs and dry grass, heard bark peeling in the stillness of the hot days, tasted dust from a willy-willy in her mouth, even as mushy snow settled over London. Funny about that, she wrote in an aerogramme home. Travel may broaden the mind but it also sharpens memory. She felt unlocked, better, now. In arthritic sentence fragments separated by dashes, a style best suited to postcards, she described Stonehenge capped with snow, fog on the M4, the mirrors of Versailles, Pozières, where Grandfather Ison had peered over the lip of a trench they called the Sunken Road, and the sea around the Greek islands as blue as the flooded shafts of the Pandowie mine. When she got home she found that every line had been published, unchanged, in the local rag: Mother, how could you, I sound like an idiot. Their first dead lamb, stretched eyeless and discarded in the dirt, distressed Anna's children. Michael stamped his foot at the crows; Rebecca turned her back on the buzzing carcass. Then Michael was killed, and every year, in the dry months, when scorching winds and willy-willies and barrelling road traffic filled the air with dust, Anna could be expected to suffer. The dust brought back her guilt. She blamed herself for Michael's death. Her husband blamed her—not in so many words, but she could sense it in him as though he wore a black hood. But he could surprise her. They were in the Land Rover. The door seals had perished and the dust poured in, bringing back her nightmare. She curled into a ball on the seat. The next moment, Sam's hand floated from the wheel and rested briefly upon her knee: It's all right, sweetheart. Anna has been gathering information about notable droughts for her Jubilee history. There is a useful quote from Grandfather Ison's journal in the family reunion book:

> 11 November, 1929. Isonville is hanging on by one small haystack and a horse trough. It is a starved and silent view we have on those chance days that are not shut down by the dust.

There will always be dust in Anna's life. Even on the coast it will find her: streetlights coming on in the middle of the day; the neighbours discussing the TV news reverently; the famous front-page shot of the cloud closing in on the city. She will sneeze muddily into paper tissues rather than soil her handkerchiefs. She will close up the house and keep a glass of water on hand, for any faint grittiness between her teeth will bring on her panic. She'll stay indoors, where she won't have to listen to other old retirees from the bush who have known the real thing.

Begetting

ANNA IDLED IN the hall outside their bedroom, waiting for them to get ready. She paged through her Bible, passed on to her from Grandmother Ison:

> The Gospel according to Saint Matthew, Chapter One. 1. The book of the generations of Jesus Christ, the son of David, the son of Abraham. 2. Abraham begat Isaac; and Isaac begat Jacob; and Jacob begat Judas and his brethren. 3. And Judas begat Pharos and Zara of Thamar; and Pharos begat Esrom; and Esrom begat Aram.

Anna, bumping her heels on the skirting board, heard: Oh Pete, I mourn my younger self. Anna peeked around the door. Her mother stood angled in disappointment at the dressing-table mirror, shoulders slumped, mouth down at the edges, her eyes gauging the swell of her hips, her middle: I'll never go back to the way I was before I had the kids. *Yes you will!* Anna jerked back, knocking her forehead. It was her father, jackknifing from behind the wardrobe door, snapping his damp towel, his baggy underpants a stripe of white at the centre of his mad dancing body: You'll always be desirable to me, Ellie. Love that bum. Love that bum. Peter, stop it. Anna saw her mother twist away, gasping, shrieking: Peter, we'll be late, stop it. Anna flew through the door at him, swinging and kicking: Leave my mum alone. She saw finally that her parents were only playing, but the playing somehow made it worse. The Fathers and Sons Association instructed the boys, the Mothers and Daughters Association instructed the girls, a lecture with slides in the Institute, the parts of the body, the changes in the body at puberty. But who does what to whom? that's what Anna wanted to know. Violet Flood was taken into care by the state. Only thirteen, she'd been doing it with shearers out on Showalter Park, charging a shilling a time. Violet resembled Chester, thin, hard and rawboned from poverty, her dark eyes expecting hurt and knowing little else. My age, Anna thought, and she's pregnant. When Dr Pirie prescribed the Pill, Anna pranced around Maxine at school: Such a relief! She could not control her limbs; she wanted to dance; she felt need and greed stir in the pit of her stomach. Slut, they called her. Am not, she said. I take it for my periods, okay? A doctor at the university health centre advised Anna to go off the Pill: Five years is a long time without a break. There are side effects and possible long-term effects. Anna stepped outside, into the sunlight, onto the Union Building lawn, and it occurred to her that she hadn't lost control but had more control now. She crossed the footbridge, light and giddy, daydreaming her way back to her room at the college. She could say to Lockie, who'd become such a pain, and say to the tutor, so inconstant and unimpressed that he hurt her every day, that she would not be making love to them for a while. Nope, don't know when. When I feel like it again. That would show them. But Lockie didn't hear the part about not making love. He heard only the part about going off the

Pill. She hated the hope that reanimated his unhappy face: If you got pregnant, maybe they wouldn't send me overseas. We could get married. Anna was able to pinpoint the conception day of her son. Sam Jaeger was a comfortable husband, a man of polite attentions, always with one eye looking over his shoulder at his parents, but Anna sneaked him away to a hotel beside the sea, and at last he relaxed, at last he wanted her. The sea wind stirred the curtains and Anna, feeling him pulse, knew at once that she was pregnant. She greeted Dr Pirie's confirmation with a mild blink and a smile. She felt taller than the rest of humanity. She drove to the six-forty acres and sought out Hugo first, she didn't know why. Because she knew he'd be the most genuinely delighted, that's why. And Hugo—sentimental, unlucky in love, exasperated with their father—needed a shot of happy news. Then emotions began to chase through Anna, leaving her bewildered, changeable, stunned. She was elated, she was flat, her belly crawled with fear. She wrote: Dear Maxine, I'm writing to ask if we could be friends again. Maxine had two boys, three and eighteen months, and Anna watched, and listened, and learned. Maxine, jiggling her youngest: Everyone's full of advice. You take what you need and ignore the rest. Like nipples, for example. I was told keep them oiled, I was told aim them at the sun ten minutes a day, I was told toughen them with an old toothbrush. She shrugged: If you're the kind who gets sore nipples, you'll get sore nipples. Anna had her baby, and suddenly found that her nerve-endings were responding to the slightest provocation. She felt a rush of milk in her breasts if Michael looked like an angel, if another baby cried, if another mother's baby suffered in the news. She found herself unconsciously rocking, comforting herself, comforting those distressed babies. Her love was boundless, and she found herself wanting another baby, half thinking that another baby might check and absorb some of that love and keep it close to home. After lunch on a day in late September, the sun shaking off winter, the welcome swallows hauling pats of mud to the battlements of a new nest above the fuse box, she began to attack Sam, slapping and tickling him, coaxing him charmed and hot-faced down the verandah steps to the back lawn, where the rose hedge screened them. They awoke to Michael on his haunches, peering at them, reaching a hand out to Sam's bare rump, while at the bottom of the hill the Mr bellowed: Sam. Where are you? Time's a-wasting. The day that Anna made love to Chester Flood, she stood on his carpet, curling her toes, watching him come up for air. He trailed his tongue to her navel, *flick*, then to her ribs. He swayed back on his heels, assessing: A perfect left breast. Not that there's anything wrong with the right. Anna pulled his head against them: I'm just glad to call them my own again. All that breastfeeding, I felt distinctly uninviting. He tugged on each nipple: You taste sweet, like a garden, like honey. Anna closed her eyes, blessing Connie, who had advised her in the ways of love many years ago. It's rosewater, she murmured. When Michael was taken from Anna, she rocked and rocked, gazing at the wall. One day Rebecca came to her, seeking a cure for their unhappiness: Mum, can't we have another baby? Anna clasped her daughter's little head to her and rocked. Last year Carl Hartwig published a special liftout in the *Chronicle* to publicise the Showalter Park sperm-bank scheme. Anna found him working on the layout, juggling bromides: the artificial lake, workmen unloading Carrera marble, Lustre 8 with a Royal Show sash around his neck, a long, low building labelled 'laboratory', straws of semen sitting in a tank of frozen nitrogen, Mrs Showalter's aquiline nose on the steps of the big house. Carl said, choosing his words carefully, not looking at Anna: It didn't seem likely that you'd want to interview Wes Showalter, given your, you know, *history* with him, so I went out there myself. He shrugged: It's quite a set-up. I'm tempted to invest. Anna said: Not me, thanks. When Rebecca and Meg have a baby Meg will be the mother. *Birth* mother, Rebecca says, holding a reminding finger in the air. Meg, spreadeagled on the hallway carpet before the sperm dies in the syringe—is that how they'll do it? Anna wonders. Or will they make it more romantic than that? Will the sperm live for a while, long enough for them to get to the bedroom, for example? Anna would like to ask them these questions. She will not offer advice. Not to Meg, the older one, who strides through life; not to Becky, who will not listen. Meg, coming back fuming from showing the baby to some friends at work: I tell you, Anna, the breastfeeding police are everywhere. Anna will rock her granddaughter in her arms, walk up and down for hours to soothe her, and, catching her reflection in a mirror, think: And I've lost my young body.

Income

ANNA WAS STARTED on sixpence a week pocket money. Then, year by year, as she grew in age and aptitude, it was increased by increments of a penny or a penny-ha'penny until finally she earned a shilling a week, two sixpences, one to spend, the other for her piggybank. This was income, not a gift. She was expected to earn it. She wiped the dishes, collected the eggs, swept the back porch, unsnagged the family's grass-seedy socks and chopped kindling for the kitchen stove. As she progressed to more difficult jobs, Hugo came in behind her, wiping, sweeping, chopping. They had cows on the six-forty acres. Anna was expected to drive them into the milking stalls when she came home from school, pull up a three-legged stool to the ballooning flank of the most patient cud-chewing cow, and strip the milk from teats that to her were like coarse-skinned, waggly dicks on a bloated sac. But her Tolley fingers proved to be useless, and so her father replaced her on the stool. She worked for Grandfather Tolley all through her high school years, every Saturday morning between eight o'clock and midday. Again she swept, but she also took inventory, restocked the shelves, and waited on customers. One day Mrs Morehead, the piano teacher, came tight-lipped and hotly tense into the shop, settled her account, and was never seen again. Her old man was caught with his fingers in the Council till, Grandfather Tolley explained. Anna froze. She drew her cloaked fear and guilt around her, waited until his back was turned, and replaced the two florins that she had pocketed from the cash register—one in her left pocket, the other in her right, so that they wouldn't clink. She kept her eyes open for shoplifters after that, even though Grandfather Tolley did not list shoplifting as one of his burdens. His burdens were freight charges, tardy payers, non payers, the lure of the bigger towns, and the contemptuous indifference of the Showalters to their massive monthly bill. They let it run up to five hundred quid, he said, then act like they're doing me a favour when they eventually pay it. If jokers came in asking for a left-handed hammer, Anna cut them dead. If little old ladies said: My, haven't you grown, or: Your mum and dad must be very proud of you, dear, Anna withered them with a stare. Then she left to study in the city and Grandfather Tolley took Chester Flood under his wing, paying Chester a weekly wage to help in the shop and putting him through a course in accounting. So there was no work for Anna in the shop when she came home during the sixty-seven drought, and work, but no income, on the six-forty acres: Sweetie, we're struggling this year. Anna blinked awake. She seemed to hear her father for the first time. She stopped dreaming and grew up a little. She returned to the university in February, when only distracted thesis writers, lost Africans and cleaners were about, and secured a job for herself in the library basement for ten hours a week. Ten hours to think in, for the work was not demanding. Ten hours to stew in, all those boys dying in that foreign war. When she applied for her first job in London, the bookshop manager in the Kings Road said: Restless tribes of colonials, then cocked his head as though another fine phrase might find its way into his mouth. He winked: So I know you'll soon be moving on, love, but you colonials work well, I'll give you that. Few people could live on what the man paid her. Anna was expected to be aggressive with the customers, to sell plenty so that she could top up her income with bonuses. Her legs and feet ached. Shoplifting gangs made snap raids on the expensive art folios, and she encountered chiselled blue-bloods—The Lady or The Hon. printed on their rubber cheques—who behaved as though the air around her were tainted. But she was finding her return ticket, here, away from her past life. Lockie and her heartache receded. She was able to stand back, assess herself, move on to other things. Anna moved on to marriage and children and hidden sweatshop labour. She discovered that Sam was paid a poor, thin, grudging allowance and herself nothing at all. I tend to the battery hens, she argued. I collect, pack and weigh eggs every day. Shouldn't I be paid something? It's all for the family, Sam's father replied. Sort of like a little communist system, Anna observed, and saw by his splutter and redness that her father-in-law was a fool and she could always silence him. Then father and son fell out and suddenly Anna and Sam knew what it meant to need money to pay the rent. At least the old system had cushioned them from some of the blows of life. When Anna first started working at the *Chron-*

icle, young mothers looked at her side-on, as if making a list of everything that marked her: A tart at school; fancied herself for going to university; her boyfriend was that Kelly who got himself killed; she came back from overseas with her tail between her legs; married into a family of religious nuts; and now she's forced to go out to work. Money in dribs and drabs, for all of Anna's life, except one day her father died and left her twenty thousand—and Anna lost the lot. Sam has been advised that the bank is forcing a sale and will appoint a manager. Anna observes, in her weekly column: Losing a farm also means losing a home, a way of life, a whole social framework. She should feel more sorry for herself, but can't forget the local kids, who leave school year after year, full of eager hope—except there is nothing to hope for in Pandowie. One or two boys have wrapped their cars around the only roadside tree in miles and it's clear to everyone that they are swelling a hidden statistic. Teenage mothers push sullen prams up and down the aisles of Tolley's Four Square Store and if they lift an item here and there, Anna's mother turns a blind eye. She has put a notice in the front window: Buy your kid a job, shop local, shop Pandowie. Anna writes: We must think laterally. It's no good finding jobs for our young people in time-honoured occupations. With tourists renting the miners' cottages in Paxton Square, and King William Street farmers snatching up our farms, now is the time to think about jobs in tourism, cottage crafts and organic farming. When she moves to the city, Anna will place small advertisements in magazines: Typing Done. She will be paid by the hour to invigilate at end-of-year exams. Anna will accept an old-age pension, a grateful government's reward for all that she has contributed to the nation, but keep to herself the conviction that she hadn't always been a worthy or a deserving citizen.

Parades

THE CHILDREN CONSTRUCTED a banner, 'Harvest Thanksgiving' picked out in scissored silver-foil letters glued to a length of cast-off velvet curtain. Their mothers dressed them in white tunics fashioned from bed linen and they wore leather sandals upon their feet. Crowns woven from straw, daisies and green crepe paper capped their skulls. Clueless, dutiful, faintly Roman and pagan, the children of the Sunday School waited for Mrs Morehead to strike the first chord on the pedal organ. They heard a wheezy blast of air, the snicker of the unoiled pedals, then a stately hymn full of weighty flourishes rattled the windows, and someone, the minister's wife, nudged Anna to lead the others down into the body of the church. Her feet glided, her back was like a reed, her hair crackled in the electric air. She sensed the vast spaces under the ceiling beams, the foolish, melting faces watching from the pews to her left and her right. In her cradling arms she carried counter-stacked sheafs of wheat, oats and barley. The boy behind her carried a bundle of loaves, Maxine behind him wedges of butter and cheese on a tray. Hugo carried honey, another kid a basket of eggs, others jars of jam, pickles and stewed apricots. Anna paraded to the front of the church, paused at a tier of planks decorated with butcher's paper, and stacked the sheafs of grain in a golden sunburst pattern against the white, exactly as instructed. She stepped to one side and took up her position beside the display. She watched the other children file down the aisle toward her. They were trampling one another's heels. It was not that they were unused to parading—they did it every day, marching into class to the beat of a slack pigskin drum—but they were unused to parading slowly. The first television set in the district was installed at Showalter Park. An antenna tower twice the height of the chimneys shone like a galvanised Eiffel Tower next to the stone cellar at the rear of the homestead. The invitation was for children under twelve. Anna sat at the back, the polished floorboards cold under her thighs, and stared out above the heads of the little kids. A bit snowy, said Mr Showalter, fiddling with knobs on the side of the cabinet. The floury images on the screen sharpened a little and he stepped back from the set. He stayed for the duration of the Christmas Pageant broadcast. In fact, Anna saw the gardener, the overseer, the stud manager, a few mothers and the cook standing behind the rows of children slackjawed on the floor. She turned her attention to the screen again. Floats, clowns, a pipe band and marching girls paraded past the cameras: Anna could feel her feet high-stepping, pointing, toe-spinning along the streets of the city. Only thirty people turned up for the march on the Raintree Corporation. It was a bad time of the year: October rains, examination blues, the risk of getting roughed up. The thirty paraded in a tight bunch, five abreast, along the centre line of Frome Street. Some carried banners attacking the government, others supported the National Liberation Front. Anna's banner read: 'Join the army today. Travel to exotic, distant lands, meet exciting, unusual people—and kill them'. The wind howled down Frome Street and twisted the banner in her hands. She saw unmarked police cars draw up beside and behind the demonstrators. There were vans at the mouth of the street. An amplified voice broke up in the wind: . . . an illegal gathering . . . the street . . . or arrested. When her children were toddlers, Anna liked to walk with them to collect the mail at the end of the Jaegers' long, rutted drive. They made slow time, the children ranging restlessly off the track or squatting to peer at ants and flint-chips gleaming like diamonds in the dust. One day their little procession met another one, a small back-blocks circus grinding past the gate. The children froze, their arms shot out: Look! A lion and an elephant in painted wooden cages, a couple of rusty cars, a lorry stacked with canvas and poles for the big top, four caravans jerking and hunting like tethered whales at the tow bars of three station wagons, and a converted milk van. The circus creaked by so slowly that the dust failed to stir, and Anna and the children saw clearly the expressionless profiles of the dark and fleshless secret people who run circuses. Anna collected Rebecca outside the high school gates and drove her to her cello instructor's house in Clare. She parked the car in the street, watched Becky enter through the side gate, and opened the newspaper over the steering wheel. They did this twice a week. Becky was Conservatorium scholarship material, according to the woman who instructed her. Today Anna was fidgety. She put down the paper, unfastened the catch on her daughter's satchel. Becky wrote with a small, precise hand. She did not doodle on her covers or in the margins. She gave nothing away to snoops. Anna sighed, pulled out one of Becky's textbooks. Becky had flagged an illustration: 'Wellington's troops on parade, Busaco'. Or perhaps she had flagged the accompanying text: English maps showed the sunken road but the French maps did not. From such discrepancies battles may be lost or won. The Iron Duke moved his troops unseen along the sunken road and in time was victorious in this stage of the Peninsula War. There have been eight Pandowie Showalter Lustre rams produced by the studmaster at Showalter Park. Lustre 7 sold for $60,000 in 1985. Anna saw Wesley Showalter lead Lustre 8 in the Copper Festival's grand parade around the town oval last year. Ram and owner looked topheavy. Broken blood vessels mapped the skin on Wesley Showalter's face and the blue and gold prize ribbon around the animal's shoulders had slipped and was dragging in the mud. They led the parade and were slow, too slow, so that a utility from the Holden dealership stalled, horses pigrooted and the high school band concertinaed into the rear of the float entered by Tolley's Four Square Store. There won't be a Pandowie show this year, now that Showalter Park has collapsed and the banks are trying to find buyers for the frozen straws of semen from Lustre 7 and Lustre 8. The 150th Jubilee Committee is clear about one thing for the Year 2000 festivities: the town will stage a procession along the Main North Road, starting at the railway station, passing through the town and finishing at the oval. Period costumes to mark the generations. Anna will drive up from the city and watch the parade from the verandah of her mother's shop. At least she will do that.

Home

GRANDFATHER TOLLEY CARRIED her through to the bathroom behind the shop, hurrying her along a narrow passageway hung with blistered brown wall panels, past shadowy door recesses, under a solitary low-wattage bulb that glowed dimly beneath a patina of singed moths and dust. He stood her in the chipped bath, stripped off her socks and shoes, dabbed at her bloodied knee, crescents of blood chasing one upon the other as he swiped at the injury with his washcloth. Wicked girl, unmanageable. Anna stared over his head at Hugo, who jittered in the doorway, his thumb in his mouth for the first time in years. Grandfather Tolley had rooms they'd never seen before. He lived in the shop, his kitchen and his bedroom. Sometimes he opened the sitting room for birthdays, Sunday teas. He was absorbed, solitary, shut in, a man who sought comfort in indirect light. It just shows you that a house is not a home, Anna's father said. It lacked a woman's touch. I lived there from the time I was a baby until I married your mother, and the only time I ever smelt baking or perfume was if one of his customers felt sorry for us and dropped by with a cake. He wouldn't know what to say to her. But we were okay. We managed. I would've liked a holiday at the beach now and then, but that was out of the question. He never ever saw the sea again. He tried hard not to be over-protective, but it wasn't easy for him, poor old beggar. A few years later, Anna's mother blinked at the dents where her bed had pressed against the carpet, at the shadow where 'The Haywain' had angled upon a picture wire, her voice bouncing from the empty surfaces: Isonville used to be my home, now it's just a house. Anna's father had one hand around her waist, another finger-hooked to a hatbox: Come on, Ellie. A fresh start. It's not as if I ever felt truly at home here, you know. Your father's place and all that. He saw his mistake, her offended spine and betrayed mouth, and tried to make it better. Catching Anna's eye: Get in the car, you kids, quick smart. Anna came home to Pandowie every Easter, every semester, every long weekend. Lockie would call for her at the six-forty acres and they would disappear for hours in his ute. Her mother said: We never see you. Can't you stay at home this once? Poor Hugo, he misses you desperately, you know, stuck here with us. He's always asking when you're coming home again. Pay him some attention, dear. Take him to the Wirrabara Dance tonight, why don't you? Mortified, Anna went in search of her brother. Fencing with Dad on the other side of the hill, her mother said. Anna climbed away from the house, kicking at dirt clods between the stubble rows: I am guilty of selfishness and self-absorption. I am a bad sister, a bad daughter. I have much to atone for. She found the menfolk in a creek where a flashflood had swept the fence away. Her father was saying: She'll do, mate. Hugo was saying: No,

Dad. It's crooked. This was the essential history between them. They welcomed her interruption. Two warm, uncomplicated smiles to light her advance through the wiregrass. Uncle Kitch chose a day in early spring for the Ison reunion. The women wore spring cottons, the men wore their shirtsleeves rolled to the elbow. Isons from all over Australia. Isons I hadn't known *existed*, Anna's mother said. She walked with Anna through the big rooms of her brother's house, smiling hellos to the thronging strangers. She went to the bathroom, came out stifling laughter: Anna, go and look. Anna looked. All through the day she came upon those message strips: Turn Off Light. Flush After Use. Keep Shut. Private, No Entry. Poor Uncle Kitch, she said. It's as if his home is a monster, devouring all of his money. Anna compiled her lists from the To Let notices in the *Chronicle* and the *Stock Journal*, piled the children into the car and drove through the dispiriting hours, crossing off one address, scribbling maybe against another. She didn't see how she could turn those empty hovels into homes. They were eaten up with weeds and salt damp. Their floors leaned. They were angled to resist the sun. Didn't these people *think* before they built? she wanted to know. Then the empty schoolmaster's house by the sunken road was offered for rent. It had been renovated by a weekending QC from Adelaide, who now wanted to spend his weekends on a yacht. This is our new home, Anna said, holding two little hands. You'll each have a bedroom, won't that be good? She watched the children, waiting for them to throw off their chains, thinking that she could relax when finally they relaxed. They stood mute and dazed, wall-sidlers who dared not stray from her side. It was their Uncle Hugo who saved them, with a little red wagon. Anna watched Michael balance on his heels and poke the wagon and swivel the handle and gauge the capacity. She saw him lift Becky around the waist and plonk her down on the tray top. He tugged the handle. Becky rocked, her eyes wide, her knuckles white: *Mikey, make it go!* The Conservatorium of Music wrote to say that Rebecca was obliged to enrol in person. We'll drive you down, Anna said, and went at once to the telephone: Sam to see Dr Slade about his back, 9.45 on North Terrace; a glaucoma check for herself, 11.15; the three of them to pop in on Mrs Mac in the nursing home around two o'clock. On the way home, Rebecca leaned into the space between the two front seats: Mother, where does it come from, your saying Home, James? Every time we go out anywhere. Anna had to think: You know, I believe poor old Mrs Mac used to say it whenever she picked us up after school. Home, James. We used to wonder who James was. The six-forty acres is home to Hugo now. Anna and Sam like to have dinner with him. He's a man alone, like many of the men in Anna's life. Alone doesn't necessarily mean lonely, he says. I'm content. He's a good cook. He's proud of his garden. He likes to show Anna the hidden folds in the six-forty acres, washaways he's reclaimed with a hundred young trees. Anna's last home will be a little place beside the sea. A home, not a house, as some of the places she's lived in have been. Even so, two or three times a year she will ring Pandowie and say to her mother, her brother: Get a bed ready. I'm coming home for the weekend.

Hair

WHEN THEIR SQUABBLING became more than a soul could bear, Eleanor Ison separated her children, sending Hugo and his bed, clothes, books and toys along the passage to the room her father slept in whenever he visited Isonville. It was a gentleman's room: a roll-top desk, rifles racked to the wall, a shell-casing brass vase from the fighting at Pozières, and an odour of old-time masculinity, composed of gunmetal, boot polish, leather and the tangy oils a gentleman might comb through his silvery hair and slap on his shaven jowls. And books at a lean above the roll-top desk. That's where you'd find Anna when she should have been collecting the eggs. She liked to clamber onto the desk and pull down the illustrated Bible, a volume of Bean's history of the war, or Mrs Showalter's little centenary memoir of the Showalter family. There—the Ison name, on page 4:

> Walter and Hugo Ison, brothers from Berkshire, took out a pastoral lease adjacent to the Showalters in 1847. The families became firm friends and neighbours in a relationship that has persisted to this day.

Anna stared at the photographs. It must have been a grim time in which to be a child. Those Isons and Showalters wore the stiff backs, starched collars and prohibitive expressions of a poor-house warden saying no to Oliver Twist. You couldn't see the mouths of the men for their whiskers. The women coiled their hair close to their unsmiling skulls. There was Leonard Showalter, aged three, in a sailor suit and ringlets to his shoulders. In the bathroom behind Grandfather Tolley's shop, Anna's hair had escaped from her ribbons and blood had pooled in her sock. Grandfather Tolley cleaned her up and patted her dry. Your mother will think I let you run wild. He fetched his oily, snaggle-toothed comb from the shelf above the sink: Let's fix that hair of yours. Anna winced. Her head jerked. She heard her tangles strain and rupture. He didn't know how to do it. He didn't know you were supposed to run your hand down the strands between strokes. Such lovely hair, he said. The same colour as your departed grandmother's, rest her soul. Lockie and Chester broke with constraints before anyone else in Pandowie.

Long-haired louts, according to Mr Wheelwright, but Anna found herself being drawn to their air of riskiness and bluff. Maxine showed Anna how to tease her hair: You back-comb it, like this, then spray it to fix it in place. They waltzed at the high school social, their heads puffed up and haloed under coloured lights. Pert little hard-faced mannequins, Anna's tutor sneered. Very pleased with yourselves. He pushed the album aside. He didn't want to look at photographs of the younger Anna. He didn't want to share in her rueful perspective. He was always losing interest in her, abruptly cutting her off, changing the subject, dismissing her. She'd return to her room at the college in tears. And there Lockie would be, patiently sitting by the front desk, waiting for her to return from her lectures and sign him in. Things had got so bad between them, and the tutor so consumed her, that often Anna forgot Lockie's existence. But there he was, and she stared at him, seeing him without blinkers. His hair was no longer or shorter than was fashionable, but, for the first time, it didn't look right. Badly cut, she decided. Ugly sideboards scything down his jawbone. And yet she'd always loved his looks. One day Anna stumbled blindly up the college steps and a stranger uncoiled at the front desk to greet her. Lockie had let himself be shorn. She recoiled. Such a naked, belligerent, ignorant and pimply bullet head. He looked so young and mulish. He looked so vulnerable, like a sitting duck. They went to her room. He tugged at her buttons: I'm off to camp tomorrow. Could be our last time. He proposed marriage again. He promised her a good life. He was afraid, and she was his salvation. No, she said, backing away, hugging herself tight. I can't. Within a year of marrying into the Jaegers, Anna liked to get away from them whenever she could. When Michael was a baby, she'd bundle him into the car and drive to the six-forty acres, where someone was bound to be at home, bound to show her some uncomplicated love, someone she could confide in: You know, Mum, for the first few months he was just this little baby, utterly dependent on me, always wreathed in smiles. But now he's developing a will of his own. He hates me washing and combing his hair. It's a real battle of wills. I can feel him trying to manipulate the situation his way. This little baby, who came from inside me, who's part of me, yet sometimes I feel a kind of coolness and irritation as if he's a separate being and I can't afford to let him control me. She laughed: What am I saying? He *is* a separate being. By the time Michael was three years old, Anna was taking him to Mr Chatters, around the corner from the Four Square Store in Pandowie. 'Barber' in a black and gold arc across the front window. 'Roly Chatterton, Prop.' Now say hello to Mr Chatters. Anna watched from a hard wooden chair. Mr Chatters never replaced his magazines. He was a neat, perfumed man, snipping at her son's head. Michael's hair fell in auburn clumps onto the sheet around his neck and shoulders. Your boy's got a well-shaped head, Anna. Gets it from his mother. Michael was killed on the sunken road a few days before his sixth birthday. Sam tried to make sense of it: But what were you doing there in the first place? Anna weighed up her options—the truth, a lie, an evasion, silence. She could say: I took Michael in to have his hair cut by Mr Chatters. Often when Anna visits Meg and Becky, she finds them tending to one another at the kitchen table, absorbed, dreamy, comfortable with her but somehow not registering that she is there. One will shape the other's hair, trace her lips, fasten dangly earrings to her lobes. I missed out on this when I was a kid, Rebecca says. Anna is compelled to protest: But Becky, you hated me fussing around you. Rebecca gazes at her levelly: I mean, a sister. Anna and her mother will become close, friends rather than mother and daughter. Anna will always harbour secrets but her mother will discover a need to unburden herself about the past, as if it no longer had the power to hurt her. I loved your dad, he was everything to me, but Rex Showalter was my first love. He had such lovely curly hair. Funny, we never kissed. The bank will foreclose. Sam will choose to stay on as manager for the new owner rather than change direction. I tell you, Anna, this bloke's got some strange notions about farming. Angora goats! Hairy bloody things. This is sheep country, for God's sake. Anna will bear with him, and, when he's gone, move to the coast. Her hair will go grey, then white. A crescent of Michael's hair in a locket around her neck, still auburn and shiny, somehow still nourished after all this time.

Hands

HANDS WERE ACCOUNTABLE, and they were nothing but trouble. Each weekday afternoon Anna wrapped Hugo's fingers in hers and led him out of the primary-school yard, past the high school, around the oval and along the footpath to Heinrich's Garage, opposite the Four Square Store. Look right, look left, look right again, Grandpa Tolley watching as they crossed the road toward him. He'd glance at the clock behind the cash register: on a good day he might be rid of them by four o'clock. Don't touch anything. But cement had leaked from a bag holed at the seam in the storeroom and the blue-grey powder felt as soft as talc under the children's palms. Dazed, they patted it, marking time until someone came into town to pick them up. Their mother, their father, or Mrs Mac. They wanted it to be their father, for he spent his long days hooked to the Stock & Station steering wheel and they rarely saw him. He'd pull up outside, bound into the shop and toss them to the ceiling, where buckets and watering cans swayed on hooks and wires. Then into the car, one gesturing hand on the wheel rim again, the other flicking up and down the homebound gears. They were not tough hands. How could they be, when all they did was steer from shearing shed to sale yards to field day, and scribble numbers on dockets and receipts? Not tough, but there came a time when he itched to squeeze them around Uncle Kitch's neck for driving them out of Isonville. Anna trembled, watching, waiting for it to happen. Her father's hands grew tough on the six-forty acres. He bought a sun-dulled International header and dragged it through wheat and barley crops at the wheel of an old Massey Ferguson. Watch where you put your hands. He was scrupulous about maintenance: those machines had to last. He'd wind up the header and lean into it with a dented oilcan until the blades whispered and the whirring cogs sang from belt to belt. One day Anna was so lost to wheat-stubble scratches on her bare legs that she failed to notice that he'd switched off and delivered silence to their corner of the world—until she saw blood drops balling like spilt mercury in the dust around her ankles and toes. Sweetheart, dig in Daddy's pocket for his handkerchief, will you, please? Anna looked up, arrested by his elbow. Blood beat the seconds, one drop after another, forming at the bony point, growing fat, quivering, falling. Hurry, sweetheart, please. Anna had never seen such hollows in his face before, such white, scooped, pain-etched angles. He didn't know it but his finger stump had glued itself to his diesely cotton shoulder and all Anna could think about was germs. Hurry, darling, please, there's a good girl. He stumbled, half crouched, to the little Austin, and slowly they drove back to the house, Anna shifting the gears for him. Oh, he said, hugging himself, oh, his face terribly white. When Lockie told Anna that she had nice hands she said: Nice? What's that mean, nice? *Shapely*, then, Lockie said, getting comfortable in his ute. You have shapely hands. Anna sighed, disorder flooding her belly, then tucked her jaw under his chin, where she could breathe him in, an essence of him aroused on the dance floor. The cooling engine ticked and snapped. Her left hand rested across her stomach and together she and Lockie watched her right, which was cupped on the leg of his jeans. He took her hand in both of his, stroking it, rolling the wrist, watching as the tendons and bones shaped themselves in the moonlight. Half crooked like that, Anna's ring finger was almost more beautiful than she could bear. She was filled with love for her hands. Lockie tensed: Your old man. They watched her father cross the moon-shadowed yard, Kip trotting at his heels, and disappear into the barn. A kennel chain tinkled. I'd better go in. One last kiss, Lockie said. At bath time Anna's son liked to slap the water, winding himself into an ecstatic release. Appalled, fascinated, he watched Anna take his fingers and munch on them. She said what everyone says: Michael, I could eat you up! Rebecca liked to ride high upon Sam's shoulders and endlessly track his jawline, bewitched by the whisper-scrape beneath her soft palms. There was nothing so commonplace as the sunken road after seasons of rain, heat and heavy trucks had scored and chopped and powdered it, but there was a day in April when Anna practically sailed over the corrugations, headlights on against the dust, feeling light-hearted, exhilarated, still wet. The drought-hollow sheep grazing upon the banks might not have existed. The boiling dust of the wheat truck ahead of her meant nothing at all. Mummy! Michael shouted, and it froze her blood. She glanced around for a second, a mere second. Oh, it's only a moth, sweetheart, it won't bite. A stupefied moth investigating the creases of Rebecca's sleeping wrist. Just brush it off her. Can't, Michael said, recoiling. You do it. It is only recently that Anna has understood that she has inherited Tolley hands.

She does not find them shapely at all—Lockie had simply been flattering her, all those years ago. The fingers are too short and are beginning to thicken, with little pouchy fatnesses developing between the joints, just as she remembers Grandfather Tolley's hands and her father's hands. Odd hands for such tall, shapely men. Hugo is the lucky one. He has the hands of the Isons, long and slender, with a shapely delta of tendons winking between knuckles and watchface. Anna can't bear to see the nicotine stains on such lovely hands. These days she cannot type for long. Her fingers fudge the keys, her forearms burn, her shoulders lock. If they knew, the locals would call it a judgment, not Repetition Strain Injury. They want the names of their forefathers to shine in the Pandowie sky, not skulk with landgrabbers and thieves—not in this, the lead-up to the district's 150th Jubilee. How could you write such nonsense? Sam wants to know. Their daughter also has Tolley hands, but Rebecca insists that she is not disadvantaged, claiming it's a myth that musicians benefit from long fingers. Her little hands quiver on the strings. Anna will melt a little, with a heartsore longing, to see her granddaughter's perfect tiny fingers clasp her forefinger and draw that hoary digit into her toothless mouth. There—a wet, powerful tug. Anna will not be toothless herself, for both the Isons and the Tolleys had good teeth in their heads.

War

THERE WAS THE RSL hall, the War Memorial in Redruth Square, Anzac Day, Poppy Day, Maxine's armless father, uniformed men frozen in silver frames upon sideboards and mantelpieces in every house in the district. There was an oak chest, passed down from the first Ison, squatting glumly in the hallway at Isonville, exactly where passing boots and the carpet sweeper might lay fresh bruises upon the old. Anna propped the hinged lid open against the wall, hooked her waist to the rim, and leaned in, parting inessential counterpanes and doilies to reveal the shoeboxes below. She hauled them out. They were marked Ison and Tolley, and linked her to her parents' youth and wartime. The little she knew of the wars of her grandfathers lay mainly on the surface: Grandfather Tolley's jumpy eyes after a night of tormented sleep, Grandfather Ison's cloth insignia, leggings, artillery-shell ashtray and purple ribbons, stored or displayed here and there about the house. These shoeboxes were a treasure trove of photographs: 'Sunken Road Trench, Pozières Heights, August 1916, looking east'. Mum, is this you? Her mother, dressed in baggy overalls, is straddling a bicycle outside a factory gate. My job, she replied, was to inspect for faulty cartridges. Every day I expected to be blown sky high. Anna also found ration books, a rail pass, her mother's identity card and a funeral order of service for 'Flight Navigator Rex Showalter, killed during air operations over Dusseldorf, August 1st, 1942, aged 22 years. Gladly he Answered his Country's Call'. Anna's mother blinked away the tears. We grew up together, went to school together, the Showalter boys, Uncle Kitch and me. Rex had been to Cambridge, he was a scientist, they even said he was prime minister material. Anna wondered: Were they meant to marry? There were letters home from Lance Corporal Kitchener Ison, stationed for the duration in a quartermaster's store outside Townsville:

> Thank you for your last. It sounds pretty clear to me that the Government doesn't have a clue concerning the man on the land. The Pastoral Industry has always delivered the goods and

> will do so very much better if not mucked about by all the form-filling that has to go on in wartime.

Anna could hear her uncle's voice in her head as she read the letter; he spoke then as he did now. Her father liked to say: Your mother's brother had a good war. Did her father have a bad one? His heart beat hot and cool in his diary:

> 28 April 1944. I await Eleanor's letters with the deepest longing. They sustain me, and as one mailcall after another fails to bring me the scrappiest communication from her I want to slink away like a dog and howl my homesickness at the jungle. 2 May 1944. We are surrounded here by Nips, as far as can be gathered thirty thousand, so why the delay, why no attempt to break through our lines? The odd one will slip through the lines to steal our boots or tucker, which are far superior, or set a shell to explode inside a tent of sleeping men. Two flushed out yesterday, a sabotage patrol. One emerged from behind a latrine, hands in the air, and got a rifle butt to the head for his pains. The other ran into a drain and would not come out again, so our chaps poured aviation fuel into the drain and tossed in a match or two.

Anna repacked the diary, replaced the shoeboxes. At the end of the decade, with a slump in prices, a credit squeeze, a couple of dry seasons, Grandfather Ison said: What we need is another war. He meant a war like the Korean War, when wool fetched a guinea a pound and even a sibling-divided family property like Isonville earned money to burn. Anna was disposed to hate a war that threatened to take Lockie from her, but the ballot was years off, months off yet, so she stored her anxiety somewhere at the edges of her mind. Besides, there was no one to shake it loose—certainly not the women in Women's College, wearing their pleated skirts and white ankle-socks. What finally did shake her was a studied act of loathing on the homebound train after her exams. A smiling boy no older than her was making his way through the carriages, talking to those who returned his smile, leaving broadsheets on the empty seats: 'Stop the Country to Stop the War'. Anna smiled back and called him by name. His father had shorn the sheep at Isonville and was still her father's shearer on the six-forty acres, a man who stood for Labor against the sitting Member in election after pointless election. They talked briefly, and the boy moved on. Almost at once he was there again, backing up past her seat, one supplicating hand raised to protect his chest from the men who were advancing on him, spitting hate and mad anger. Freedom of speech, he said, but they ground his leaflets and bumper stickers into the floor and finger-jabbed his ribs. Leave him alone, Anna said, and one man, beer-fed and knotted with hate, leaned his face into hers: What's it to you, slag? Pure, useless, helpless indignation rose in Anna and she pursued the pack, which shrugged her off and trampled over the boy, tossing him aside. She helped him to stand, then sit, peering at his damp eyes and dust-smudged face. Animals, she said, but he shrugged and smiled lopsidedly: Oh well. It was as if he knew too much about the world. Anna knew too little, and what she was beginning to know she couldn't put a name to, but she did know that it was fierce in her heart—fiercer, when the boys from home began to die. When her son was born she made it a rule: no guns, no uniforms, no war toys. But what was the point? She saw the crazy light in his eyes, the gun in his fist and his lust for blood whenever he played with other little boys. Only three boys from Anna's class had been spared by the ballot from fighting in Vietnam. One of them was Chester Flood. When Anna met up with Chester again, a part of her hoped that his good luck might rub off on her. The other part sank into his arms, forgetting everything. Chester was a relief from the Jaegers.

He was a beautiful, bold, unnerving, quicksilver lover, a reminder of the love she had lost. She has never forgotten those distorted faces on the Pandowie train. She sees them from time to time, most recently on the evening news, chin-jutting, spitting in the faces of women attempting to lay wreaths commemorating the rape of women in wartime. Anna telephoned the little house in North Adelaide: Is Becky all right? Was she hurt? A little shaken, Meg replied, spitting chips, but basically okay. More and more women will rise to the position of prime minister or president in the years to come, and some of them will propose or wage war. Anna will listen to the arguments—a woman like that is a traitor to her kind; a warlike disposition isn't the exclusive province of men—and find little satisfaction or relevance in either position. The point is, she will say, war makes us all hateful.

Fire

DROUGHT, PESTILENCE, FIRE. There was a summer heralded by unwanted December storms, which chased one another in from the west, flipping the Showalter Park Cessna onto its back, stimulating the wild grasses, pinching the wheat crops where they stood. When the sun reappeared in January, bringing a long run of summer heat, it was too late—the government silos brimmed with worthless grain and Isonville lay tinder dry, wide open to the first spark. What were you doing out there? Anna demanded. Hugo stood sullen and mute. She shook him. His pocket rattled. You've been playing with matches again. Hugo threw his forearm over his eyes and shrank back: Don't tell. But why should Anna tell? She wanted what he wanted. Show me, she said, and he dropped his arm, and relaxed, and gradually the lineaments of his mania reappeared and he turned and led her through the grass, away from the house with its knowing eyes behind the candy-stripe noonday blinds. They had been taught to strike away from the body. It's gone out, Anna said, staring at the match on the ground—but it hadn't, the sun had robbed the tiny flames of colour, that's all. Then, before their eyes, the flames had shape and colour, eating swiftly through the grass, leaving ashen shapes like black and grey after-images in the dirt. Hugo danced at the edges, panicky, elated: Don't let it get away! She felt it, too, a fire-lick in her belly. That was on Isonville. No playing with fire on their six-forty acres, where everything was precarious. When the little Austin truck had had its day, her father didn't dump it in the creek or sell it to a wrecker but stood a two-stroke pump, hoses and a couple of 44-gallon drums of dam water on the tray and called it his fire plant. One late February evening, when the superheated air had been gusting for forty-eight hours without a break, Anna saw her father stop in his tracks, tip back his head, and sniff the wind. I don't like it, he muttered. She was halfway across the yard with him, Kip dancing around their feet, tormented by the flap of mutton in his hands. It's a bad one, he said, moving on to the kennel and the chain. Anna paused for a moment in the darkness, spooked now, the night assuming lost cries and flickers around her. She followed the jerking torch into the shed. She wanted to know what it was her father had seen or heard or smelt on the wind, but then she came upon him in one of his old, comforting postures, down on one knee, crooning as he clipped the chain to Kippy's collar, and the world righted itself again. They returned to the house, arm in arm, discussing her coming year in the city. The call to save the town came at one o'clock in the morning. Pandowie, nineteen miles away, with a fireglow in the black hills behind it like a war, or hell, or a city of brawling nightclubs. They had scarcely reached Dead Man's Corner in the little Austin when Channel 7 waved them down. Lose any stock or property, anyone hurt, anyone killed? reporters wanted to know, swarming around the truck. Anna's father stared at them, a terrible stare. Finally he snarled: We're here, the fire's way the hell over there, *you* work it out. Ghouls. Morons. A little village of headlights and trestle tables had been set up in a dry creek bed in a forgotten gully deep in the hills, and for the next twelve hours Anna and her mother helped to make sandwiches and mugs of tea. The men were called the menfolk. They drove in, dog-tired, stopped for a while, drove out again. Anna stared after them, dreaming that she stood on a tilting deck, hosing down the flames, but she liked it with the women too, a place where she heard things she realised she was hungry to hear. One day in August, Lockie drove down to the city to show her his call-up notice. Burn it, she said, stung into taunting him by the expression in his eyes, his queer, dreamy pride and hunger, his bitten, angular, country fingers. Burn the fucking thing. She made to snatch it from him: Here, give us it. You're sick, he said, jerking away from her, they've twisted your mind, and suddenly ugliness and struggle were there in the room with them. When Wesley Showalter paid Sam to cut up and burn a massive pine tree that had split and collapsed in heavy winds, Anna took the children to see the bonfire. Suddenly she remembered Hugo, his matches, and anxiously searched the faces of her children as they watched the flames. Nothing abnormal; they hadn't inherited that mania. The flames reduced the old tree to a bed of coals and a wall of heat. Anna stood watching with her children. Behind them the stud cattle watched. Still smoking, Michael said, two days later as they made the school run on the sunken road. And the cows and heifers were a few metres closer. On the third morning they saw the cattle standing around the ashy remains like spokes in a wheel, facing out, tails up, squirting long, hard and steamily upon the coals. It must be nature, Anna said, and it became something to giggle about over the years. Anna had assumed that she was done with fiery love. That part of her life was over and it had been fiery enough to last her forever, all that passion and pain. Someone solid and dependable, that's what she'd needed after Lockie died, and that's what she'd got in Sam Jaeger. But the body mends, or some states are temporary, for she woke up one day wanting to burn again. It was a disappointment she hadn't counted upon, Sam's muted needs. Companionship was all very well, but it was hard to let go of her need for passion. And where was the companionship now, anyway? Along with his emotional and sexual thrift, Sam was obsessive, he couldn't sleep, he was eaten up inside with hatred for his father. Anna is writing about fire for the town's Jubilee history: The Ngadjuri used fire to regenerate the scrubland. George Catford, founder of the Pandowie Lode, died when he fell, intoxicated, into an open fire. Fires burned in the mine shafts before the waters came. Fires lay waste to our livelihoods. We are forged in fire. As she writes, she wonders if anyone is interested. When Anna stays with Meg and Rebecca in the city, they might return from a draughty concert hall on a wintry night and stand before the gas heater like the three monkeys. Rebecca says that this is the only time she can see the benefit of wearing a dress, for she is able to bunch the skirt around her waist and roast the backs of her thighs. Anna will have central heating in her house beside the sea. A thermostat will cut in and out and warmed air will whisper in all the rooms. Bushfires on the evening news, that's the closest she will get to naked flames when she is old, and she will never be quite warm enough.

School

DURING THE COURSE of each long summer, Anna and Hugo pushed at the boundaries on their bicycles, drawn farther and farther away from Isonville by unanticipated bush tracks, gates, mine shafts and washaways, yet always they returned to the old school ruin on the sunken road, where the spirit of their mother still moved within the crumbling classroom walls. Nettles and licheny stones covered the rotting floorboards. A tilting chimney, a door frame, two window frames, three half walls and rudimentary roofbeams suggested the shape and dimensions of the old school, while the mind's eye, and their mother's kitchen-table stories, supplied the rest. Faded blackboard paint remained on one of the walls, and whoever those final pupils had been they had left a perfectly proportioned yellow alphabet across the top and the twelve-times table down one side. The desks were long gone. Only the schoolmaster's residence remained intact. Showalter Park sprawled a few hundred metres away across the lucerne flats, the homestead screened by lawns and a box-hedge from a chapel, a woolshed, a dairy and a scatter of stone workers' cottages, shearers' quarters, barns and workshops, set among red gums, pines and weeping willows. A sufficient number of cooks, servants, stablehands, stockmen, blacksmiths, well-sinkers and gardeners and their families had lived on the property before the First World War to warrant the school. Showalter Park had been a self-supporting feudal enclave, and the Showalters and their practices were considered, by Government House aides-de-camp, to be a suitable diversion for circulating earls and minor princesses. By the early thirties, when the Showalter boys were riding to the school in a horse and sulky driven by the children from Isonville, the school belonged to the Education Department. Anna's mother tapped her finger on an old photograph: It was the Depression. There were only ten pupils left. Me, your Uncle Kitch, Wes and Rex Showalter, the overseer's kids, a couple of sharefarmers' kids. Kitch and I would collect the Showalter boys and park the sulky in that little stonewalled paddock at the back of the school and let the horse go. Rain or shine, five days a week. By jingo, those frosty mornings could bite. I get chilblains just thinking about it. Habits of contempt and cruelty at the high school enabled Anna and the others to ignore Chester Flood. He had no parents; he lived at the convent; he had the skinny, raw-boned cast of someone born to poverty, dirt and cunning. Five out of ten; nought out of ten; two out of ten. Twice he was put back a year. Ink stained his fingers and sleeves; his trousers were holed and shiny, revealing his hard, brown, possibly grimy flanks. Mr Wheelwright bent Chester Flood over a desk and cut him with a whistling cane. Anna stopped breathing: Chester held out until the fourth cut, then lifted his bony, martyred skull and cried out, a long, throaty cry of protest and deep, deep pain. Anna was impressed by his close and very human flesh and odour, his snuffling tears and nose-wiping misery. Yet he remained invisible, and Anna and the others saw him beaten so often that finally they failed to register that it was happening. A tutor at the university left his desk one day and crossed the room in front of Anna, saying: Let's give ourselves some privacy here. She heard a faint snip: he'd locked his office door. She looked up and saw the heat and gleam of powerful feelings on his face. He hovered a moment, then pulled an office chair close to hers. Their knees touched, precipitating in Anna a breathless, anticipatory paralysis. He leaned close to her, vinyl squeaking under his rump. The man was notorious, and Anna waited. When his warm, dry hands picked up her wrist and kneaded the tendons in her forearm, she closed her eyes briefly and swallowed. She heard his low, goading voice through the veil of her emotions: I read your article in the student rag. What could you possibly know? You are an empty page waiting for experience to write itself across you, and the sooner the better. Have you ever had an idea of your own? That pretty head of yours is full of refectory talk, correct me if I'm wrong. Anna heard his loathing even as his warm hands crept along her compliant upper arms. When he had reduced her to tears he began to kiss her, a hundred highly charged bites and lip-pulls on her neck and earlobes. She was dependent, submissive, emotionally captive. Then the phone rang and he exhaled involuntarily and Anna smelt an old, old corruption working inside him. But still, he took her to his house in Unley and she went willingly. When Anna married and had children, one of the burdens of her existence was the interest her parents-in-law showed in the spiritual growth of their grandchildren. They were appalled to learn that the primary school did not offer religious instruction of any kind, let alone instruction in the many faiths of which they disapproved. They undertook to guide Anna's children in spiritual matters, and soon Rebecca and Michael were clapping hands for Jesus and reading comic-strip moral tales printed on blurry cheap paper. Anna's husband is on the Parents and Friends Committee for the high school these days, a body that quivers with responsibility now that the government has given local bodies the right to determine who will teach their young. Sam's eyes burn: We don't want any ratbags on the staff. What have you heard about So-and-so? he'll ask—which Anna takes to mean: Is So-and-so left-leaning, ambiguously single or tinged with foreignness? Among the illustrations she has collected for her history of the town is a photograph of pupils outside the Showalter Park school in 1879. There are a couple of gawky eighteen-year-olds towering above the little kids. Maybe one of them is Elijah Ison, son of one of the original Ison brothers. Elijah later joined the Pandowie Social Improvement Association:

> It is a grand opportunity for a young fellow from the Bush to improve himself in moral and intellectual matters. I recited Elegy Written in a Country Church-yard by Thomas Gray, a capital piece, and got taken to task for standing incorrectly.

Anna will regret that she didn't finish her degree. She will enrol in the University of the Third Age and start again. It will be unkindly put to her that women undertake further study in order to leave their husbands, but Anna will need no such artificial means. Died when he was fifty-three. Heart attack.

Naked

BODIES WERE HIDDEN from view and so Anna imagined them. From a sketchy beginning—Hugo's description of a pale, loose, globish bottom briefly glimpsed when Grandfather Ison undressed in the light leaking through the bedroom door from the hallway, pom pom pomming as though he hoped he were not being observed by the little boy in the corner bed—Anna constructed the old man's thick legs, padded grey back, drum-tight, hanging, hairy stomach, thin white arms abruptly sun-browned from wrist to fingertip, and a generalised dark accumulation at the mid-point of his body. She saw her mother once, full length from the rear, towelling herself dry in the ladies' bathroom along the corridor from their rooms at the Delmonte Hotel. She registered these things before her mother shyly dragged a satiny flowered robe over her dampness: streaked, mottled pink skin, a wet shoulder blade missed by the towel, knobbly bones revealed along the bent-over spine, a referred jelly shake of thigh and buttock as one dried foot and then the other landed solidly upon the squelchy floor tiles. She only ever saw her father's torso. It was broad, vulnerably stippled with freckles and moles, moving minutely as he scraped a cut-throat razor over his whiskers in the mornings. Hugo's body was about as relevant to Anna as her own. The children enticed their cousins to the old school at a bend in the sunken road and ordered them to strip, squat open-legged for inspection, urinate, defecate, Anna cool and curious, Hugo bow-shouldered and shivering, the bobbing eye of his finger-thin stem like an extra, eager spy at the proceedings in the cobwebby ruin. Anna found little privacy in the boarding house of her mother's old grammar school. Bodies, morning, noon and night—in the showers, in the changing rooms, in the narrow shared territory between each pair of iron cots. Convinced that her breasts were too small, the thatch at her groin too sparse, her cleft as featureless as a little girl's, she shut herself in a lavatory cubicle and perched upon the closed lid with a mirror. Suddenly there were footsteps inside the bathroom and the sounds of shouted laughter, flushing water, doors and singing, then silence, then another burst. Anna breathed shallowly, encouraged into a sense of hidden sin and power, and watched her fingers. Wonderfully, she saw herself grow and open. She was reminded of unfolding flowerheads and rock-pool anemones, the dewiness on their bracketing lips. She decided: Not different, just a variation. She ran away home, and within three or four years they were calling her experienced, loose with her body. Exaggerated, unfair, but Anna learned to live with it. One thing that she wanted, apart from love, was to see a boy stand unselfconsciously naked in the sunlight. The boy who could do that would be one she could love, and who would love her. But all Anna got was the darkness of the back roads and the impatient clankle, slap and zip of unbelting jeans. Nothing to see and nothing worth looking at—not until Lockie made love to her in long grass on the Razorback. Anna's English tutor took her to his house in Unley. The people there smiled in a sleepy dope haze, elbow-propped on cushions on the floor, and waved her in. The tutor rested the back of his head on Anna's thigh and stared glitteringly up at her. He was putting it on, trying to look demoniacal. Anna watched closely when a new joint went around: handle gingerly, draw back in hyperventilating huffs, snatch away from the mouth, hold in for several seconds, then release. She applied the yellow body paint to the tutor's chest and stomach. Another woman there decorated his cheeks and forehead with broad strokes of red and blue. A third striped him green and gold from his hips to the blades of his feet and threaded gold glitter foil in the tangled hair between his legs. That left his genitals unpainted, a sad bunch of cold-shrunken lumps. The three women seemed to sober simultaneously, to draw back from him. He said plaintively: Anna, won't you finish me? Anna thought guiltily of Lockie, of his beauty. She didn't know that Lockie had followed her to the house. In the morning he confronted her: Two-timer. He said: You're drifting away from me. Then he was gone to the war and she had no word from him for months, only the card describing the sun-shot South China Sea. She evoked his body in her mind's eye. In her worst moments, parts of him were torn away under the impact of landmines and sniping bullets. The son Anna gave birth to five years later was part of her cure. First the crown of his head, playing hide and seek with her in an angled mirror, and to get to that point she cried out, moaned and huffed for almost twelve hours, sometimes directing unregretted snarls upon the nurses, whose ministering hands had become a torment. Finally she pushed, and at last she saw all of him, gliding out of her in a heaven-sent rush. Sam leaned close to her and articulated carefully, as if she were deaf or feeble-minded: He's perfect! A perfect little body. Well done! They called him Michael, an old Ison name. Anna often caught herself beaming at him entranced—his arms and legs stirring the air, his edible fatness. Sometimes it seemed a pity to clothe him, although he did look fine in clothes, in baby clothes, toddler clothes, the shorts, shirt and sandals he wore on his first day at school. She kept these things for some time after the accident, until Sam told her not to be morbid. When he said: Pass them on to Maxine's kid, Anna wondered: Does he ever think before he says anything? And so her body abhorred his. Sam rarely wanted her anyway, but, whenever he closed in, she grew agitated, her trunk and limbs hunting for a way out before freezing finally, waiting for his touch. She wondered: Does my body bear the mark of my loss? People stare at me on the street—do they know from gossip or does my body betray me? Rebecca and Meg like to shower together, soak in a hot bath together, the door open so that they can draw Anna into their conversations. Anna is accustomed to it. Meg, she's noticed, is big-boned, swaggering and strong-looking, her body apt to wrap itself around little Rebecca and never let go. It seems to Anna that, for Meg, lesbianism is a sexual expression; for Rebecca, political. When Anna sees Sam naked now it's when he's tossing his workclothes on the laundry floor and stepping into the back-porch shower stall. He's getting paunchy, more and more like his father every day. She wonders what else stirs him now, apart from his dream for the 150th Jubilee. She supposes that he will grow old and begin to shrink, as will they all. Anna will visit her mother in the retirement home behind the Pandowie Hospital and one day happen to see the old woman dart with a giggle from the bathroom to the gown behind the bedroom door, and be struck by how youthful the naked body may seem, even after eighty-four years of gravity.

City

THEY ALL FELT the push and pull of the city on the coast. Grandfather Ison retired to Burnside when his daughter married the Tolley boy from Pandowie; Grandfather Tolley depended upon a distributor in Hindley Street for his weekly film canisters; books from the sandstone library on North Terrace were parcelled up for the children once a month; Stock & Station obliged the children's father to attend head office from time to time; and the family holidayed at the Delmonte in Glenelg every January. When the children were small they were taken to see the lights of Rundle Street, where the big department stores sat like bishops and sniffed as you passed through their doors. The city had embraced neon, the merchants scribbling and stamping their businesses with it. Names stuttered and glowed in red and white behind plate glass, climbed external walls, or popped hoarsely above the heads of the country women who had come down for the sales, one arm herding their cowed children, the other locked on their shopping bags against purse-snatchers and undesirables. At night, Rundle Street swam in neon. Rubbernecks crawled along in their cars. Anna discovered that if she were to blink her eyes rapidly and sway her head, the neon stretched and yawed like molten elastic. One night she felt cut down and tossed aside as if she were nothing. A car crammed with wild children pulled up alongside the Stock & Station Holden at a traffic light, and Anna made the mistake of looking at them. Dreaming, floating, cocooned in metal and glass, she believed that she was joined to all the children in the world. But, in the crowded window opposite her, three long, livid tongues rolled out and membraned the glass, three pairs of cross-eyes looked into her brain, three mouths were prised wide and wetly open. Anna gasped and looked away, shocked, hurt, defenceless for the first time. Normally she had plenty of nerve—after all, she had roamed the back roads seeking her father and seen dead and dying lambs and the flickering tongues of tiger snakes—but no one had been unthinkingly cruel to her before. The blood rushed to her face and she was deeply ashamed. Sometimes her father drove them to a cracked brick house in Mile End. The back yard faced a railway line and the house and yard seemed to crouch and slink away from the constant iron thunder. It was never spring or autumn in that place, only scorching mid-summer, and Anna sensed that the man who lived there, her father's offsider in Borneo in 1944, had slipped in the world and had farther to slip. He had a twangy voice riddled with sullenness, a face tucked and pillowed from the beer. She played quietly in the dead grass with Hugo, while the wives struggled to find a common ground in the shade of the verandah and the men drank themselves into risky moods. A kind of raucous irony and scorn came over her father when he was drunk. He liked to drive back through leafy suburbs in search of victims, shouting insults at pedestrians who seemed too buttoned-down or too good to be true. It aroused the children. They saw surprise and offence in the receding faces as the car accelerated away, and crammed their fists in their mouths to smother their snorting laughter. Even their mother was aroused. She slapped him affectionately: Peter, you'll get us arrested. But somehow their delight in him always spoilt the mood. He'd scowl and shut down abruptly, as though displeased that they could be so easily diverted. When she finished at the primary school, Anna was sent to her mother's old grammar school in the city. You'll be able to say, My mother was an old girl. The school hummed with the untroubled assumptions of caste and privilege, where wealth came second and intellect third. Black cars whispered along the bordered drives and shoe leather snapped on the polished floors. There must have been streets and houses beyond the ivied perimeter wall but Anna couldn't see them. She was served pâté on a sliver of toast in her housemistress's room and didn't know what it was. Even sprawling on the grass was beyond her. She didn't have the style for it. She was in a well-watered, green, ascendant world and seven days later she ran away from it. As the taxi downshifted for the descent through the Pandowie Hills, Anna leaned forward to peer at the wheat stubble, someone's dust-scribbling farm ute, a sparrowhawk floating in the air currents, the meandering stonewall fences, and finally the blue-grey bends and curves of the sunken road far in the distance. There, she said, pointing her finger. When she turned eighteen she didn't want to leave Lockie, but she couldn't wait to leave the bush. The city, the idea of the city, excited her now. Besides, Lockie was only three hours north by road. On the day on which paint was splashed over her face and clothes and the placard wrenched from her hands outside the Raintree Corporation, Anna saw the hate-filled faces along the footpath and remembered the children who had spoilt the city lights for her, twelve years ago. She remembered the howling pack in the Pandowie train, pursuing the shearer's son. Anna's parents insisted on a slap-up wedding in Adelaide, in the well-bred Burnside church where Grandfather Ison was still remembered by all the old sextons and vigorous powdered widows. Anna glowed in her wedding dress. Sam looked crisp and vivid, his white shirt, his black suit and tie. But afterwards, as the big hired saloon crept away along an elm tree corridor, Sam's hand landed on Anna's knee and she saw how scoured and raw it was, a raw-boned bushman's hand that was nothing like Lockie's. She thought: Lockie and I would have had a romantic, irregular, disastrous marriage, full of lies and vows, and it would have been all I ever wanted. She wondered: What sort of children will Sam and I have? They made many trips to the city to seek a cure for Rebecca's asthma. Their daughter had inherited, from the Isons, allergies to everything around her: animal hair, house dust, yeast, dairy foods, pollen. The specialist swung in his swivel chair high above North Terrace: Also, don't let her get excited. Ideally you should move to the city to live. Anna gazed past his shoulder to the spires of the Cathedral, which obscured the red-brick wing of Women's College where she'd had a room and read arguments for and against the existence of God and made love to Lockie twice a month. She didn't speak. She went home and said to Becky: You're getting an education. Well, Rebecca knew that anyway. Rebecca studied at the Conservatorium and bought a house of her own and suffers now only when seasonal winds blow dust and pollen from the inland across the city. Many of Anna's contemporaries have sold out and moved to Brisbane and Perth, seeking sunshine and burgeoning economies. According to the latest census, over two thousand young people have left rural areas for the city. Anna's twin cousins have married a pair of Adelaide suits and so the Ison name will die out when Kitch and Lorna die. When it's time for Anna to leave she will settle for a place close to the wind-whipped sands of Henley Beach. She will find herself thinking more and more of that city woman, her grandmother, taken by a shark long before she was born.

Dress

WHENEVER ANNA'S MOTHER and her dressmaking friends settled down to sew and gossip, the supple nouns and verbs of a co-existent language floated there in the room with them: fittings, patterns, sizes, measuring tape, buttons, cotton reels, balls of wool, leftover material, sewing-machine burr, pins-in-the-mouth murmurs, the clack of needles, and the eyes-narrowed, calculated final assessment of a dress, a pullover, a blouse. Anna stood on a kitchen chair and they turned her around and around, tucking and pinning. Everything has to be red with Anna at the moment, her mother said. When the dress was ready, Anna raced to the other end of the house. Mrs Mac leaned her rump on the sink and said: Aren't you the pretty one? With a huge, hammering heart, Anna glanced down and slowly, slowly, smoothed the cloth over her thighs. My party frock, she said, and in the mirror the skirt frothed about her knees, concealing, revealing, concealing. Auntie Beulah? she said, swishing inches from her great aunt's tartan rug. She said it again: Auntie Beulah? Like my new dress? But the old woman's watery eyes were watching her lost love and she was singing to him, so low that Anna could scarcely hear her. Mrs Mac wheeled Beulah into the sun. You mustn't mind, dear. She's wandering a bit these days. Anna stood and thought about that, the tips of her fingers seeking reassurance from the red cherries on the white collar. She had imagined saying to Great Aunt Beulah: See, the belt goes through here. See the buttons? See the cherries? Mum embroidered them. Then for a couple of years Anna wanted to dress only as a boy. She had a rough and tumble life and felt too skinny, too gawkish, too false, to wear a dress or a skirt and blouse. Twelve, thirteen, fourteen. Suddenly Anna had legs and a drowsy, catch-breath appreciation of them. Her legs drew the gaze; she drew the gaze. She wore tights to school, a tanning shade of brown, with one dazzling white knee truss to reinforce the effect. She sat where Lockie could watch her during the grinding hours on the Bitter Wash schoolbus, perched opposite him on the sideways-facing seat above a rear-wheel arch, tormenting him by bunching the slippery purple and gold folds of her uniform about her thighs. The netball changing room was the science lab. Boys might catch Anna and Maxine there, framed in the window, slow-handed, grinning a wide-eyed O of mock dismay. Anna's mother said: For the ninetieth time, there simply isn't the money. It's been a bad year and Dad wants us to make economies where we can. And so Anna blamed him, too, for letting her appear in a home-made gown at the high school ball. She could not see the quality of the cut or the fabric, or the skilled hand, only that the gown was not shop-bought. Nothing would make her beautiful, so what would make her uglier? Lashing eyes and a tongue that could cut to the bone, that's what. When her father asked her to dance the Pride of Erin, she folded her arms and stared fiercely at the floor. Then for the next two hours she flung herself into half a dozen self-abasing back seats in the chilly car park while the band played softly inside the hall and warm shapes revolved behind the yellow windows. Anna greatly loved a black cotton jumper but it betrayed her in the end. She wore it next to her skin at lectures and whenever she went home to Pandowie. One twilight Saturday she returned to the house with chattering teeth, her arms wrapped across her chest, and met her mother's long, unblinking, expressionless gaze as Lockie tooted goodbye outside: Anna, it might interest you to know that your jumper is inside out. For exercise, for a distraction, Anna attended dance classes in an upstairs studio along a forgotten alley behind Victoria Square. Here she flexed as though she were naked, her bare feet slapping down upon the varnished floorboards. A woman called Connie remarked, admiring her: They must have had you in mind when they invented the leotard. The dress Anna wore to the Showalter Park field day was for Chester Flood, not the field day women. At two o'clock she poured a final cup of tea, draped the apron over a fold-up chair and slipped away from the catering tent to hunt for the children. By half-past two she was soothing them to sleep on Chester's bed: Sssh, darling, a little nap, and then we'll go home to Daddy. She joined Chester in his sitting room. She removed her shoes. She curled her toes in the thick pile of his carpet, turned her back, lifted the hair away from the nape of her neck. They didn't speak. Chester's hands flicked down her back, freeing buttons one by one along her spine. The dress sighed to the floor. Suddenly Rebecca appeared in the doorway, knuckling her eyes: Mummy. Anna took her to the bathroom, then back across Chester's long carpet to the bedroom, and when she returned to Chester's warm arms the world had tilted a little. Did she . . . ? I don't think she saw anything, Anna replied. But I'll make it into a game in the car going home, so she won't know who she's seen today or where she's been. For a long time after the accident, grief and mottled legs eroded Anna's confidence. Sam said: You're incredible, you know that? If I mention that I like you in dresses, you assume I'm saying you look bad in pants. And all these dark colours all the time. Snap out of it. They were days of struggle. Anna's mother came by with the old sewing machine: At least let me show you how to run up a dress. Anna made skirts, workclothes for Sam, little dresses for Rebecca. She saved hundreds of dollars that way. When Rebecca grew touchy and particular, she taught her to sew. But it was more than simply teaching Rebecca how to sew. Theirs was a relationship weighed down by complications. Anna wanted her daughter to stop settling that fatalistic gaze upon her, and she wanted her daughter to know how to fend for herself, take responsibility, pay her own way. Rebecca made dresses if she had to, but mostly she made shirts and trousers. She grew into a quick, slight, moody woman, suited to pants and jeans. If she can get away with it she wears loose black pants rather than a dress when the orchestra is playing. Rebecca and Meg don't hide anything from Anna. For example, Meg is interested in inversions. She stages parties at which everyone must wear a dress. She likes to experiment in low-key S&M with Rebecca. It's the marginality I like, she tells Anna, the tinge of danger, the eroticisation, the giving over of the self when I play-act and dress in chains and leather. But we don't hurt each other, nothing like that. Anna will dress to flatter as she grows old. She will argue that she doesn't see why she shouldn't display some flair and style in her declining years. Old women in humdrum situations like to watch the young ones parade in their new clothes, but Anna's attitude is: Not me, sister, not me.

Running

A FRESH START somewhere new—that's how Grandfather Tolley, irreproachably polite, avoided the unwelcome question. His questioners would nod thoughtfully in Tolley's Four Square Store, and put two and two together: the taciturn man with his city clothes, the motherless small boy—obviously he's running from something. Grandfather Tolley didn't tell them that he was placing a specific memory behind him, an image of his young wife flailing in the red-frothed shallows, bewilderment on her face, then fear and shock, then her eyes dulling, dulling. She ran out on him: She died having the kid—both neatly accounted for his gloominess, his presence in the town. Not that the circumstances mattered; something bad had happened, and he'd run from it, simple as that. And so the shark-snatch story remained a family secret. Anna's other grandfather had also run away from heartbreak. Family and strangers conspired against Grandfather Ison during the Great War, leaving him propertyless and obsessed with property. He left to make his mark, inched his buckboard through the saltbush and mallee scrubland near Pinnaroo, broke an axle, and wept. After the rolling guns and mud of the Sunken Road Trench at Pozières, and the chattering of his five sisters, he'd never heard such dense silence. After the neat geography of the trenchlines and his wife's and his children's chubby curves, he'd never been in such a tangled, stringy, monochrome place. Nothing would yield to the match or the axe. A voice told him that he should provide. Another told him that others had done him wrong. Louder, more insistent, was the voice that told him he was not up to it. What made Anna run? A permanent dissatisfaction, to begin with. As soon as she was capable of toddling on bandy legs she wanted to venture beyond the hedge at Isonville, drawn not so much by the promise of the world as by her father's unaccountable absence every day. She saw him disappear in the Stock & Station car after breakfast, and it was a rare and precious evening if he were there to read to her at bedtime. She hooked her fingers to the thick, white, plaited wires of the garden gate and screamed inconsolably at his departing dust. But someone always carted her struggling into the house and her toys, and the memory faded—until the next morning, when her father betrayed and abandoned her yet again. Once it was Dr Pirie who brought her back, rumbling over the corrugations on the sunken road in his mud-splashed black Humber. Uncle Kitch and Aunt Lorna spotted her from the overseer's cottage and telephoned the big house, grimly satisfied, for although they didn't have a proper home they did have ginghamed twin daughters who never roamed. Dr Pirie encountered Anna on the road for a second time, the mail contractor once, and twice strangers delivered her to the Pandowie police station in Redruth Square. She never did find where her father had gone. Later Anna developed a private running, to places in her head, away from her squared and regulated back yard. Or she'd give herself up to the animistic fig and apricot trees and be unaware of the stonewall perimeter fence or what lay beyond it, so fully absorbed was she by a ladybird, a chip of flint or a broken-backed sparrow's nest. Buoyed by their first good harvest on the six-forty acres, Anna's parents sent her to boarding school in the city. She was twelve years old. She shared desks with twelve-year-old city kids, farm kids like herself, and hard and knowing kids from the remote station country, boarders since the age of five. Anna reasoned that the object of the school was to break her spirit. The staff obliged her to be a young lady, the other boarders a teary wretch. The world was a bigger place than Anna had supposed it to be. It was full of swifter runners, more fluid minds and longer ancestries than she could claim. On Sunday morning, when the two hundred boarders filed through the leafy streets from the boarding house to the Cathedral, Anna hung back, edged away, found a taxi rank. Pandowie, she said, and the driver blinked: Oh yeah? Who's paying? My father. Yeah? Who's he when he's at home? We have a property, Anna replied, and saw deference and calculation form in the man's eyes. Three hours later she was home, spinning giddily in the push and pull of everyone's dismay, guilt, outrage and admiration. The taxi man accepted a cheque. Anna was home. She caught the Bitter Wash schoolbus at the end of the potholed drive now, and a wildfire of whispers spread from her notorious centre.

Later, when the kids from school began to die in the foreign war, boys she had teased and kissed and ignored and endured, Anna was poised to slip away. Then Lockie died. She fled; her mind retreated. She came to a place where the black layers of self folded upon each other until she had only an intermittent and fragmentary awareness of others. It was like a rehearsal for dying. Voices reached her through the fog: *Face up to it; don't run from it.* She wasn't running—she was fading to nothing like condensation on a window. Six weeks were lost to her, a catatonia induced by a loss she thought she'd never bear. But she had a return ticket, time gave her a return ticket, and she was Anna again. She did not refer to this time as running away, or even as getting over a loss, but simply as moving on. Later, when Michael was killed, she would not have been able to run away even if she'd wanted to. She had a family to consider this time. Just the other day Sam said, picking his way through the words: There was a time early on when I thought you were long gone. He shrugged: I even wanted to run off myself. But you and Becky have made life worth living, you know that? Anna opened and closed her mouth, her defences gone to nothing, and realised that it would once have been a burden, hearing him say that. She wrapped him in her arms and they swayed clumsily together. She often finds herself examining that term: running away. Three sets of neighbours have sold out or walked off their properties and gone to live in Queensland, most of the district's school leavers head straight for Adelaide every year, and last week a young mother drove to the Showalter Hill lookout, ran exhaust gases into the interior of her car with a length of hose, and gently killed herself and her baby daughter. Running away? Anna has considered the separate heartaches of her grandfathers and herself, and examined the times when she had gone looking for love to replace love that had grown pinched, bad or nonexistent, and is of the opinion that there is no such thing as running away. Or rather, she can hear someone like Meg correcting her: *Running away? A value judgment.* Anna will leave for the city when Sam dies, and be told by some of the locals that she's another one running out on the district, but her line will be: Why endure the unendurable? From time to time she will disconcert her loved ones with this notion. For Anna it will be enough if just one or two of them take her advice and move on to something better.

Christmas

ON CHRISTMAS DAY, the Tolleys, the Isons and Mrs Mac groaned around the table in Beulah's half of the big house. It was a day of blind eyes, blind to Mrs Mac's singing, Eleanor Ison's one cigarette of the year. Anna and Hugo liked to watch their mother puff and giggle through a couple of sherries, well-being rising pink from her breasts to her throat, highlighting her cheeks. Then the old ones died and Kitch edged Anna's family out into the cold. Now there was only Grandfather Tolley, and he drove out to the six-forty acres or they carted a cooked turkey to his house behind the shop. Anna's mother didn't abandon her Christmas Day cigarette and sherries, but the flush at her throat lost its innocence, apt to grow hard red with hurt and anger: My own father, my own brother. How could they do that to me? The Tolleys were on the guest list for Christmas drinks at Showalter Park because Wesley Showalter and Anna's mother had grown up together. They came to the main gate. Holly. They drove in. Christmases at Showalter Park had once intimidated her father. Until he owned the six-forty acres, he'd been forced, on Christmas mornings, to endure the drunken back-slaps of

Wesley Showalter, who boxed him around the compass on three hundred and sixty-four days of the year, arranging the sale and shipment of the Park's hoggets, ewes and rams. But the six-forty acres made him almost an equal, on those white-cloth, long-tabled Showalter Park lawns on Christmas mornings. He even bred from a couple of bottom-of-the-range Showalter Park rams. Anna was not prepared for her first Christmas Day with Lockie. She sat mute, wide-eyed, stirred to the core, as love and discord raged about her head. Lockie had a chain-smoking, corner-of-the-mouth father, a heavy, slippered mother who shouted dear at her above the racket, and a Queensland heeler stretched out on the dark pantry floor. He had a tribe of little snatching brothers and sisters, and uncles and aunts who lashed out to cuff whining earholes and skinny bare legs. And he had Chester Flood, who had no love or family of his own, only district gossip and an orphan's bunk bed at the convent in Truro Street. Anna nodded at Chester, who sat as patient and unblinking as a hunting bird, family life whirling around him and brown beer bottles accumulating on the kitchen table. She gazed at him covertly. He was here, he was clearly Lockie's friend. It was as though she were seeing him for the first time, as though the stigmatised kid at school had been someone else all that time. In the first year of her marriage to Sam Jaeger, Anna installed a new kitchen range and her mother's recipes in the transportable home at the lip of the gully and offered to do the Christmas cooking. But she hadn't counted on Mrs Jaeger: You'd better let me do the turkey, dear. I think I'd better do the pudding this year. Dad likes a skin on his custard. Do I detect rum in this, dear? Anna was offended. She refused to see it as Sam urged her to see it, a blessed release from labouring for hours over a hot stove on Christmas Eve and Christmas morning. She saw it for what it really was, an exercise in power and control. Anna could never please Sam's mother, even if she were to clap hands for Jesus twice an hour. So why did she continue trying to please the woman? Every Christmas Day, exactly at noon, Anna and Sam loaded presents, ham and a potato salad into a cane basket and stumbled down the stony hill behind their skipping children. Into the scorching kitchen. Mrs Jaeger would peel back the linen teatowel and sniff at the potato salad: I'm not sure if there's room on the table for all this. They chewed stolidly through the hours. Even Michael and Rebecca grew quieter, quieter. The music of Christmas in those stern years was a knife clatter on the best china, liquid jaws, the toe of Becky's sandal ***kick kick kick*** against the stout, impregnable leg of the Jaegers' dining-room table. Anna saw the years fall away from her father's face when he inherited Grandfather Tolley's shop, quit the six-forty acres and returned to the town. Tolley's Four Square Store beat warmly between the Tourist Office and the fish and chip shop in the main street, a place for Daily Specials and catching-up over morning coffee. It became customary for him to stay open late on Christmas Eve with a promise of presents and Santa Claus for the little ones. And so Anna was hurt and bewildered when Sam offered to plump himself up in a red coat, britches and a cottonwool beard and canter up the main street at dusk on someone's old pony. It seemed insensitive of him, so soon after Michael's death. She read it as a slap in the face, as a reminder that she was forever guilty. Why isn't he thinking of our son, she wondered, why isn't he still stunned with grief, why isn't he like *me*? It's okay, it's okay, Maxine said, comforting her, leading her away from those clamouring sweet faces and indulgent mums and dads. When Rebecca acquired a house and a lover, she invited Anna and Sam for Christmas lunch. Sam arrived in a state of great agitation, unable to meet Meg's eye, shaking her hand gruffly before setting off at once to examine the house, oil a hinge, change a tap washer, rap his knuckles against the plastered walls. Meg shrugged at his busy back and grinned at Anna, a warm, faintly sad and mocking grin: Classic displacement behaviour, she said. There won't be Christmas drinks at Showalter Park this year. The locals have had their fingers burnt, and many of them want only to break the test tubes, thaw the embryos, run a plough over the landing strip and dig up the parquetry floors. Until Sam feels more comfortable, he will find excuses not to spend every Christmas with the girls. There will be a ewe down, a windmill broken, the threat of dust and fire, and so Anna will make the six-hour round trip alone, grateful that he isn't with her, yet wishing that he felt he could be. When he is gone from her Anna will prepare cold Christmas lunches, not hot, and people will nod, very sensible, but she will be just as happy to spend the day alone. She will send cards to Maxine on the Gold Coast and Chester Flood in Victor Harbor, and ring them before nightfall on Christmas Day if the lines are not tied up. There will be a stretch of time in which Anna views her teenage granddaughter with distaste at Christmas time—her bad skin, her sulky gracelessness, her tossing presents to one side as if to complain that her grandmother and her two mothers owe her something, but it won't last.

Trains

IT BEGAN WITH a rolling mutter in the rails, faint at first but rising rapidly, as if an electrical storm had mustered behind the Razorback and begun to pour along the valley floor toward the town. The children stood rooted to the buckled station platform, stupefied and afraid. Iron ground hard against iron; Anna's ears rang with it. Soon even the light was ploughed under. She felt a spasm in Hugo's tiny hand, then nothing, only a tingling sense-memory in her empty fingers. She looked around for him wildly, began to run. She found him in the baggage room, trembling in a head-concealing squat beneath the solid redwood counter top. Outside, the engine rumbled past the ticket office, the waiting room, the signal box, before flattening into a string of red carriages, glass-rattling and benign, with drop-jawed, frayed-collared faces elbow-propped here and there upon the varnished windowsills, staring out, registering nothing. Don't cry, Anna said, I'm here, it's all right. She heard her mother's conking heels behind her. I've found him, Mum. Let's wait here, shall we? her mother said. They listened as couplings took up the slack beyond the gloomy walls, a fussy shunting in the two-line yard punctuated with timorous pauses and incompetence. When the train drew away they returned to the light. Maxine's father was there, his black uniform cap gleaming plastically above his dead white forehead. He helped them down the steps with a hand to their elbows and a little pointless laugh: Mind how you go, Mrs T. Opposite them, marooned on a shunting line beneath the wheat silos, a single carriage waited. The children and their mother stepped carefully over the asphalted rail ties. Anna looked left and right for runaways and soundless beasts. Up into the carriage. They were not the first. Other mothers waited with new babies and fretful small children. Aunt Lorna looked up, mute, exhausted, quickly grievous, the twins clutching her knees. Whooping cough, she said, as if Anna's family had it easy in the world, in the big house across the creek from her on Isonville. The nursing sister twitched back a curtain. Who's first today? she demanded, grim and brisk, stuck in this backwater for the day. When it was their turn, the children's mother explained that Hugo could not get his breath at night. Try a eucalyptus inhalation, the sister suggested. Then she paused: Mrs Tolley, this is the Baby Train. Hugo's rather too big now. It's not fair on the other mothers. Sometimes, far away across the lucerne flats, Anna watched the goods trains crawling north into the dry wastes. Once she lost count at seventy-nine carriages and her father explained that the Electricity Trust had erected a town overnight upon a seam of desert coal. Hugo built a winding track around blue-metal boulders collected from the driveway and over icecream-stick bridges. He funnelled pebbles into the tiny open ore carriages and on the days when the asthma clawed at his throat he might viciously stage a derailment and trample progress into the dirt. In Anna's final year at the high school, a handful of teachers took the seniors by train to Sydney, then up the eastern seaboard to the tropics. It was winter; the train's heating often failed in the night hours and Anna and Lockie slept shoulder to shoulder under a Black Watch blanket. But she could not sleep. There was a niggling, an irritation, a sensation close to appetite and provocation. She rolled with it, the endless growl and shimmer of the massed iron beneath her groin. She parted her legs a little; her eyes rolled back; her lips peeled slowly open. It rose floodingly in her and she gasped. She reached for Lockie's fingers and showed him how and where she wanted them. There was no light, only a moongleam at the edges of the flapping window blinds, but sufficient to show Anna a glint of envy and acute attention in the kids sitting opposite her, awakened by something, alerted to something. She sometimes thought of that night—a night in the education of her senses—whenever she rode by train through the tunnels under London, the metal ceilings and curved-glass walls tightening around her, the hand straps clinking like sounds from a bad dream above her, the human odours and viciousness aroused by timetables, IRA bomb threats and eyeball-to-eyeball intimacy with sour strangers far beneath the city. No one ever talked. A man with an unlit cigarette between his lips had it snatched out and ground into the floor by a man who screamed and pointed at a no smoking sign. That was enough for Anna. Coming halfway around the world had cured her of her grief. She went home, got married, had a son and then a daughter. The son was captivated by trains and ducks. Trains rumbled through his books and toy cupboard; a slow duck circled in the air currents above his bed; a train freize ran from door hinge to door latch at chest height around his room. Whenever Michael saw a real train he reached out his arms to it. His real prize was his Uncle Hugo's old train set, delivered to him on his fifth birthday packed in the original boxes. Anna looked back down the years but failed to remember the icecream-stick platform, the water tower, the signal box and tiny station clock. The Pandowie line is closed now, replaced by the Adelaide to Broken Hill bus, which stops once a day outside the Four Square Store in the main street. One day dealers will tear it up for the value of the scrap iron and sell the sleepers to landscape gardeners, but meanwhile the 150th Jubilee Committee has restored it temporarily to relive the days of steam. During the months of spring, the original engine and two items of rolling stock run between the town and Last Hope Pass, where the pink-smudge ranges roll on forever across the desert. With any luck, Sam says, we'll still be running her in the year 2000. Sam and other dignitaries dressed themselves in period costume for the inaugural journey and the mayor made a speech. Anna has written a five-hundred word history of the train and its pioneering times, printed up by Carl Hartwig at the *Chronicle* as a folded-twice free pamphlet for the tourists. She will ride the train once a year until the service is cancelled. It will be fun: open windows, the smell of the wildflowers on the claypan flats, cinders in the eye. She will never again take a bus anywhere. She'll rarely fly. Even with bullet trains and whisper-quiet cushioning, the old appeal will be there.

Poverty

ALWAYS WITH US, like the poor, her father sighed. It was just an expression, applied equally to droughts, punctured tyres, bad-penny types like the clerk of the council who'd been caught with his hand in the till, but Anna fixed on that word 'poor'. She pictured an ordained society, clean people going about their business, except that among them were the tolerated poor—ten per cent or so—who could be identified by the dark cast of their faces, their grimy hands, their air of shuffling helplessness—if the people around her were to be believed. Just an expression, yet Anna took it seriously. Did her father mean that the poor could not help being poor, and it was therefore pointless for the rich to help them? What of George Catford, discoverer of the Pandowie copper lode, left destitute and unacknowledged apart from his twenty guineas? She'd heard Grandfather Ison, Great Aunt Beulah, Uncle Kitch and plenty of others say that it was their own fault, the poor. No elbow grease, slack bootstraps and something inborn. But, as Grandfather Tolley observed: You can afford to say that if you're born to rule. I advertised for a shop assistant when I came here at the height of the Great Depression and over two hundred people applied. You can't tell me it was their fault they were poor. The Isons and the Showalters, they've always had a cushion under them. Anna knew of one genuinely poor family. When the Floods moved into the district, people drove past for a look. The Floods rented a house where the Terowie road intersected with the railway line, a redundant railway ganger's house a car's length from the level crossing, so that the thundering goods trains broke in upon their dreams. A dark-haired, thin, unsmiling father, a broad-beamed, lardish mother, and nine torn-skinned, restless, grimy children. They struggled. Grandfather Tolley paid Mr Flood to unload the weekly deliveries and the Showalters paid him to clear weeds and stones from their landing strip. Mrs Flood took in sewing. The boy Chester was composed of fleshless cheeks, hard, angular, dusty bare legs and arms, and hatchet-trimmed straight black hair. The smell of him leaked from his gappy pants and holed shirts. Until he got wise to everyone he'd dive for a dare through the fences at school or plunge impossibly from rail to rail down the monkey bars in sharp, black intensity. The father and the children looked half-starved. The mother's bulk was the bulk of white bread, child-rearing and possibly cheap sherry, although no bottles were found in the ditches at the end of the town, and the family was never seen in the Bon Accord Hotel. The Tolleys were among the few who saw good in the Floods—Mr Flood might have been threadbare but he was always decently turned out, Mrs Flood finished Anna's ball dress beautifully, and the children were not deliberately bad or stupid, simply reeling from ten schools and towns in seven years. And those children were fast on their feet: if not for them, Pandowie would have come last in the school sports. But the Floods were lightning rods for calamity. Mr Flood was decapitated by a crop duster's propeller on Showalter Park, and Mrs Flood died soon after, possibly of a broken heart. The children were suddenly grown-up and wary before their time. The government stepped in and placed them with strangers. Only Chester and Violet stayed in the town, wards of the convent. Anna went through the next few years blind to them, until a department car one day came for Violet, and the district buzzed: She was doing it with shearers and shedhands for a shilling a time. When Grandfather Ison died, leaving Anna's mother nothing and no house to live in, the Tolleys began to enact a life that was like a rehearsal for poverty. The six-forty acres was no Isonville, and now there was a mortgage to boot. Then a second mortgage. No more casual trips to the city; no more little gifts just to say I love you; a second-hand school uniform for Anna, dry-cleaned but still inhabited by a stranger's body; a vegetable garden; a rickety desk for Hugo from Pandowie Collectibles. For ten years Anna's father made do with the little Austin. He patched boards as they broke on the tray, replaced bare tyres with worn tyres, decoked the valves himself, let the registration lapse. Once as sleekly black as the Showalters' Bentley, the little truck faded to the mossy greys of the hillside rocks. He liked to say, after Anna had run away from her school in the city, that he hadn't known how he was going to afford her fees anyway. But they were not poor, merely careful, and occasionally living on a knife edge. Anna learned more about poverty from Lockie's family. She was sixteen when she met them and by the end of the summer knew these things: you stole a little—a sheep here and there, a battery out of a car, a can of petrol siphoned from a neighbour's bulk drums; you let things 'go'—fences, bores, engines, tyres; you bought on the never-never; cash deals only, no cheques or receipts to bother the tax man; you shot rabbits and pigeons; you did not read, did not travel, did not hope. But still you knew everyone's business and were afraid of no one, as you smoked and winked and took the mickey in the thick hours of evening, seated around the gouged pine table where family life was lived. Strategies, in other words, not only for putting food in your belly but for seeing you through times of emptiness, when things are apt to look skewed against you. When Anna married Sam it was not only material poverty that her father-in-law forced upon them—ensuring that they would not fritter away all that he'd achieved by the sweat of his brow—but also a poverty of the spirit. If the Jaegers ever laughed, it was grimly satisfied laughter. They wouldn't allow themselves to spend much in the way of love. Whenever Anna wrapped Michael and Rebecca in hugs and sloppy kisses, she heard disobliging sniffs high above her kneeling body. Sam had inherited his parents' emotional thrift, but he tried, at least he tried, snatching hugs and pecks from the children when his parents weren't around. The Jaegers would have robbed the children of wonder and magic if Anna had not been so vigilant. She sang with them on her knee, filled their heads with stories and nonsense, and encouraged them to step into the pictures in their bedtime books. She wanted richness in their lives. In a recent article for the *Chronicle*, Anna has written: We must recognise and help the hidden poor in our midst. Now she can't walk down the street without someone staring hotly: I'm not poor, how dare you. Anna wants these people to see their situations with fresh eyes, but she's fighting a losing battle. Even the most desperate would rather get behind the 150th Jubilee celebrations than be informed that they need not accept their plight. The old-timers say it's sad to see an Ison turning her back on the district, as though they believe that Anna thinks she's better than anyone else, and the kids who hang about on the footpath outside the cheerless Community House seem to thrust their lower jaws at her as if to say: What would you know? When Anna retires to the city she will become accustomed to the motionless shapes of homeless men and women. They will be there in the sand dunes, under the jetty, on the leeward side of the breakwater, in kiosk doorways when she goes on her early morning walks, each one uniformly brown-blanketed or grey, their heads hidden, silent as she passes at a respectful distance. Another of her father's expressions will come back to her: There but for the grace of God, et cetera.

Music

THEY FOLLOWED THE organ at church, and had a mantel radio, but the children wanted music they could make. They spent the drowsy afternoons in Beulah's half of the house, where the pianola rolls were stacked in a sideboard so grim that it swallowed all of the light. While Hugo wrote 'clean me' in the dust next to the crystal decanter, Anna opened the doors and rummaged around for 'The Rose of Tralee'. There was something about that song, but she could not remember what it was. Since the children's legs were so short, Mrs Mac wriggled her rump onto the stool and pumped the pedals for them. Soon her thundering back and haunches were rocking, her big head tipping like a metronome. She crossed her arms like a potentate. Magic! she cried. No hands! as the keys tocked magically up and down the keyboard and the children bared their teeth. But, behind them, Great Aunt Beulah began to cry. Anna turned, begged: Please, don't cry. I can't help it, Great Aunt Beulah said, it's that blessed song, it brings back memories. At once Anna's tears began to spill. She had delivered her great aunt a cruel, unthinking unkindness. My true love, said Great Aunt Beulah, forbidden to me by my father. Anna offered to change the roll. No! said Great Aunt Beulah. Let me hear it. Back where the light was warm and strong, the children's mother said: Of course you may, my darlings, and after school the following day Anna and Hugo enrolled with Mrs Morehead, Pianoforte Instruction To All Levels. *Clunk* . . . panicky search . . . *clunk*, went Anna's Tolley fingers, while Mrs Morehead, a raw-nerved woman with feelings close to combustion, hovered at her elbow with a knuckle-rapping ruler. Mrs Morehead, wife of the clerk of the district council, bitterly confirmed in her opinion that fate and a husband had delivered her to a hellhole. Then Mr Morehead's hands were found in the till, and the Moreheads moved on. When Anna turned sixteen she was permitted to stay out until midnight one night a week, which meant the Pandowie drive-in or the fortnightly dance. She was there when Lockie Kelly and Chester Flood staged a coup at the Wirrabara hall. They were tired of foxtrots, quicksteps, military two-steps, The Pride of Erin. Drive fifty miles for that once a fortnight, fifty miles back again? The Masonic Hall had a fast waxed floor but the dancing couples trudged around it like convicts in irons, as sluggish as the Wirrabara Inkspots, three after-work farmers who plonked themselves on the stage like old labourers at the end of the day, expressionless, immobile, scarcely moving their arms, the music leaking away when it should have been stirring the blood. Mr Riggs on piano, Mr Phelan on guitar, Mick Molloy scratchety scratch on the drums. They counted: One two three, one two three; everyone counted, inducing a mass trance, the same thing every fortnight. But Lockie and Chester showed them, leaping onto the stage at the end of the first bracket, belting out 'Eight Days a Week'. Anna came awake on the waxed floor. When Mick Molloy emerged from the supper room, a lamington speckling his ruffled shirt, she watched for fireworks, her eyes bright and hopeful, but it was all right, Mick swallowed and joined the boys as though they had delivered him from the dead. They formed a new band. The Wirrabara Dance became sixty-forty after that, a little waltzing bearable if you could stomp and shout as well. Anna became a kind of lead-singer's moll. She liked it. On the day that Anna's future husband took her home to meet his parents, she was warned: They're a bit, you know, fanatical, so we'll slip away if it gets too much. Anna shrugged. She'd heard whispers about the Jaegers, but clearly Sam wasn't like them. His mother clasped Anna's hands and sighed, as if to search her soul: Mr Jaeger and I have found the Lord, my dear. We hope that you may too, in time. Do you sing? A little song around the piano? Sam cut in: Mum, we'd better go. The father rumbled then, black as night: Come on boy, you've only just arrived, and Anna saw a side of Sam that she wanted to make better—his hunted, half-way-there rebellion. So they sang, a couple of harmless songs as a polite nod to Anna's secular self, a couple to sow the seed, clapping hands for Jesus. Afterwards Sam said: Sorry about that. No need to be, Anna told him. But that was the one and only time she sang with them, and the Jaegers came to give her glance-away looks of deep deep sorrow, to lift their noses as though to catch a whiff of corruption, the Devil's slick tracks, upon her skin. But she could never entirely escape their grim joy in a grim God. Now and then, as she rattled the ice in her sundowner on the verandah and the deckchair canvas creaked to her weight like a ketch at sea, faint voices raised in joyous song drifted up from the stone house below. There were always cars grille-to-grille in the Jaegers' yard at times like that. Anna liked to train the fieldglasses on them: New South Wales, Victoria, Queensland. They were the Logos Foundation. There were not many of them but they reached hands across the miles. Later Sam's parents formed a splinter group that called itself the Church of the Creator. Later still they joined the Ascension League. Along with every other disappointment that she causes her husband now, Anna puts herself out of reach, loses herself, when she's at the keyboard of their old piano. Sam complains that she becomes too detached, he doesn't like it, but it's more than that—he doesn't want her to walk where he cannot follow. He doesn't want her to go the distance.

They've had a call from Rebecca. She's agreed to perform a recital during the Copper Festival: Nothing too demanding for you lot. 'The Four Seasons', 'Fiddler on the Roof'. No-one loves a smart-arse, Becky. Anna's hands will seize up as the years go by. She will rely increasingly upon tapes and compact discs and borrow operas and ballets from a video library. The technology will change and she'll struggle to keep pace with it. An old woman, laying bare a box of switches and dials on Christmas morning: It's lovely, dear, thank you. Grandma's very pleased. If you'll just show me how to work it?

God

IF ANNA HAD been a boy, the Methodist congregation might have remarked upon her godliness and not only upon the godliness of her brother. She wore her red Sunday School dress, and she mounted the pulpit confidently, clasped the dark wood, leaned into the stifling air: The word of God is like an auger, drilling out the badness in us all. But Anna had over-reached again. The congregation yawned, ricepaper fans whipped before crepy necks, and fingers tugged at collars and ties, and when Anna saw her father glance doubtfully at his finger, cut off by an auger, the words died in her throat. She felt blood rush to her cheeks—Miss Smartypants, guilty of trampling her clodhopper boots over someone's feelings again. She stepped down. Hugo took her place. The dear little boy, whispered the congregation. His gaberdine suit, his angelic smile, his voice as clear as a bell: The lesson for today is. Anna suspected that her mother pictured him in a clerical collar. She saw her mother blink, a handkerchief balled in her hand. Every Sunday after that,

Anna fought against buttons and bows: Is the Queen going to be there or something? When Anna was fourteen, Maxine urged her to join Youth Fellowship. I can't stand that God stuff, Anna said, but Maxine said: It's not like that, just a short prayer, a bit of a discussion, then table-tennis, charades, dancing to records. Reverend Allen leaned forward in his fold-up chair, his freckled, thick and hairless forearms solidly upon his knees, and looked around at the semicircle: Tonight we're going on a moonlight ramble around the town, but first let's spend a few minutes discussing what it is we should look for in a marriage partner. Those drones, their sweet voices piped up: a Christian, honesty, goodness, good manners. Anna lifted her chin: Physical attraction. She faced them all down. They hated her, those buttons and bows, but she had an unexpected ally, for the Reverend Allen held up his palms: Just a minute, everyone. Anna's right, physical attraction *is* very important. Suddenly Mrs Allen was there in their minds, eight months pregnant. Then they walked in the moonlight. Country towns hug the earth at the fall of night. A distant screen door complained on its hinges, a streetlight hissed and popped, the moon caught the glass shards in the roadside ditches. Otherwise there was only the darkness, their scratchy footsteps where the bitumen became dirt and gravel, and spurts of conversation which faltered under the ear of the stars, the ear of the Reverend Allen. Then the air got to their spirits; nothing could keep them down for long. Anna and Maxine swaggered shoulder to shoulder down the centre of the road while boys drifted across in front of them, slowing, slowing—like Anna and Maxine, those boys were scarcely breathing by now—until there was the unmistakable poke of superstructured breasts between their shoulder-blades. They bounced away again, back into the night. The syllogism was framed like this: A large family is a poor family; a poor family is a no-hoper family; therefore Lockie was the son of no-hopers. Anna's father did not quite come out and say that Lockie was also a Catholic. Look at that, would you?—the shells of cars rusting in the yard, fences falling down, skin-and-bone sheep panting in the dirt around the scummy troughs. Priest-riddled, ignorant and superstitious. Anna flared: I don't care, you can't stop me from seeing him. But God came between the lovers in unexpected ways. Lockie, it's yours and it's beautiful, Anna told him. It doesn't put you off? Of course not, she said. She didn't tell him that she felt wonder, curiosity and a kind of heat in equal measures. She heard a faint *phsst* and saw the gluey mass flip and flip out of him, splashing onto his stomach. He groaned softly, turned away, cleaned himself. A little death. What's wrong? Nothing. Anna pursued him: What's wrong? This, Lockie said, guilt, misgiving and desire heavy in his face. What we just did. In her room at Women's College he would restlessly pick up and set down one book after another. *Arguments For and Against the Existence of God*: You're leaving me behind, he said. Then, blurtingly: Marry me? Lockie, come here, come on. But Lockie lolled in pain against the door. Anna's children were christened by the Reverend Allen. He muttered automatically under the domed roof of the Pandowie Methodist church and traced a damp fingertip over their foreheads. Their responses were typical. Michael opened his eyes for a moment, closed them, and briefly wriggled his arms and legs, but a drop of water ran cold and unwelcome from Rebecca's temple to her ear, and she heaved and roared to be free. A few months after Sam broke with his father, Mrs Jaeger wrote to Anna: I felt I must send you this little book, dear, with a sincere desire that it may open your eyes. Mr Jaeger and I were thirtyish before ours were opened. You will probably be bemused, to say the least, if you have never heard what the author has to say. Believe me, it is all one big conspiracy. Mr Jaeger and

I were horrified when we learnt the true extent of it, which, of course, is never revealed in the popular media. I find the ABC particularly biased and I listen for the alternative viewpoint but it never comes, and never anything remotely uplifting. Even the wildlife programs refer to evolution and the earth's age as billions of years, when scientists whose work goes unrecognised put it at no more than 10,000 years. It is sad that people have used their own free will and turned their backs on a mighty God. Don't let this happen to you, dear Anna, for the Lord will have the last say when he says, Enough! My love to my darling grandchildren. When Mr Jaeger died, the cars with the out-of-state plates appeared in the Jaegers' yard overnight. Those holy rollers, fumed Sam after the funeral. The bastards have been helping themselves to the old man's petrol and diesel. Anna said: I'm surprised the pumps weren't padlocked, and got a dirty stare. Those holy rollers also had an eye on the farm, but they didn't know what Anna knew, that the Jaegers of this world might give up their souls to God but never their worldly goods. Rebecca has begun to attend a little High Anglican church in North Adelaide. Meg affects amusement, but Anna can sense the chagrin under it. According to Meg, Rebecca is pretty well representative of the congregation—a few gay academics, a few yuppies, no one younger that twenty or older than fifty, dress casual but expensive. Meg laughs, a harsh bark in the little house: The new face of the church. I myself haven't the time for self-examination. Anna doesn't know her daughter, and wonders if that matters. She doesn't ask, she doesn't meddle, but she does wonder what drives Rebecca. She wonders if it has anything to do with that old wariness, Becky's watchful gaze from the passenger seat. Anna will grow old wondering it. For her part, Rebecca will not forsake her mother, but she will keep a door closed between them.

Names

ANNA ANTONIA ISON Tolley. She was named Antonia Ison for her mother's mother, who had set out with nothing but a baby and grit to bring Grandfather Ison back from his darkness in the mallee scrub. Anna? Another family name, dear. Mr Wheelwright rapped his cane on the wall map. Yarcowie, Caltowie, Terowie, Edeowie, Booborowie, Tarcowie and our own Pandowie. What do these names have in common? Exactly. And the *owie* means? They didn't know—this short, compact, natty stranger from the teachers' college had to tell them: It's a word used by the Ngadjuri people to refer to water, a place of water. Anna perceived dimly that she belonged to ransacking inhabitants who had forgotten history, who had no use for it, since they knew the cost of everything and the value of nothing. Bit of a pinko is he, your teacher? Uncle Kitch wanted to know. The words 'Tolley's Four Square Store' were painted on the main window of Grandfather Tolley's shop and raised in plaster above the shopfront verandah cap. The name Tolley was rendered homespun and unassuming by his storekeeper's apron, his long, taciturn face, his newness in the district, and not even his son's wildness had been able to untame it. The Isons and the Showalters, on the other hand, had left their mark on the landscape itself: Ison's Creek, Showalter Hill. Toward the end, Anna and Lockie seemed to scrap all the time. Anna wounded him with names, she couldn't help it, and, wounded and confused, Lockie looked for ways to wound her: Okay, what's the difference between the North Vietnamese, the Viet Cong and the NLF? Names, names, names. Anna blithely turned the subject around. She was an accomplished sidestepper. Yet Lockie had hit home. He was a country kid who read the daily paper and listened to the news, while she was a sojourner at the university, someone far from home and full of useless passion, someone who could not keep pace with the issues or the names on the refectory table broadsheets. But, if Lockie knew many little things, Anna knew one big thing, and it blazed inside her: The war was wrong. Her husband's name for her was sweetie, and her parents-in-law called her dear. She found that she'd married into a family that didn't listen. But they did talk, constant, niggling, contestable, branch-line conversations that left her exhausted. Since they didn't listen, they didn't notice that the poor dog answered to two names: Sam called her Bluff, the Mr and Mrs called her Hilda. The Jaegers left Anna gasping for air. That's why she strayed. The school run, work, shopping, field days, diversions to see Chester Flood, that's why Anna burned up the miles and drained the fuel in Mr Jaeger's bulk tanks. Chester stood back in the shadows that day, waiting for her. She whisked Michael and Becky in from the car, down the corridor, onto his bed. Now, close your eyes, my darlings. Where are we? Who's that man? they wanted to know. Shhh, sweetheart, close your eyes. A quick nap and then we'll go home. Afterwards, in the car, Anna played riddle-me riddle-me ree with her children until she had filled their heads with names. She said: When we get home to Daddy, who shall we say we saw today? Every name but Chester's. They were pushovers, her children, they wouldn't give her away. Anna had them so bamboozled that they might even doubt that Chester and his house existed beyond the traces at the edges of their dreams. As though to suit his name, Michael was steady and uncomplicated. He laughed easily, a gurgle when he was a baby, an infectious chuckle when he was a little boy. Rebecca grew into her name. She approached it as she approached everything, with suspicion, saw that it fitted her, and remained dark, European, unreadable, refined to the farthest degree. Sam's parents insisted on being called Nana and Pop, names to make an Ison shudder. One day Anna walked down the gully slopes to the stone house to ask for an envelope, but the Jaegers had gone out for the day. Well, Anna was family; she would simply find her way to the nerve centre and help herself. She had never been inside old man Jaeger's study before. Her father-in-law liked to pounce on every phone call she made, every pair of shoes she bought for the kids, every mile she drove, yet look who he was giving his money to: Voters' Policy Association, Christian Institute for Individual Freedom, League of Rights, Australian Heritage Society, Christian Rural Action. The Mrs belonged to something called the Lilac League, hearts of iron inside lilac twinsets. Anna has noticed that the children of the district call her Mrs Jaeger these days, not Anna, a clear sign that she's passed into the middle years of her life. Sam frets whenever he's reminded that the old names are dying out. He likes to list them a little wildly: Your uncle Kitch is the last Ison, the Showalters have left the district, Hugo is the last Tolley, and Becky's the last Jaeger. He's bewildered by Rebecca's announcement that she and Meg intend to have a baby: Will it have your surname or Meg's? Both, Rebecca tells him. What about this sperm donor fellow? He's given up all claims, Rebecca replies. Discontinuity, delegitimisation, no wonder Sam's head is spinning. The 150th Jubilee Committee will commission a plaster replica of the gravestone on Ison's Creek, but then discover that neither the full inscription nor the shepherd boy's surname had ever been recorded. Some committee members will swear that George Catford, discoverer of the Pandowie lode, had carved the stone, until Anna shows them the inquest report, dated 1851. Anna will not be called Nana, Gran or even Grandma by her granddaughter, just Anna. She won't be remembered as a town bike, a ratbag, a selfish cow, a hard-faced bitch, an old bag, just Anna-who-knew, even if she didn't necessarily know what name to give to it.

Films

THE PICTURES CAME to town because Grandfather Tolley suffered. He stared from his shop verandah at the sharkfin Razorback, and suffered. In spring, when the flowering grasses tossed and surged in the wind like whitecaps on the sea, he remembered his wife and he suffered. Your grandmother liked a good film, he said. She'd take herself off to the Henley Beach Odeon and forget herself for hours on end. Anna watched him on the verandah, staring out. She wondered if he was running a film through his head, grainy villains and lovers in improbable stories to drive that cruising shark away. Then one day he began to take himself off to Adelaide every so often, but he wouldn't say why, not until he turned up with a certificate, a rented projector, and a second-hand screen, fine-webbed with cracks and curling at the edges. The posters arrived on the Monday train, the film canisters on the Friday train. A display case on the wall of the Four Square Store announced: 'Pandowie Pictures, Forthcoming Attractions', and every week children dreamed beneath the fly-specked glass, provoked by flared nostrils, guns, surrendered white throats. But, within three years, the folding chairs proved to be too hard, the distances too great, the menfolk too weary, television too appealing, and so Grandfather Tolley closed the Pandowie Pictures and set up a lending library behind the racks of canned peaches, a place where Anna would conceal herself from the world. The winding blade of the auger took more than the tip of her father's finger. For a while during the long year that followed, it also claimed his spirit. He asked: Why did I ever take up this game? In the chilly winds of July and August his aching fingers crept blindly for warmth deep inside the folds of his coat. The evenings around the sitting room fire were dark and long, and he was a reproach to his wife and children, a shuttered figure who stared at the coals for hours at a time through the stubby branches of that throbbing, never-warm hand. The family watched him. Anna's mother wanted to say: Snap out of it, Pete, and she wanted to reassure him that she didn't consider it a step down for her to be an Ison on Isonville one minute, a Tolley grubbing for a living the next. One bitter night, when they should have been a comfort to him and he to them, they left him to his discouraging fire and negotiated the mud and the washaways on the sunken road to attend a charity screening, Doris Day and Rock Hudson on a tiny fold-up patch of white in the Ladies' Auxiliary supper room. There were husbands there but no other children, and Anna saw that her mother felt it keenly, imagining stares and whispers. The family bought a television set. It was a poor, weak, grey-faced thing in their sitting room, for power to the house came from a bank of 32-volt batteries partly charged by a wind generator, and on gusty nights, when the freelight propeller howled and shifted in the inconstant wind, the tiny screen swelled and shrank, swelled and shrank. The little towns of the northern highlands lost their drive-ins and cinemas one by one until only the Pandowie drive-in struggled from one year to the next. Blushing, steadying Lockie's fevered head between her hands, Anna said: Please, don't hang my pants from your aerial. She waited, her heart thudding, steeling herself. Would he laugh? Ignore her? A voice called softly in the darkness; someone in the next car shifted on creaky seat springs. Lockie mattered to her—the others hadn't—but was it a mistake to let him know that he mattered? She didn't really know him. She wondered what he had heard about her. They had been seen driving in, his mates had seen him with her, and all bar Chester Flood had given him the thumbs up: In like Flynn there, old son. Lockie was backlit by the screen towering above them; the speaker crackled on the window next to Anna's ear. She turned Lockie's head so that it caught the light: Lockie? You won't, will you, please? There were boys out there who had made a trophy of her, all shiftiness and hunger, but she didn't want to be *his* trophy. She wanted to see love suffuse his face. When Grandfather Tolley died, Anna's parents handed the six-forty acres to Hugo. He blinked. He flexed his wings. He pulled down the rotting shed, straightened crooked fencelines, planted trees, finally scrapped the little Austin truck. A skylight and a glass wall to brighten the living area at the back of the house. A thirty-metre-high VHS/UHS antenna with booster boxes and coaxial cables to pick up the special channel. For weeks he was devoted to a series upon the American Civil War. The book was on his coffee table, next to an overflowing ashtray. Anna spotted Sunken Road in the index:

> Of the fighting in Maryland, the bloodiest was at the Battle of Antietam on September 16, 1862. At one point Union troops came in behind Confederate sharpshooters stretched out upon the Sunken Road, which was to the north of Sharpsburg, and, in the words of a newspaper man from Washington, fired down on them 'like sheep in a pen'. Thereafter the Sunken Road became known as Bloody Lane.

Sometimes Anna borrows *Breaker Morant* from the video library in Hugo's shop, just to see Rebecca and Michael, who had been extras in one of the crowd scenes, a pair of small, knickerbockered, bonneted figures standing hand in hand as the troopers rode out onto the veldt and a brass band pomped away in the old rotunda outside the Bon Accord in

Market Square. Sam had been hired to play a Boer guerilla, a distant, bearded, blackcoated horseman riding along a slope of the Razorback, but the director had left him on the cutting-room floor. Sam claims that Anna is obsessed, but it's he who is obsessed, recording the deliberations and activities of the 150th Jubilee Committee with his video camera. Now and then Anna's mother's old voice rasps on the line: Could you tape the late film on Channel 2 for me, dear? Technology will defeat Anna too, eventually, and she'll turn to Meg, a woman of hip-swinging flair and confidence, for advice on how to preset the tuning and the timer.

Cars

THIS FUNNY, JOUNCY old goggle-eyed truck was called a buckboard. Anna liked the sound of it: buckboard, buckboard. At the bottom someone had printed, in scratchy black strokes with a broad nib: 'Setting Out, October 1920'. The children wanted to know where Grandfather Ison was going, posed like that with one foot on the running board of his buckboard. He was unrecognisable, every feature leached from his face by sunshine and over-exposure, and the photographer—Grandmother Ison?—had caught her own shadow in the white foreground. Anna traced her forefinger over his supplies, a number of boxy tarpaulin shapes heaped on the tray top together with coils of fencing wire, a crosscut saw and axes. He had hooked a corked jute waterbag beneath a bulbous headlight. Must have been quite a journey, Anna said, and saw her mother's eyes lose focus and swim down the decades to a time of pain. The children strained to hear her: Something terrible happened. Your grandpa was very bitter after the war, felt he'd been cheated out of his rightful inheritance. He took up a block in the mallee country, sight unseen, and was supposed to send for us but he never did. No town, no post office, no one to inquire on our behalf. The weeks went by. My poor mother: she bundled Kitch and me together and we took a train to Pinnaroo, borrowed a horse and cart, and drove off into the scrub, looking for him. He was deranged when we found him, almost out of food and water. It was awful land and he just lost heart. He felt he'd failed us and was too ashamed to come home. Anna sighed. The leaves of the album were cardpaper the colour of charcoal, and she prowled through the years. Grandpa Tolley, looking tall, thin and high-strung, one hand propped on the bonnet of his wartime gas-burning Austin; the family's new Zephyr roofracked with cases, beach balls, buckets and spades; Hugo overflowing his pedal car on the side verandah at Isonville. The main street of Pandowie was one big verandah to Hugo, that's why Anna always clasped his fingers tightly. He yanked, she yanked back, almost wrenching off his arm, just as Mr Showalter blared by in his glistening black, snout-up Bentley, drunk again, missing them by inches. The Showalters were loved because of that car and hated because of it, often in the same breath. When the Redex Trial passed through the district, two cars rolled on an elbow bend in the sunken road, leaving angry paint scars on the cutting wall and an impression in everyone's ears of glass splintering, metal peeling open. One by one the girls in Anna's class turned sixteen and one by one they began to ride in the passenger seats of their boyfriends' utes, falling naturally into an easy, sleepy, casual acquiescence as if they belonged there and had never not been there. Anna loved the smell, compounded of sun-baked vinyl, grease and Lockie himself. She would not be two seconds in his passenger seat before she bared her legs, propped her bare feet on the dashboard and planted her hand on his thigh. They both loved the liberated, elastic, half-zed of her legs. Later, whenever Anna drove a car, she noticed that a man would never settle comfortably in the passenger seat. She drove Lockie's ute to the Wirrabara Dance and he crossed and recrossed his legs, folded and refolded his arms. She drove the tutor to the Law Revue and he rode as though in alien hands, as stiff as rope. One of the many things that Anna's father-in-law controlled was the cost and type of car that she and Sam would drive. Mr Jaeger would come to her, waving a list of figures in her face: According to the speedo, you've driven three hundred miles since last Tuesday, two-ninety-five the week before that. How come? Where would you be going, to clock up that sort of mileage? Surely not your job at the *Chronicle*? Young wives, they shop three times a week when once should be enough. Always dropping over to see their mothers. Do you think we're made of money? I've a good mind to padlock the bowser. Anna told him that she had a good mind to padlock the car so he couldn't spy on her. Showalter Park has gone to the wall now and the receiver is selling off the property's vehicles. Trucks, utes, vans, station wagons, all in good nick. Unfortunately, however, even despite a fresh paint job, the Showalter Park logo seems to persist, like a bad memory, on many of the driver's doors around town. Anna has seen her mother delivering groceries in an ex-Showalter Park pick-up, faintly embarrassed and faintly defiant, as if to say that she hadn't circled in at the kill when the Park went under the hammer, but so what if she had?—the Showalters had brought a lot of the locals to their knees. Anna will drive along the sunken road after it has been newly sealed, its elbows straightened out, and find herself braking unnecessarily sometimes, bad old hazards and memories still haunting her. Was it here that I had a blocked fuel line, just when I needed to accelerate out of danger, or was it here? She will continue to run a car until, at her annual driving test, an examiner shakes his head over her hearing, her eyesight, her response time, her stiff neck. Her granddaughter will drive her around after that, Anna marvelling at the girl's languid wrist-flick turns, her easy windmilling style. Shopping will be a cooperative effort for Anna and her neighbour. One will reverse the car, the other will guide her: Bit more to your left, straighten up, mind the tap, whooh! 'Woman, 84, Killed. An 84-year-old Henley Beach woman was knocked over and killed yesterday when her neighbour, 87, was attempting to reverse out of the driveway of her home'. Three lines at the bottom of page three and it could well be Anna.

Writing

WHAT'S THAT YOU'RE writing there? Anna lived in the world but she also lived in her head, and if she withdrew too often, books were snatched from her hands, fingers were snapped before her eyes, voices scolded: Daydreamer. What are you thinking? What are you writing? When Anna voyaged, wearing her various costumes, everyone said: Wake up in there. They said: Play with your cousins. They said: It's bad manners. They wanted her to be engaged—if only they knew that she *was* engaged. When, in a caprice of love, her mother posted 'Kip', by Anna Tolley, 8, Pandowie, to the children's pages of the *Sunday Mail*, Anna took her writing underground. What was she writing? She was writing a letter to June, her penfriend in England. June was her cover story. June also became an unwanted obligation. Anna didn't like June. She didn't like writing to her. She could picture June's weak eyes, her mother's perm, her father washing his Morris in his shirtsleeves and braces. They had little to communicate to one another once Anna had evoked Isonville and June the Holly Hill Estate, Leeds. June's letters caused Anna to mince around the house: Oh, Mummy, Hugo is ever such a horrid little boy. Kids from Texas were never listed among those seeking pen-pals, only Junes from Leeds. Anna loved two men and she hurt them sorely with her pen—Lockie, who'd described for her how the dawn broke over the South China Sea, and her father, who'd had her in his thoughts as he watched his sheep die on the verges of the sunken road. If the editors of the student rag hadn't been so offhand with Anna, it might not have happened. Their approach with her was: You can clean the paste-up bench, maybe review the odd film, so Anna submitted a thousand words attacking conscription and the Anzac myth, and they led with it in the next issue. She posted a copy to Lockie and the silence stretched between them. She posted a copy home and heard bewilderment and offence. Anna was saying *Look at me*, wanting Lockie and her father to see that she was someone special, not someone they could fob off with automatic or absent-minded love. She was saying *Look at me*, unaware that they would always look at her. Then the boys from home began to die and her pen dried up. She fled the country. She recovered her voice, but it was slow, slow. It was a halting, fragmentary, pen-slashed voice: Dear Mum and Dad, Taken off the plane at Frankfurt—very security conscious—suppose you can't blame them—opened my camera case gingerly—expecting a bomb?—most unnerving—why me?—travelling with two Kiwis and they weren't hassled—must have the eyes of a fanatic. When she married Sam Jaeger, her father-in-law, blind to who she was, urged her to write to the papers, to businessmen, to bishops and MPs. He stood in her kitchen and boomed: Dear Chief Commissioner. We, the undersigned, are strongly in favour of a more energetic police action to put down the anti-Springbok rabble once and for all. We won't be sorry to see a few police batons in action, if that's what it takes. Totalitarian forces like these seek, through infiltration and subversion, to destroy the values of our Christian way of life and sacrifice our freedom on the alter of atheistic materialism. Sign at the bottom, girlie. Carl Hartwig offered her two days a week at the *Chronicle*, proofreading, writing up the Strawberry Fete, the Red Cross Flower Show, the dusty April field days, the Copper Festival, hatching, matching, dispatching. Her income helped to tide the family over when there were no odd jobs for Sam in the district. All these years later, Anna is still writing about fetes and weddings for the *Chronicle*, but Carl Hartwig is also giving her space for feature articles and local history, based on material she's been collecting for the 150th Jubilee book. It's going to be an opinionated book, and some of her opinions are finding their way into her weekly column.

> Sir: The residents of Pandowie and district do not agree with Mrs Jaeger as stated in The Chronicle on April 4 that 'Pandowie is dying'. We are of the opinion that a newspaper report should be interesting and informative, based on fact and worthwhile news, but her article was neither interesting nor informative. The townspeople are not all old, as she suggests, and even though family farms are falling into the hands of the big concerns, and landholders in the area, of which Mrs Jaeger's husband is one, are getting fewer in number, community groups such as the CWA and school welfare are still able to accommodate 1200 people for lunch during Merino stud field days in April of each year. The Pandowie Red Cross flower show is renowned as one of the best in the mid-north. Pessimistic criticism of this nature is not welcomed by people who are proud of their heritage and working to maintain a town which has survived for 150 years and will thrive for many more to come.

Anna and Sam have received a letter from the bank in which a faceless suit-and-tie has written: We regret to advise you. How dare they? Sam wants to know. He flicks the letter with the backs of his fingers and blinks away the tears. We bank with them for twenty years and they let us know by *letter*? They can't even talk it over with us first? As Anna's eyesight fades, as she begins to miss grease spots on the benchtops, she will put away her stamps and envelopes in favour of the telephone. Every home will be blessed with gadgets that make writing redundant and she'll talk to her daughter and her granddaughter on a flickering screen. She will continue to mark appointments on the calendar and fasten messages to the refrigerator door, but she won't see what her granddaughter sees, handwriting that unravels as Anna approaches the grave.

Siblings

ANNA WAS TRYING to understand: Grandfather Ison and Great Aunt Beulah are brother and sister? She grew restless and meditative on her father's lap, her brows drawn together, as all human patterning realigned and rearranged itself in her head. She herself was a sister, with a brother. She began to sense that she was not unparalleled and unprecedented in the world, that the people around her were not there simply because she stood at the centre but were caught in webs of their own. She wanted to know more. There was plenty to know. Grandfather Ison had *five* sisters, in fact. Anna came eventually to understand that Grandpa-and-his-sisters was a story full of trouble and strife, but she wasn't interested in the quality of the links between them just now, only the type. It would be fun to have a sister. We'll see, her mother said. Who's *your* sister? Anna wanted to know. I haven't got one; I've got a brother, your Uncle Kitchener. Again Anna frowned, absorbing this new tie. She twisted back her head, stared up at the underside of her father's jaw: Have you got a sister or a brother? He had not. He also was motherless, his mother taken by a shark when he was a baby. Peter! You'll give the child nightmares! Able to go no farther than Grandfather Tolley in her contemplation of her father's line, Anna turned back to the Isons. She stared at her little brother. Hugo was stretched cheek-down on the hearthrug, running a tiny, wheel-less metal truck across the toe cap of their father's leather slipper. She rearranged the players. She imagined that Hugo was her Uncle Kitch, a small boy ready for bed. Her mother, sitting in the club chair on the other side of the flames, became Grandmother Ison. Her father, murmuring into the hair at the back of her neck, became Grandfather Ison, and Anna herself, the child in his lap, became Eleanor Ison, a little girl ready for bed. Anna wanted to know why—since her mother and Uncle Kitch had grown up together in this house—did Uncle Kitch now live in the overseer's house across the creek? Because I was the first to get married, and when you kids came along we needed the extra space. But Uncle Kitch is married with kids now, so won't he need extra space too? He certainly will, Anna's father replied. Anna's father often said one thing and you heard other things behind it. Four years later, Kitchener inherited Isonville and moved his family into Beulah's half of the house. His rift with his sister, his hungry presence on the other side of the dividing door, drove Anna and Hugo into taking long bicycle rides through the back country or to their mother's old school on the sunken road. They felt free and venturesome. Then one day their cousins begged to come along with them. They were twin girls, with thin, straining, overwashed print cotton frocks on their sturdy frames and identical expressions of envy and glum anxiety on their faces. They had no thoughts of their own and understood nothing. Outside the schoolhouse, Anna and Hugo dismounted from their bikes and watched the sisters wobble toward them through the tossed-aside blue gravel at the road's edge, flushed and damp, afraid of missing out. A lazy kind of badness crept in Anna's blood. She infected Hugo with it. They took the twins through the gap in the crumbling wall and seduced them out of their hot dresses and bike-seat wrinkled pants as though they had been rehearsing this for all of their lives. Dazed, overheated, always wanting more, the twins dogged Anna and Hugo through the summer. There was always Maxine in Anna's life, but she wanted a sister. She learned at first hand that a friend may be treacherous, a friend may reject you. She fell out with Maxine and had no one until Lockie Kelly came along. When she first met his family she came home to tell of it with the light of their careless, raucous, even-handed love still burning in her eyes: He's got *four* brothers, *two* sisters, *endless* cousins. But, like a slap in the face, her father said: The Pope promises them extra points in the afterlife if they breed up big. Anna flared: So how do you explain Grandpa Ison and all his sisters? Anna's father couldn't explain it. He didn't bother to try. He turned the page and smiled a smile of wisdom and secret intelligence that made Anna burn. At least she didn't have a falling-out with Hugo over the six-forty acres. She had no right to expect half of that poor, stony country: it was too small; he'd worked hard ever since he left school; she'd seen enough heartache and strife between her mother and Uncle Kitch. Sometimes Anna wonders how things might have been between Michael and Rebecca if Michael had lived. Should she and Sam have had another baby? I begged you, Mum, remember? I was so lonely by myself. Anna tries to remember. Maybe Rebecca would have been happier, less on her guard if she'd had a brother or a sister to love and care for through her young years. Anna will draw closer to Hugo and her mother. They will be all she has left of her own young life. She will return to Pandowie every few months and see that nothing changes, even as everything changes: the unvarying beat of the town and her family there as the old certainties crumble.

Sport

WHEN THE FIRST Eighteen played at home, cars and utes by the dozen parked snout first around the oval's perimeter rail like stubby spokes on a huge hub, like beasts crouched at a waterhole. Anna and Hugo stood on the front seat of the Stock & Station Holden, bumping their behinds on the seat-back. Their mother sat next to them, lost in a book propped open on the steering wheel. When the horns sounded the children stiffened, searching among the men streaming onto the field for their father, who wore the purple and gold of the town, the number 12 stitched to his back. But Pandowie lost the toss, obliging them to kick against the wind, and so the children's father, stationed on the flank at the far end of the field, looked tiny, unused, disappointing. That changed at quarter-time. Suddenly he was right there in front of them, ceaselessly patrolling and dashing, sometimes climbing the sky with a leap-twist, riding the backs of slower men to snatch the ball. The children could scarcely breathe. They clambered out of the car, leaned on the rotting white rail, straining to touch. The men were massive, thunderous. The damp earth rumbled under them and the children heard the vicious punch and slap of bone against bone. They feared for their father. At half-time he trotted to the car to gulp water from an enamel cup. The spell broke. Anna recoiled from him: so much taut, white, mud-splashed, damp-hairy flesh; his cyclonic breathing; the spray of sweat and snot from his hot, elated, angry, heaving face. Another man leaned to ruffle her hair, enveloping her in a stupefying animal fug: Your dad's a wild man, missy. The children's mother played tennis in the summer months. Again Anna noticed that dislocating transformation. Her mother, dressed in tennis whites, wasn't as huge, snorting and destructive as her father in his black shorts and black sprigged boots, but she did seem larger, powered by strong, quivering, naked thighs. Anna reached out her fingers to the tracery of red and blue veins, the dimpled, follicular flesh, but did not touch. Then, fully dressed, they were her parents again, smaller and more accessible. The long skipping rope rose, arced, dropped, snickered on the schoolyard asphalt, rose again, dropped again, in a hypnotising, metronomic beat. Anna and Maxine, face to face outside the ring, began to nod, then rock and sway minutely, finding a sympathetic pulse-beat in their veins. Together they stepped into the blur and began to skip, a tidy, efficient, one-two of their feet, their skirts breathing around their knees, Anna's plait knocking gently against her spine. Without warning they clapped palms, twirled one hundred and eighty degrees, twirled again, clapped again. Anna felt buoyant and weightless, attached to the earth only by her need to rebound from it. It was known in the family that Hugo was clumsy, a dreamer. He tripped on his laces. He gazed beyond the school grounds as balls trundled past his dreamy legs. But he tried. He might come home and say: Dad, I got eight kicks today, which Anna knew to mean: Dad, I didn't cry today. At the end of her first year at the university, Anna said no to blazered Americans selling encyclopaedias and caught the train home to Pandowie. She slid easily back into Lockie's sinewy arms, but was not so certain how old friends would receive her. Her year away, her ticking mind, were a burden here in the wheat and wool country. I'm available if you need me, she told the tennis captain. That was on Monday. On Thursday she drove into Pandowie and checked 'the board', a glass-fronted public-notices cabinet bolted to the outside wall of her grandfather's shop: Last week's results, next week's teams, premiership table. She had not been picked. That meant one of two things: there were plenty of better players available, or she was being told that she could not expect to step willy-nilly back across the barrier she had set up when she left the district. Anna waited. Two weeks later, her name was there, Pandowie vs Wirrabara. She drove to a dusty crossroads on a baking plain. The tarry court surfaces jellied under the hot soles of her sandshoes, while panting sheep watched the play from the poor shade of half-a-dozen pepper trees. Across the road was a tiny Methodist church, set behind a stonewall fence in the corner of a crop of unharvested wheat and star thistles. In the four hours that Anna was there that afternoon, three lonely cars shuddered by in roiling clouds of dust, spinning small stones like missiles against wheel arches and into the powdery roadside grassheads, and she knew that nothing had changed. She lost interest. When Rebecca was old enough for Saturday sport and week-night practice, Sam was the one to drive her there and back. He was not a peaceful guardian. If Becky revealed a torn knee or diminishing ardour, his ambition for her grew more pronounced. He pounded the sidelines, snarling: Get in there, Beck. He arrived home, swollen with outrage: Some brat's mother had a go at Becky today. When Rebecca finally quit in favour of the cello, Sam mooned about, full of unfocussed energy and rage, so Anna steered him toward the bowling club. He seemed to sigh with relief—the wobbling, measured pace of the heavy fat clumsy balls on the grassy links, an opportunity to bitch and yarn with friends and strangers, the anticipation leading to the Association Championships every March. He is the club president this year. He holds great expectations for the Year 2000 Jubilee Tournament and has posted invitations to championship teams and individuals from all over the Commonwealth. Anna stares at the exotic postage stamps on the replies that have begun to arrive at the house, and often catches herself thinking that Michael would have enjoyed fixing them in his albums. Sometimes Maxine, decked out in her whites, urges Anna to join. Anna shakes her head. Her argument is that the local clubs don't need her, they need kids who will stay on in the district. She writes: Young people are traditionally the driving force behind our sport and social clubs but there is nothing to keep them here, and so we are suffering a tragic loss of youth leadership. The closest that Anna will get to sport in the years to come will consist of listening to Rebecca's good-natured objections to watching Meg play soccer on run-down ovals in distant suburbs on squally Saturday afternoons. All the devotion and energy of Anna's ageing neighbours to bowls, organised walks and winter swimming will fail to move Anna, who will walk at her own pace, and die in her own good time.

Books

THEIR FATHER CAME home dog-tired every evening, often after they had gone to bed, but he never failed to read them a bedtime story before sitting down to his lamb chops—by now oven-husked, in a sludge of gravy—bread and butter, sugar-steeped black tea and tinned peaches or apple crumble. He'd appear grinning at their door, lower his creaking bones on to the end of one bed or the other, and feel for a small foot beneath the covers: My darling first-born, my precious second-born. Anna and Hugo stirred, scooting upright to the heads of their beds: Read us a story. Okeydoke, and he'd page mutely through their creased, friable, cottony boardbooks, sigh, deeply dispirited, and end up spinning them a story of his own. Anna learned to read early, hungrily and well. Her books were passed on to Hugo, and from him to the Pandowie orphanage, where children like Chester Flood might read them. Anna lowered her concealing wings of hair into her mother's childhood books—thick-papered English hockey stick and Empire stories—and dreamed her way into the colour plates. She ran about in a gym slip with flying ribboned hair, dodged spears on the frontier, grappled with swarthy spies on the running board of a touring car on a mountain pass in a small, fir-tree Balkan state. She soon left her friends behind, she left the school library behind, and began to sneak into corners with books from her mother's bedside table. She read like a fast, hungry vacuum, sucking in dizzying, rousing, half-understood characters and notions. All that indirect talk, all that flesh made willing and weak. Her mother found her one day and half-heartedly tried to prise the book from her hands: Sweetheart, I want you to understand, life's not like that. Not like what? Her mother's face, pink and hesitant, grew sharp and certain at last: Loose morals. There were other clipped and pointless lessons over the years. When Anna started at the university there were five hundred eighteen-year-olds enrolled in English 1. She floundered. She understood one thing in the books she was expected to read, her lecturers and tutors another. She felt that she must have been only half alert all those years ago, curled up with a book in a corner, or that she had somehow missed half the lines on the page. When she lay waiting through the slow months for her first child to be born, her blood beat slowly within her. Only mustard pickles and manor-house mystery novels would stir it. The mysteries were delivered by the boxload from the lending library that Grandfather Tolley had set up behind the canned peaches in the Four Square Store. Her mind would wander from time to time. She'd put a book down and ask herself: What if? What if this were Lockie's child kicking in my belly? If Lockie had not been so cruelly taken from her, that is. She'd lost six weeks of her life when it happened, had lived six weeks of a parallel life. According to a flick-page magazine in the doctor's waiting room, something similar had happened to Agatha Christie. Anna went very still when she read that. She felt a kind of elation, a connection in time to the heart-ached author. One day Mr Jaeger came to her with jars of relish from the stone house in the gully below and placed half a dozen slim, cheap pamphlets in her lap. Then he stepped back, struck a commanding pose against her patchwork valley view, and pointed, his finger quivering at the books, her womb: Things you should know, now that you are about to bring a young one into the world. The lines in his face were like cracks in concrete. She glanced down, saw *Conspiracy* and *Elders of Zion* among the obscured titles. Her father-in-law counted on his fingers: The family, Christianity, private enterprise, non-interference from government, insularity in world affairs. One finger bored at the baby within her: There is a nexus between communism and Jewish internationalists, did you know that? I suppose you were taught by pinkos and Jews at the varsity? The Jews, he continued, counting again, have been responsible for the Russian Revolution, most of the recent wars, organised crime, feminism. Did you know—he delicately lifted a wilting pamphlet from her lap—that Hitler was part-Jew himself? The bastard son of Baron Rothschild? His extermination policy was financed by wealthy Jewish internationalists, for devious ends. Anna manoeuvred her heavy rump to the leading edge of the chair, planted her hands upon the armrests, hauled herself to her feet. The pamphlets spilled to the floor. She kicked them flying, stumbled and swayed: Get out, get out, get out. You . . . are . . . poisoning . . . me. There was a time when books were an unsafe subject around Anna's daughter: Mother, you are part of the straight hegemony. Have I read this, have I read that, dead white males, living white males. The system has colonised me; I wish to decolonise myself. Anna believed that Rebecca was unhappy. She could not say: You'll meet someone soon, but it was what she thought. Then Rebecca bought a house. Anna helped her unpack, and the woman there in her daughter's kitchen that first morning had clearly stayed the night. They broke for coffee. Where to begin? Anna relaxed. Let them break the ice with me. She watched the stranger obliquely. Where Becky was dark and darting, Meg was slow, tall and lazy, a blue butterfly the size of a thumbnail where her flaming hair touched one bare shoulderblade. Finally, Meg blew a wobbly smoke ring toward the ricepaper shade: Have you read, she said, naming a Chicago private eye, and Rebecca and Anna leaned forward, eyes alight. Now the three women swap books and argue that so-and-so's latest book is not as good as her first, her most recent. One of Anna's disappointments as her eyes grow weaker will be the limited range of large print titles in her local library. She will spend more time thinking. She will attend the monthly meetings of a reading group from time to time but come away irritated with the know-all women, the sweetness-and-light women, the women who talk only about their children.

Dancing

GRANDMOTHER ISON LOVED to dance. She was more spirited than the Isons, who were dour, pessimistic and hectoring, the slow flame of grievances nudging their hearts along. Even though Great Aunt Beulah wore her down, cruelly pleased to have someone at her beck and call, Grandmother Ison danced to remind herself of who she had been before she married into the Isons. For a start, she was not born to be a Methodist—she liked a sip of sherry and she loved to dance. Try to imagine that these crossed sticks are swords, Anna dear, she said. Hands on hips, back straight, on your toes, knees high, this is how we do the Highland Fling. Anna wore a heavy pleated tartan skirt, white socks, black shoes; her ribboned hair bounced against her spine. The skirt flowed, divided, lifted and fell, and for the first time in her life she sensed her body, its grace, ease and arrogance. Bravo, Grandma Ison said. Anna's mother confided: She used to teach me too, on the quiet. It's not that my dad was against dancing, but he'd grown up in a very strict household and never really approved of it, so Mum and I used to practice in the woolshed when he wasn't looking. I would love to have gone to balls and dances when I was a girl. I'll take you dancing, Anna's father said, and he whisked the children and their mother off to the Woolshed Dance at Showalter Park. The woolshed, a dark, echoing, six-gabled stone chamber the size of half-a-dozen houses, with stands for sixty shearers, was on the National Trust register. Nothing would ever crack or shift it. As two hundred pairs of feet stamped upon the hardwood floor, and dust and cigarette smoke gauzed the air, Anna and Hugo dangled their legs over the edge of a wooden platform and watched the women spin their skirts, the men their glossy shoes. Behind them the band sawed and thumped. Anna itched to dance. She rocked on her haunches, bobbed and swayed, then stood, and felt her feet begin to move. She danced through the evening, a solitary figure caught in the repeating rhythms of the greasy night. She turned thirteen and was not convinced of her beauty. Long, angular, small-handed, composed of hipbones, ribcage, elbows and ankles—who would want her? Besides, there was the question of her luck and of her unlucky age, thirteen. But she did not want Mr Wheelwright to pair her at the last minute with a boy who had a pocked, milky face and hadn't had the courage to ask that singsong question: Will you be my partner for the Polonaise? She reasoned that if no boy was going to ask her, she would do the asking. Six weeks before the high school ball, she asked a boy from the schoolbus on the Bitter Wash line, and he blinked, sidled past her, side-mouthing: If you like. The school's tennis courts were weeded and swept, a record player was set up in the corner, and the Head quivered upon a wooden chair above the snaking line of couples: Remember, your parents will be there, Mrs Showalter and her son will be there, the mayor will be there. I'm counting on you not to let the school down. The Polonaise is a stately march, children. Flow with it, heads high, bodies graceful. At the mid-point of a long winter, when the women of Women's College seemed closed-in and crabby, the street rallies futile and Lockie touchy and easily hurt, Anna sought to clean and sharpen herself. The leotard folded into almost nothing. None of her friends ever went near the draughty back streets of the city, where poky shops dispensed tattoos and fast haircuts, and light-stepping, big-bellied, beehived women ran first-floor dance studios, classical and modern. Anna dipped, whirled, leapt, and heard her bare feet slap convincingly on the varnished floor. It gave her courage; it gave her shape. Connie said, as they showered and changed after class: Coming for a drink? It was an unlikely friendship. Hard knocks had scored lines on Connie's face, encouraged a wry, dry rasp in her voice. She smoked and drank and took taxis. Anna was not long married to Sam Jaeger when the town council voted to bring the Mechanics Institute up to ballroom standard. The floor proved to be fast; crystal chandeliers distributed the light. Now there was a reason for a Tennis Club Dance, a Football Club Social, a Cricket Club Hop, and a New Year's Eve Ball to outmatch the one in Yarcowie. Anna had not seen Chester Flood since the old days. His white dress shirt looked very white, his black suit very black. The old, assaying stillness and concentration were still there, and she saw that he was better looking than she'd remembered. He drew back his head to smile at her, witty, courteous and shrewd, his hand firm in the small of her back when they danced. Complicated feelings of loyalty, luck and dishonour made her feet fast, her colour high, her eyes alive, her body half-yielding. She floated home, and Sam said to her at the wheel, as the headlights played over stone walls and foxes on the prowl in the starlight: I saw you, don't go thinking I didn't. You and him and that bloke who got killed, you were pretty tight in the old days. There are not so many opportunities for dancing any more. The policeman has given up on the Blue Light Disco, for the kids want booze, amphetamines, video clips and something to sharpen their hopes for a job. The Bowls Club Social is coming up next week. Anna has promised a potato salad. She likes to dance with Sam, his slow, sturdy, regular beat, and with her brother, who is jokier, clumsier, a familiar slice of herself. The 150th Jubilee Committee has pledged a Gala Ball for the Year 2000 celebrations, maybe an Olympic athlete to present the Belle and Beau of the Ball. In the years to come, stiff, creaking gentlemen will sometimes take Anna to a supper dance, where the music will tinkle obligingly. Her granddaughter will enrol in a Saturday morning ballet class, but, soon after managing the splits, lose interest in favour of horses and charms for her bracelet.

Reunion

TEETH-STAINING TEA IN bone china cups, Anzac biscuits, service medals clanking on Grandfather Ison's dark suit and on their father's sports coat. Even their mother wore a tiny red and gold cloth badge in her lapel. Waiting, in the house in Burnside, until it was time to take a bus in to the Cross of Remembrance. Parking will be hell, Peter, Grandfather Ison said. He had the bus timetable open upon the table. Pom, pom, pom. The children's father stretched his legs, leaned back in the little kitchen chair, clasped his hands behind his head. Smoke wreathed about his sun and smile-crinkled face, and his cigarette bobbed: Good to catch up with the blokes again. Grandfather Ison stiffened. His spine seemed to say: No slouching, not in this house. No talking around a cigarette. Remember who you are, remember it's the Isons you married into, remember what this day represents. It was a day of reunions, but Grandfather Ison wanted it to be a day of mourning. Even Eleanor, his daughter, was going off with her pals from the munitions factory after the ceremony. Anna saw her father snap forward in the chair, swing around to the sideboard and silence the radio: That's better. Couldn't hear myself think. Grandfather Ison swelled: Good God, man, that was a Bach mass. Behind her husband, swirling in her apron, the cake tin in her hands, Grandmother Ison twinkled, a silent message directed at Anna: Your dad likes winding your grandpa up, doesn't he? It'll be a relief when they've finished their tea and left the house so we can have the place to ourselves. The only gift that mattered on Anna's twenty-second birthday was unexpected and unintended: Hi, Anna. Coming home at last, April sometime. Be good to catch up with you. Guess what—they gave me a stripe. Yours etc., Corporal Lachlan Kelly, esq. She turned the card over. Rice and misty saw-teeth mountains, and a kid with a water buffalo. A flicker of outrage: Vietnam's being torn apart by war and they're still making postcards? Not Lockie's fault, though. They'd be reunited soon and that's what mattered. They would start anew. He still wanted her, didn't he? He'd written to say he was coming home—that had to mean something. And he hadn't needed a lucky wound to bring him back. On the morning of the reunion of the Isons, Anna made a potato salad, sorted, weighed and packed fifty dozen eggs, filled the car from the bulk fuel tank, cleaned the children's shoes, got herself and the children ready, and read to them until Sam came in from the paddock. She imagined her way into her mother's skin, walking through the big house on Isonville again: I've been there a few times in the past year, you know, helping Kitch get his facts right for the reunion book and writing letters to far-flung Isons, that kind of thing. I must say I feel better about the bad blood between us. But I've never been invited further than the kitchen. Lorna's a difficult woman. Did you know yours is an old family name? Anna. Hugo's another one. Rebecca. Michael. Old Mrs Mac's been invited. And a million Isons. Kitch has been marvellous. He actually dug up an old photo, it had on the back 'Ison's Field, Berkshire'. Makes you think, doesn't it? That's how Anna's mother had been babbling on for the past few months, and Anna could see now that it was simple excitement. Her mother was a forgiver. So long as Kitch doesn't have a go at me about not checking Chancery records for him, Anna told herself, then maybe I can forgive, too. Anna stared around the heads of her children, beyond the verandah railing, focussing on a flash of windscreen glass in the Jaegers' yard below. Sam and his father, back from the paddock. The father saying something, laying down the law, Sam turning his back, stamping up the track toward the house. The sooner we find somewhere else to live, the better, Anna thought. Sam stormed up the verandah steps: That's the last time I talk to my old man, the last time I work alongside him. I'm cutting myself free. As of now, I'm a separate person. We'll never be reconciled. But then Michael was killed. Sam grieved. He looked accusingly at Anna: What were you doing on that part of the road, anyhow? He wanted his mother and his father around him. He was away for most of the day. Anna and Rebecca heard the thin slam of the Land Rover's door just as the sun irradiated the clouds behind the Razorback and died. Rebecca ran to him and he swept her up. Anna remained where she was; she knew that she must seem cold and staring to her husband and her daughter, but she had no light left in her. Sam hesitated in the doorway, finally bursting out: I had to come home. I couldn't stand it any longer. They had their holy rollers there. Wanted me to sit around in a circle with them, holding hands. Said we were going to thank God for taking Michael. And his voice cracked. Rebecca's arms went tight around him. At least Sam had the love of a daughter in his life. Reunions, anniversaries, get togethers. Anna was reunited with Maxine, but not with Lockie. On the twentieth anniversary of the Hammersmith house, she was not at the base of Nelson's Column, and nor, she supposed, were the New Zealanders who had taken her in. Tonight Anna is on the telephone to North Adelaide: They've even planned a high school reunion. I tell you, Becky, I'm getting tired of the word Jubilee. You're a cynic, Mother. I liked that school. I wouldn't mind catching up with everyone again. Becky, you hated school. No I didn't. School was an escape. Anna swallows. She wants to cry. She doesn't know what the truth is about some things, any more. She doesn't know if Becky's being tactless or intending to wound. Anna's frame will shrink and her bones grow brittle, and she'll wonder, when the time comes: With whom, in death, shall I be reunited? Will Michael still be five years old with a smiling dimpled chin, or will he be middle aged, as I am old? Will my grandmother bear the wounds of those tearing teeth? Will she like me? Will the other one want to dance?

Drunk

MRS MAC WAS shickered again. The signs were her rousing laughter and the ebb and flow of poorly remembered songs at the other end of the house. The children's mother confirmed it: Shickered again. She would never apply so hard a word as *drunk* to Mrs Mac; nor would it occur to her to mislead the children. Mrs Mac sometimes had a little too much to drink—a sad, sad affliction for poor Mrs Mac. The single bottle of Southwark Bitter in their own fridge and the decanter of visitors' cream sherry on their sideboard were not the same thing at all, for these bottles were scarcely ever opened and the children had better remember that. Their mother's giggling two glasses on Christmas Day didn't count, either. Anna kept to the winding path between the hollyhocks and lavender, listening to Mrs Mac, listening to the satisfying crush and snicker of the white pebbles beneath her sandalled feet. She rounded the corner, where the subsided ground had sucked the glassy cement of the verandah with it, and found Mrs Mac planted unsteadily in carpet slippers outside Great Aunt Beulah's bedroom window. Mrs Mac's eyes were glittering discs, her lips wide and wetly open over her shifting dentures. She bawled: Now Jim poor soul's got a belly full of coal and he corfs up lumps of coke, oi! Come on, youngster, with me now. La, la, la et cetera, oi! Anna watched, closed-in and silent. She wanted some sort of showy disaster. She couldn't see any bottles nearby. They would have been inside the house somewhere. The evidence was all in Mrs Mac: Bad-tempered old cow, your Auntie Beulah. Thinks her shit doesn't stink. Whoops! Pardon me, your highness. One year the children of the primary school were enlisted by the returned servicemen of the district to collect empty bottles for Legacy. Remember the widows and fatherless children, the RSL president cried above a blustery northerly, and grades five, six and seven were waved through the school gates with chaff bags upon their backs. Anna and Maxine paired off to search the grassy ditches and thistly culverts behind the Stock & Station sale yards. They came back with eight bottles, a wheel-less toy and a mud-and-horsehair bird's nest dislodged from a tree by the high winds. They sniffed at and upended each bottle before placing it in their sacks. They giggled, fancying that the sharp stale beer whiff had unhinged their senses. Anna staggered in the roadside gravel, bawling: He wears gorblimey trousers and he lives in a council flat! She roamed the back roads behind Isonville and Showalter Park on her bicycle, the pannier hooked to her handlebars so full of bottles that she had to fight to steer a safe line between the potholes, sleepy lizards and heat-snapped fallen branches. The mail contracter slowed to pass her, then accelerated grimly away, his springs creaking, the dust of the sunken road wreathing about her head. She saw him stop at the Park's massive stone gateposts, lodge the gaol-sewn mailbag in the box, whine off down the road again, and, just as she drew adjacent to the curving drive, Mr Showalter himself was there to collect the mail. He didn't see Anna at first. His hand went in, came out with the mailbag. Again he reached in, and this time he had a bottle of whisky, a handy pocket size. Anna saw a flash of glass and then the bottle was inside the concealing folds of his jacket as her squeaky wheels betrayed her on the road. He knew that she'd caught him. He winked, his puffed, rubbery features bunching like a glove, then grinned, his bloodshot eyes disappearing: It's our little secret, he said. Just you, me, the mailman and the gatepost. But his drinking was not a secret; nor was the fact that his friends and acquaintances delivered bottles to him on the quiet; nor that he could be a menace at the wheel of a car when he'd been drinking. For a time at Women's College Anna drank until she lost consciousness. They all did it. A kind of drinkers' club existed and they might play poker, and smoke and swig down beer and cheap wine, for twelve hours at a stretch. Anna fell in slow, sleepy, smiling, good-natured stages toward oblivion. She was not an argumentative, bitter or lashing-out drunk. But then one of them pitched head first to the ground from a second floor balcony and was paralysed for life, so they disbanded the club and nobody spoke of it again. Anna learned to pace herself. Two drinks were generally sufficient to relax her clenched jaws, her tight stomach muscles, and drive the demons away. Two sundowners on the verandah, watching Sam, her husband, dust-scribbling on the tractor in the valley below. She almost loved him then. Wesley Showalter was clearly three sheets to the wind before lunch on the day a stud breeder from Dubbo wrote out a cheque for thirty-four thousand dollars to buy Pandowie Showalter Lustre 6. The women of the Ladies' Auxiliary kept their distance from him behind the trestle bench in the refreshment tent—he was very fumy, very noisy, and rough with it. It was the same every year, the biggest field day in the state, let down by Wesley Showalter himself. His movements during the afternoon left gaps of an hour or so unaccounted for, but a sharefarmer from Yarcowie remembered seeing him fishtail away from the big house in the dusty Bentley at about four o'clock and disappear on to the sunken road, probably bound for the Bon Accord. Anna's Jubilee history is thematic, not chronological, in structure. She's found this in *The Park: the First Hundred Years*, privately published by Mrs Showalter in 1950:

> A great many of the shearers and hut-keepers are the off-scourings of English prisons, and a more insolent set of scoundrels you could not find. They are much given to spending all of their money on drink and bad women, but there are few good men of the labouring classes hereabouts, and, from their long servitude on the Sydney side, they all know a good deal about sheep.

These days Anna may have a glass of wine in the evening. Possibly two, if she's in the city and Meg and Rebecca have taken her to a restaurant. It's always Meg who orders the wine. She's a frowner, never satisfied with the wine list. Rebecca drinks mineral water. She tasted an alcoholic drink once, and hated it. Anna will find a nightly Scotch more satisfying as she grows rounder and more creaking and puts her feet up at the end of the day. It will be a 'thing' about her, known to the family. When those closest to her fly back to the country from abroad they will always be carrying a duty-free bottle of Glenfiddich for Anna, who will want to share it and want to save it.

Secrets

GREAT AUNT BEULAH cloaked herself in secrets. They were all she had left. Secrets kept her out of the grave and were her chief weapon—in her feebleness, trembling and reliance on a keeper—against first Grandmother Ison and then Mrs Mac.

Come here, dear, she would say, drawing Anna to her like another secret: We don't want that old bat to hear this, do we, sticking her nose in where it's not wanted. Anna glanced back over her shoulder. Surely Mrs Mac had heard? Yes—you could tell by her tipped-up nose that she had. Beulah's clamped claw trembled on Anna's forearm as if to shake her apart: I had a lover, dear, forbidden to me by my father. Such a fine-looking man, riding up the drive on his horse to see me, grinning to beat the sun. And sing! She lowered her voice: I would sneak out after dark to be with him. He wanted us to run away together. He said: Don't tell your father. But I did, I don't know why. Don't you make the same mistake, dear. The lost weeks of Anna's grandfather in 1920 was another incident in the secret history of the family, and Anna's mother did not reveal it until he was dead. She said: It's not that he went mad, you know. It was just a breakdown, the sort of thing that could happen to anybody. Imagine the pressures he was under, the disappointments, stuck for weeks on end in that godforsaken place with no one to talk to. It's no wonder he lost track of time. But you're not to think that that kind of thing runs in the blood, Anna, and there's no need to repeat any of this. Anna reared back. As if she would! Anna herself was full of secrets and always would be. She gave up none of them, secrets confided or her own. Lying and evasion are components of secrecy. Whenever Anna got into trouble she'd spin explanations and excuses so elaborate and confounding that her accusers would soon abandon grilling her. Yet she was struck by how easy it was to free others of their secrets. Anna was a listener, always watching, thinking, making connections, and she had only to sit and stare at the eyes to hear all there was to hear. It was not only children, drunks and adulterers who wanted to confide in her. Most people felt the burden of their secrets and gave them up with a sigh the moment Anna pinned them with her clear, unblinking, acquitting eyes. But Lockie found out about the tutor. One night he followed Anna to the house in Unley and kept watch on it until the dawn, shivering grimly behind a dewy windscreen and putting two and two together. Your secret life, he said sourly. Anna retorted: At least I don't sneak about. He scowled: Anna, listen to yourself. What do you think screwing behind my back is if it's not sneaking about? She folded her arms: Who are you to talk morals? You're about to go off and learn how to kill people. He went away to camp, he sailed for the South China Sea. She didn't see him again. There was only a postcard, an exhilarated postcard that left her feeling oddly abandoned and outpaced. Habits of secrecy and evasion were necessary if Anna and Sam were to contend with Sam's parents. They learned to conceal what they had spent their paltry allowance on, to conceal their only holiday together, their thoughts, even their children. One day Mrs Jaeger abruptly ceased her endless polishing and stared fully at Anna, her face twisted in fury and impotence: You're a sly one. I don't understand people like you. Anna made love to Chester only once, but once was enough. It was a terrible secret. Perhaps even thinking about him to begin with was enough to count as a dangerous hidden fact. She happened to read in a magazine at the doctor's that in three out of four couples one partner harbours a secret which, if revealed, would destroy the partnership. Anna snorted, startling the others in the waiting room: Don't reveal it, then. Rebecca was eighteen when she telephoned to say that she was bringing a friend home for the weekend—and oh by the way, the friend was a woman and they were lovers. This last bit was muttered hurriedly and there was a click and then the dial tone as Rebecca broke the connection. Anna thought, irrelevantly: My daughter has no skills for this kind of thing. The revelation itself affected her not at all. Anna didn't mind, she wanted only for her daughter to be happy, but irritation set in: Does she expect me to tell Sam, or does she want it kept secret from him, or does she want to tell him herself? No, she wants me to tell him. And when I do, he won't say anything. He won't know how to deal with it and so he'll not deal with it. Beyond being faintly embarrassed when Rebecca and her friend are here, he'll say and do nothing to acknowledge the fact that he knows, or that he cares. It will be as though Rebecca has a secret life, in a parallel time, and he need never be aware of it, if it's not brought to his attention. And bringing it to his attention will practically entail sitting him down and stating it slowly, loudly, clearly into his face. Why do that? It would only hurt everybody. And what of the grandparents? My mother will be okay about it but the Jaegers won't. I shall never tell them. I'll leave that up to Becky. Anna did tell Sam, it was not mentioned again, and things are mostly okay now. Sam has jokey phone conversations with Meg whenever he rings Rebecca, so that's all right. A few weeks ago there'd been something he wanted to get off his chest. Anna had waited patiently, and one evening, as she was sorting through photographs from the Public Record Office, he said hesitantly: Anna? Yes, my love? He swallowed: I've some bad news. Uh huh. In a rush: I borrowed against our place and sank it into that breeding scheme of the Showalters'. We'll maybe get back two cents on the dollar. The world is teeming with secrets but few of them surprise Anna. She will play 'Can You Keep a Secret?' with her granddaughter and enjoy her visits to Pandowie, where she will listen to the stories Hugo and her mother have for her about the people she grew up with. She will hear a secret that will leave her feeling numb with pity and love. Her mother will ask, unexpectedly: Were you involved with Chester Flood at the time Michael was killed? Kind of, yes. Silence for a while, then: It was understood that Wes Showalter and I would get engaged. But I was more interested in Rex. We used to meet in secret, but the war took him to Europe and he was lost over Germany. After that I couldn't marry Wes. Funny how things turn out.

Food

FOR EGGS THE households on Isonville relied upon half a dozen black hens. A faint, engrossed scratch and murmur filled the daylight hours, a perpetual background busyness beneath the wiry hedges. At sundown the hens bobbed spastically into the open and crossed the yard to the wire-netting pen and sheltered roosts at the rear of the house. It was Hugo's task to toss them kitchen scraps at night and Anna's to collect the eggs in the morning. Two generations ago an Ison had planted apricot, apple, quince and fig trees to screen the big house from the overseer's cottage. The families rarely ate beef. A ewe or a hogget, butchered once a month, provided chops, liver, brains and leg roasts. They got milk and cream from a couple of Jersey cows. The children often felt a kind of slathering avarice for scalded cream. There were occasions, abundant springtimes, when the milk tasted of the wild-flowering grasses that had begun to choke the paddocks. Anna grew carrots and radishes in a narrow strip of weedy soil beside her father's tomato vines, sweetcorn and sandy lettuces. One numbing and bitter day in August, when the windborne rain slanted far into the shelter shed and the ground was as hard as iron, Anna gave up her school lunch to Chester Flood. He sat with everybody but he had no lunch box open upon his knees. The nuns had dressed him in patched shorts and a threadbare grey pullover, and Anna couldn't bear to see the purple cold-bruises on his shanks or hear his helpless teeth. He ate the jam sandwich; she ate a rock bun; neither said a word. Anna wrote about race relations on the frontier for her honours research project. According to Mrs Showalter's old family memoir, the Protector of Aborigines had toured the district in 1842:

> Consequent upon the presence of great numbers of cattle and sheep hereabouts, the chief food of the Native, namely the kangaroo, the emu and the wallaby, has been unprocurable and so he makes armed attacks upon the hut-keepers, carrying off livestock, occasionally with the loss of life on both sides. I have communicated with representatives of the northern tribes on the subject. They acknowledge having attacked the flocks, claiming *shipi paru padlotti* (a longing for sheep's flesh). I advised them to desist, for they risked rendering themselves obnoxious in the sight of the European and liable to persecution and abuse. I am now satisfied that they fully understand the nature of our laws and punishments on the points of theft and murder, and expect no further trouble from them. Indeed, one settler has made tea, flour, sugar and tobacco available in exchange for labouring duties, the Native proving to be most adept at hauling stone, and on occasion a lubra will deliver a wild turkey and be paid in flour, which she gobbles from her cupped hands.

Anna's tutor had never heard of the book: Indulgent family history, privately published—how can you be sure it's accurate? he demanded. Is there any real analysis? Anna's job in London entitled her to luncheon vouchers, issued in bundles of five on payday once a week. Her pay was mean, the luncheon vouchers were mean. One voucher, exchanged for a thin, cramped wedge of sandwich or an apple and a finger of stale cake was not enough to take away her hunger. She needed food to fill her up and she needed it to help her forget. When she had been married for five years and the children were toddlers, her twin cousins, the daughters of Kitchener and Lorna, had a double wedding in the garden at Isonville. A vast striped marquee crowded the lawn at the front of the house, the canvas bellying and exhaling as a hot northerly blew in across the lucerne flats. Anna sat with Sam, Hugo and her parents at a trestle table next to the bridal party and picked at cold chicken and potato salad while Hugo sneezed and wiped his scratchy eyes. Anna drank too much and took showy risks on the portable dance floor, her way of fighting down old grievances. She had not seen her uncle and aunt for many years and rarely since the day they'd forced her family out. Kitchener and Lorna had prospered at Isonville, but there were no sons to carry on the Ison line, only sons-in-law from the city, sleek men who would carve the property up when Kitchener and Lorna died. Anna could see her mother thinking these things, see the complicated memories and hopes in her face. Then Uncle Kitch appeared at their elbows: I was thinking about an Ison family reunion, this time next year. What do you think? Eleanor? Care to help me arrange it? The field days every April were pretty daggy, in Anna's view. She always helped with the catering, more as a way of gathering information for the *Chronicle* than as a commitment to the district. She didn't notice Wesley Showalter's drunkenness this time: she wore her new dress and was daydreaming. Should she go to Chester naked underneath? She beamed across the cups and saucers and plates of scones in the Ladies' Auxiliary tent, confusing the orders and blushing at the frankness of the scenes playing behind her shining eyes. She did see Wesley Showalter at the funeral, four days later, staring abjectly at the ground. He thought that he was fully culpable, but Anna knew better, Anna shared in the guilt. She should not have been coming home from seeing a lover or enjoying the lingering sensation of him on her skin but concentrating on the shapes coming toward her through the dust on the sunken road. Years later, something happened to cure her of her guilt. To celebrate Rebecca's acceptance as a student at the Conservatorium, Sam and Anna arranged a meal out at the Bon Accord Hotel. Dinners there were a joke, everyone knew that, but that was part of the appeal. The steaks came drenched in gravy on chunky white plates and Rebecca's salad was awash in vinegar. That awful man, Rebecca said suddenly, and Anna looked through the smoky alcove to the front bar. Wesley Showalter stood there swaying and shouting, his heavy face red with power and unhealthy blood. He recognised her, went still, then began to elbow jab through the smaller men until he was framed in the alcove and finally booming above them, dipping alarmingly at Rebecca: You've grown, girlie. Rebecca shrank away from him. He stood at a rocky attention again: Worst day of my life. Should've stayed at home. Anna understood that he meant the day he slammed her car into the rock face. They stared at him. After a while he wandered away. Last week Anna put it to the Jubilee Committee that tribal seeds, berries, grubs, tubers and insects should be included in a proposed display of the district's foodstuffs. Her suggestion was approved by a vote of seven to six, but only after some forceful lobbying on her part. Today she is making notes about the double suicide on Showalter Hill for her column in the *Chronicle*. The Red Cross had stepped in with food and mugs of tea after the funeral, but Anna finds that she cannot bring herself to mention their generosity or the funeral itself, not when the suicide is clearly an indication of a deep malaise: The government would do well not to ignore the level of disenchantment of the people who make the nation's food, and we would do well not to place all of our hopes in the Jubilee festivities. As she learns to cook for one, Anna will find herself eating less and better food. She will learn to make small economies. One of the pleasures of her life will be to buy fruit and vegetables fresh from the market gardens that ring the city, for fruit and vegetables at Tolley's Four Square had always displayed the wear and tear of storage and transport and were rarely a pleasure upon her tongue.

Hate

BEULAH IS EASY to hate, hard to love, Grandmother Ison said. The old cow. Anna gave the appearance of not listening, of absorption in her crayonned chimneys, smoke and hillsides. In the armchairs above her bowed spine her mother said: Don't let her get to you, Mum. It's eating away at you. Grandma Ison shifted her careworn, bony frame. It's a trade-off, isn't it? Beulah rescued us after your father's breakdown and now she's extracting her pound of flesh. Literally. Hateful old cow. Anna looked up. At once her grandmother said: Sharp ears. How would you like to dance the swords with me again, sharp ears? Four years later, when the old generation had died out and everything had gone to the son and nothing to the daughter, Anna's mother said: I want to remember my father with love but it's hard not to hate him. She said: I want to love my brother, but tell me how I can. If he would just give us something, release some land to us. Didn't I count? Don't I count? An unfamiliar harshness had entered her voice, as if she were edging warily through treacherous new emotions, hate and envy and a sense of deep, deep offence. Hate rose easily in Anna's heart on her mother's behalf. She treated Uncle Kitch, Aunt Lorna and her cousins with disdain. If they happened to inquire, in their side-door manner, how the house-hunting was progressing, the hate came back to bite her, sidling in on her flank when she least expected it. She came home from school one day and saw the dog stretched where there was no afternoon sun to warm his bones. Kip, she called. Kippy. He lifted his tail once and let it fall. He was disinclined to stand. Anna's fingers flew over his fur, encountering blood, while his snapping jaws tracked her hand apologetically. Did Auntie Lorna do this to you? Bloody bitch. Anna's quick mind aroused hatred. She was hated for experimenting with boys. She met the hateful sneers and curled lips face to face, silent and proud, and understood that envy breeds hatred. So did difference, so did fear, so did public display. Think you're so smart, said the faces lining Frome Street. Think you'll be allowed to do this when your slant-eyed friends take us over? Join a circus if you want to make fools of yourselves. There was bewilderment in her father's letters: Do you really hate us? What did we do, for you to hate us like this? *Talk* to us, sweetheart, he said. Lockie said: You're filled with so much hate. You spout love of mankind but it looks like hate to me, your face all twisted up. Anna put both hands to her cheeks, suddenly aware that he was right, that something like hate was wrenching her mouth into hateful shapes. She counted to ten and said evenly: What do you think you're doing, learning to kill people, if it's not hate? Lockie's finger quivered: Quit it. Just you quit it, twisting words around. Must've been mad, thinking we'd ever end up together. Anna married into the Jaegers. Such hatred. It simply poured out of her father-in-law, a leaning-forward, voice-lowered, eyes-narrowed assumption of a common ground between them: You can tell by the nose if there's a dash of the Jew. Crinkled hair, your black. The complexion—you can tell a lot from the complexion. A dash of the Abo—look for a thickness about the lips, the spread nostrils. Would he be Greek or

Italian, that new bloke in the bank? Turkish maybe? Same bloodline. Sam hated Anna for a while when Michael was killed. He blamed her. He was too grieving and too polite to say so, but she knew. Hate need not be showy; hate may burn coldly, forever. At first, Anna didn't hate Wesley Showalter. She allowed him a certain right to venture out at the wheel of the black Bentley that day, just as she'd allowed herself a secret elation from being with Chester Flood. And there were simply too many other factors involved for Anna to blame Wesley Showalter alone: water in her fuel line, the choking dust, the hungry sheep, the blind corners of the sunken road. But she did eventually learn to hate him. He had been born to rule, and no matter what tragedy or mistake he caused, he would never lose that assumption or the power it gave him. He'd never learn; he'd never truly be sorry. And so she felt hate; her frustration and her impotence bred hate. One day a stockman on a station property behind the Razorback entered the homestead with a hunting rifle and shot dead the manager and his wife. The district said instantly: Probably she wouldn't sleep with him. Or she wouldn't leave her husband. The papers printed his likeness: skin pasted to the bone. Half a day later, fear set in under the swift shadow of the Showalter Park Cessna and the beating rotors of the police helicopter as they crisscrossed the dry country behind the Razorback. The killer had been seen crossing the Murray, passing through Gawler, slipping among the quartz reefs on the Razorback itself. The women and children of the outlying stations began to drift into the town, making for Tolleys Four Square, where Anna's father served free coffee and made them shiver and laugh. Crazy, they said of the killer; he was crazy with jealousy. That's what love can lead to. But Anna thought it might have been hate. She imagined the cold, unloved, whitewashed walls of the stockman's quarters, the yawning gulf between the stockman and the world inside the big house. Then someone found the man dead with the rifle between his knees in the property's Land Rover on the bank of Ison's Creek. He was coming to kill me, Aunt Lorna shrieked. Stupid woman, shut up, Anna's father said. The stockman shot himself because he hated what he'd done, said the sages of the district, but Anna doubted that too. He'd got rid of the focus of his hate and left himself with nothing. Carl Hartwig is rubbing his gingery hands together over Anna's latest observation in the *Chronicle*: Some of the Showalter Park workers have spent the greater part of their working lives on the stud. Is it any wonder that they felt intensely proud of its origins and heritage, the world-class reputation of its wool clip, its vital role in Australia's merino industry? Now they are dismayed, as we all are, to see it go so rapidly under after almost one hundred and fifty years of hard work. And not only the workers. Many of us had a stake in the Park's new technology and have lost our life savings. It's as though an admired parent has shown us feet of clay. The excesses are hateful: the flights interstate, the frequent trips overseas, the wholesale gutting of the big house to make way for costly renovations, the lavish parties, the extravagant colour brochures, the annual Field Day circus. And how have the Showalters atoned for everything? By running a brokerage firm called Golden Fleece from an Edwardian mansion in the Adelaide Hills, leaving we here in the mid-north to pick up the pieces. The letters are pouring into the *Chronicle*: Does Mrs Jaeger hate us, writing these things about us? Maybe she hates Australia and should go and live in certain countries to our north where she can indulge her hate. What we want, in this lead-up to our Jubilee festivities, is positive thinking and selfless love of town and district, indeed nation. But I'm only pointing out, Anna begins, but Sam, or someone in the street, is always cutting her off, spitting hate in her face. So much hate. The locals listen to idealogues on talkback radio or on mail-order audio-cassettes, and Sam has invited a soapbox thumper to address a Save Australia rally on issues of moral decline, the right of citizens to bear arms, the immigration crisis. And so Anna admonishes herself: Keep your head down, your mouth shut. She will become a good hater. She will enjoy hating, learning that there is no profit in hating for personal reasons but plenty in hating for the common good. Politicians, posturing fools, people in the public eye.

Water

CLEAN WATER, BORE water, rainwater, fresh water, water supply, out of water, wrigglies in the water, don't waste water, tank water, water under the bridge. The four figures circled the house—the man on the verandah roof, keeping to the capped nails where the beams ran beneath the corrugated iron, the children and the dog below him, metres out from the walls so that they could see him clearly. When he stopped, they stopped. He carried a zinc bucket and a painter's trowel. Metal scraped against metal and Anna's flesh crawled with it. Her father finished scooping up the rubbish in the rainwater gutter and tipped it into the bucket. Dirt, straw, petals of old paint, leaves, mud-encrusted feathers. He moved on a short distance, scraped again. The iron sheets of the main roof overlapped unevenly where they hung over the guttering, leaving points like hidden razors to snag the skin on the backs of his hands. From time to time he wiped the blood on his trousers, and Anna imagined the blood falling into the gutter, the rain washing it into the underground tank. Beside her, Kip yelped and circled in the dirt, wanting the man to come down from out of the sky where he did not belong. Hush, she said. Another, smaller, ground-level roof concealed the underground tank, an echoing chamber the size of Anna's bedroom. Padlocked doors kept the children out but there was an open porthole in the low wall just above the ground, breathing cool, damp, ancient exhalations at them and frequently sounding a piping note deep down in the blackness. Anna knew all about water. She owned a plastic stencil of the country. You placed your pencil hard against the outside edge, starting at Cape York Peninsula, and traced around the coastline crinkles to the Gulf of Carpentaria. Scored inside the stencil was a short, hooked channel, the river system, but not long or broad enough to be considered one of the major rivers of the world, according to Mr Wheelwright. She lived in the driest state in the driest continent in the world, a fact she was not allowed to forget. Mr Wheelwright ran the tip of his cane down the wall map: Goyder's Line. To farm outside it meant risk and heartache. Old-timers joked: I've been watching that cloud on the horizon there for the past ten years. Often the rains came too little or too late. Once a severe frost gripped the mid-north. Forgotten washing hung as stiff as washboards on back yard clotheslines and pipes burst, freezing the water-spray into diamond-winking ice necklaces under the early sun. An underground tank was not enough. Isonville had two above-ground tanks sitting on mossy railway sleeper stands for backup in the dry seasons. One tank was minutely holed and the seepage had calcified over the decades into a lumpish formation that invited the tongue on hot days. The children were warned not to climb into old refrigerators but they were never warned not to explore Ison's Creek. They sent boats into the current. In winter they measured the high-water mark in the pasted grasses high on the bank, and in the drought years they trudged over the tocking dry roundstones in the creekbed. To Anna's knowledge, flashfloods had never reached as high as the headstone of the drowned shepherd boy. When the family moved to the six-forty acres they ran into water trouble. There had only been an old bachelor on the place before: A man, Anna's father said, who was a stranger to bathwater. One narrow galvanised iron tank, scarcely big enough for an old cracked-brain bachelor let alone a family. The children went with their father to a clearing sale and came back with a second-hand rainwater tank roped to the tray of the little Austin. There was a dam in the paddock behind the house, fed by a poor suggestion of a creek. All the history seemed to vanish from Anna's life in that salt-damp house, which had no decent creek, no grave from the last century, no line stretching from 1850 to the present. She started to go out with boys. They took her to the old mine above the town. Eyeless sheds, rusting hoppers and pulleys, nude stone chimneys, heat-buckled railway tracks, hillsides sliced open across the grain, and no trees, only wiregrass tussocks and red dirt anthills. But there were the bottomless shafts, flooded for over a century, the water as blue as sapphires. You sat in his seat and dreamed your way into the blueness, wore the blueness maybe as a dress or a ring, or plunged unheedingly into it, in a shimmering dive from the rocks, seeking the rapture of the deep, while all the time his thick fingers probed and he gave off ignitable, eye-prickling fumes of cheap aftershave. They were beefy, loose-lipped redheads and towheads, those first few boys, and they put Anna off big men for good. Anna's end-of-year exams marked the start of the bushfire season. She always came home to swot, counting upon the familiar beat of the farm to see her through the temporary madness—feed hay to the sheep, check the bores, help mend a fence, fill the 44-gallon drums of the firefighting plant with water pumped from the dam. She lost concentration one day, framing an answer to daydreamed attacks on her stance against the war, and allowed the mouth of the inlet hose to sink into the mud. Her father jerked it out of her hands, looking at her curiously: Wake up, missy. At first, when Anna married into the Jaegers, she liked their orderliness—tidy sheds, well-oiled machinery, no weeds, a clean canvas spout on the fire water tank at the gate on the main road, clean bulk containers of diesel and petrol for the farm vehicles. That's why she didn't expect the car to have fuel-line trouble. Rainwater, old man Jaeger explained, pointing to the cap on the massive tank above their heads, and he proceeded to show her how to remove the fuel filter and the float bowl in the engine compartment and blow the water out. Anna was appalled: You mean each time the car stalls, or chokes when I try to accelerate out of trouble, I'm to get under here with a handful of spanners and fix it? Wouldn't it be easier all round if you were to fix the seal on the overhead tank? Dollars and cents, girlie, the old man said. A bit of grease won't do you any harm. Now that Showalter Park is in the hands of receivers, *Shame File* reporters have been snooping around, splashing the excesses over the front page of the Adelaide dailies—two 300 SEL Mercedes saloon cars, marble quarried in Italy, a spa with gold-plated taps, a ballroom with a white grand piano, not to mention the artificial lake. A swimming pool, fine, but an actual lake? Meg will have an ultrasound at eighteen weeks. The foetus, swimming in its amniotic sea, will resemble nothing so much as a cartoon figure reclining in a hammock, according to Anna. She will move to a house by the sea and Maxine will write from the Gold Coast: Why not get a place near us? But the Gold Coast isn't Anna's idea of the sea. She will walk shoeless on the sand where her grandmother was lost and let the water paint her feet.

Stone

THE CREEK WATER ceased to flow, stilled into pools, and finally, in mid-summer, winked into nothing, leaving tumble-smoothed stones clustered pink, dry and testicular on the sandy bed. The stones clocked satisfyingly under your feet. When the water was high, the children sought hand-sized flakes of the serried rock that skeletoned the country around Isonville. Crouch close to the lapping water, draw back the hand, and throw, encouraging a final spin with your fore-finger, and see it skip-slap across the water, finishing in a juddery display like a kind of emergency braking on the surface. The headstone of the shepherd's son was in fact one massive flake of the same dark rock. Lichen crawled across the chiselled face, filling the grooves and channels that spelled out the boy's name, and his fate, and the father's appeal to God. Anna once noticed a hint of fretting where the stone leaned out of the grass. Her fingernails itched. She dug them in, pulled, and dislodged a segment of the shep-herd's prayer. Hastily she pushed it back but it failed to hold and slipped into the grass. Anna's bad luck, bringing bad luck to others. She never touched the headstone again. Trucks came to the Isonville homestead with gravel every few years and her father helped the men shovel and smooth it along the front drive from the roadside gate to the house. Until the pastelly blue chips of stone were packed down, they seemed to choke and bind the tyres of the children's bicycles like a river of molasses. On the six-forty acres there was no flash long driveway, just a rutted, potholed track. And, in all of the paddocks, unforgiving ranks of white quartz had been pushed to the surface by ancient movements of the earth's plates, treacherous reefs of it concealed in the grass. Heart-breaking country. To farm it efficiently, Anna's father was forced to terrace the steep hillsides, winding his tractor and plough around the stone islands in nervy concentration, full of fear that he might topple the heavy machines, desperate not to waste an inch of the undernourished soil. Their house sat squat and solid at the base of a windy hill on which one last bent-over tree seemed to crawl for shelter behind a fringe of licheny quartz. The masons who had quarried the blocks must have been beefy, sweat-flipping, careless characters, Anna decided. The stones were all sizes and bore unmistakable chisel and crowbar gouges. To prettify the walls the builder had cemented the gaps and scored the wet cement with orderly horizontal and vertical lines. One of the first things Lockie did was take Anna up onto the Razorback. He brought her to a cave, no more than an eye socket in the hillside. She saw lizard shapes, spearheads, stick humans, stick kangaroos bounding ahead of them. I was going around my traps, Lockie said, saw this eagle disappear, and hey presto. Anna peered deeper into the cave and saw the twigs of a nest. It won't attack us? Wrong time of the year, Lockie said. There had been a local tribe, the Ngadjuri, according to Mr Wheelwright, but no guesses as to what had happened to them. Seven years later Anna feared that the rock paintings would be discovered by some heavy-footed actor or producer or clapper-boy or director. She sat in the car with the children and watched the cameras track Sam and the other locals as they staged a Boer charge along a down slope of the Razorback, and willed them not to roam, not to get curious. Mummy, why are you crying? Michael wanted to know. Nothing, she replied, knuckling her eyes. A memory, that's all. When Grandfather Tolley died, Anna's father inherited the Four Square Store and called a family conference. Anna's mother whispered in the kitchen: Do you know what finally decided him? He was working the top paddock and first blew a tyre on the tractor, hundreds of dollars for a new one, then broke an axle of the header on the same blarmy rock. The last straw as far as he was concerned. On the afternoon of the Showalter Park field day, Anna encountered dust. It lay thickly in the deepest channels of the sunken road and swirled about her windscreen. Behind her, in the back seat, Michael cried out, alarmed by a moth. Ahead of her there was nothing, only dust eddies, until the black Bentley appeared, its raised snout and arrogant headlamps bearing down on her from out of the laden air. Anna had been taught not to brake sharply on loose surfaces. She would steer her way out of trouble. She turned the wheel, planted her foot on the accelerator. But the engine faltered. Watery fuel entered the carburettor and the car kangaroo-hopped for a short distance and then they were being sideswiped by the Bentley. They rolled, the car uttering a long, protesting moan, and when it stopped and the wheels were spinning and the strained welds had relaxed again, Anna heard one of her children crying. Rebecca, afraid but unhurt, was crouched confusedly on the side pillar, wondering why the seats and doors and ceiling had rearranged themselves. Near her feet, Michael's window glass had folded inwards over one of the fallen rocks at the edge of the sunken road, like a web-patterned final pillow for his head. The Jubilee Committee intends to restore several sections of the old stonewall fences in the district, using mud and lime to bind the stone in the traditional manner. The most intact section meanders over paddocks and gullies from Isonville to Showalter Park and one wag has painted 'The Great Wall of China' on it in acrylic white, knowing how much that will irritate Kitchener Ison. On one of her visits back to Pandowie, Anna will load a few stones from Ison's Creek into the boot of her car. Small, interesting, colourful ones for the mantelpiece, large ones for a rockery in her tiny garden. One stone in particular will fascinate her granddaughter. No more than a thumbnail-sized, dull-looking pebble, it will darken dramatically when the child places it in her mouth.

Blood

GRANDFATHER TOLLEY BONE-CREAKED down to the level of her head and tut-tutted with a vast khaki handkerchief at the welling blood on her kneecap: You're just like your father. He was always into everything, couldn't take my eyes off him for a second. Anna let herself go slack. Her head lolled on her neck and her trunk loosened as her grandfather's kindly, panicky, cuffing great hands comforted and supported her and staunched the blood. She felt blood in her sock, thick and wet. She had been watching it tick out of her knee just a moment ago, before her grandfather's bulk broke in upon her dreams. Hugo watched nearby, appalled and elated. I warned you two not to go near the barbed wire. Wicked, wicked girl. Both of you, wicked. It's dangerous—very sharp, full of germs, God knows what else. What if you'd bled to death while my back was turned? Life is a very fragile thing. Anna let him pat her leg dry and heard him spit onto his handkerchief and rub it around the cut. She looked out over the floor of his shop and saw the shelves and goods suddenly gleam and quiver as vividly as knives and glass. What will your mother say when she comes to pick you up? She'll think I haven't been taking proper care of you. When the Floods came to live in the town, the oldest boy would do anything for a dare. He'd dive out through the strands of wire in the schoolyard fence and dive back in again, flushed and elastic and untiring, a new boy unloved and in need of an audience. But the grin that split Chester's narrow face and his throaty man's laugh took on a desperate, unrewarded edge as the children began to lose interest and drift away. He rallied: Look, I'm bleeding. Anna drifted back. She put her hands on her knees and peered at the gash on his thigh. It looks deep, she said. Does it hurt? Doesn't hurt. He was beautifully brown from the sun and a dusting of dirt, and Anna felt an appalling need to reach out and touch his dark rich blood before it dried, envying him, for she was pale, a little freckled, an unlovely bleeder. Bad luck that bit of wire hooked me, Chester Flood said. Anna stiffened. She didn't say where the bad luck had come from. There was no telling when her bad luck might jump from her on to someone else. It would happen without warning, a disaster out of nowhere, a shift in the alignment of time, place and people, over which she had no control. Her bad luck seized her father, shoving his poor hand into the whirring auger of the harvester and slicing off the top of his finger. What if her bad luck had been very bad that day? He would have lost his arm, lost his head. Think of the blood then, missy, he said, winking at her from his pillow. Hush, Peter, stop teasing the poor child. Anna held his hand and kneaded the grainy dry palm. Ahh, that's better, he said. The middle finger, swaddled in gauze and smelling of the hospital, stuck out fat and long, as if the doctor had enlarged it while her back was turned. The boys from home began to die. By November Anna had attended three funerals. On Remembrance Day she bought a red poppy, then thought irrelevantly: Do poppies grow in Vietnam? Would poppies grow where the blood of those boys has stained the soil, now that the Americans are dowsing the jungles with defoliants? Finally Lockie was killed, just when she thought they might get over the bad blood between them. The first thing Anna's future father-in-law said was: Fine family, the Isons. I had a bit to do with your grandfather over the years. Fine man. He means fine blood, Anna thought. He's pleased as punch that Sam's marrying someone with Ison blood in her veins. She supposed it was inevitable, given that farming people saw everything in terms of bloodline. There was good and bad blood, weak blood, healthy blood, and tendencies in the blood that might appear without warning in future generations. Sure, Anna had suffered a breakdown when Lockie was killed, but she was also predisposed to it, like her grandfather before her. Mr Jaeger warned her about the blood of the Jew, the Negro and the Chinaman. Weaken our bloodstock? she inquired, raising her eyebrow, and he clapped his hands in delight: Exactly! There was very little blood in the car or on the ground. Anna forced herself to lift her son's head from the cradling rock—very little blood. His eyes were closed, his fingers curled in a loose fist near his cheek, miming sleep. Well, of course, she realised, as she gazed at him later in the casket, how could there have been blood if his heart were still? Her own blood stopped then. It was fifteen months before she needed a tampon again, time enough for the long-forgotten spare one in her bag to have broken through the cellophane—promising, she told her mother, all kinds of toxic shock. What did you do? I was only spotting a bit, Anna replied. Nothing too alarming. I got home before it got too bad. Her mother looked away, down through the years: The body will do that. When we had to leave Isonville and find somewhere else to live, I stopped bleeding for a while. Rebecca, so slight and obsessive, started late, and bled sporadically and inconclusively, but the moment she found someone to love her, the blood flowed strongly, richly and on time. Sam will grow increasingly obsessed with names and bloodlines—old names dying out, bloodlines coming to an end. Until he actually sees Meg and Rebecca with their baby, and melts under all of their smiles, he will explain hotly to Anna why it is that he can't feel a family connection to them: One, it's not our daughter who's giving birth, so there's no blood connection; two, it wasn't a natural act of conception; three, there's no father, just two mothers. Anna will give up telling her brother to quit smoking. Toward the end he will cough up blood. Anna will call him from time to time and urge him to sell the farm and move in with her: Where I can keep an eye on you. No thanks, he'll say. I'm staying right here where the air is clean. It will seem to Anna when she is old that her blood is slower, darker, heavier, winding down as she winds down, ceasing altogether in certain parts of her legs and in the backs of her hands.

Funerals

GRANDFATHER ISON DIED in comfort in Adelaide but the family had him carried home for burial to his beloved mid-north, in the cemetery behind the open-cut mine, where his sister Beulah, his wife Antonia, and the generations of Isons before him had been buried—where the season seemed always to be high summer, the red dirt unforgiving to picks and shovels, the bull ants quick to rise up and bite, the mourners stunned by the heat. Anna looked down at her feet. Ants. Fast, hardy, segmented black scratches swarming over the caps of her shoes and on to her socks. She kicked, stamped her feet, raising a dust cloud. Keep still, Aunt Lorna hissed, her face unreadable. Anna shook off the last of the ants and kept one wary eye upon the ground and another on the rear doors of the Pandowie hearse. Uncle Kitch, her father, Mr Showalter and three men she didn't know were shouldering into position under the coffin. Now they had begun a slow march with it to the grave's edge. Anna glanced at the faces around her, to see who was crying, or should have been crying, or was faking it. Then, in October, Beulah died and there was another funeral. Anna's mother said: Poor old girl. When her father had died she had said: Poor old boy. Four years later, a school project took Anna back to the cemetery to find the headstone of George Catford. She searched, but he wasn't there, and wind, rain and the erupting roots of the pine trees had long ago toppled all of the old headstones into the nettles, so she went to the tourist information office next to the tractor dealership in the main street. The man there dug up a facsimile of the November 1851 edition of the *Chronicle*:

> Coroner's Inquest—Death of the Discoverer of the Pandowie Mine. An inquest was held on Friday, 21st inst., on view of the body of George Catford, who met his death under the following distressing circumstances:- The deceased, who was the discoverer of the Pandowie Mine, was engaged in cutting wood in the Pandowie Scrub for the Copperworks, and had come into Pandowie for the purpose of obtaining a settlement for his work. He was last seen alive on Tuesday, the 18th inst. about 2 o'clock p.m. by a man of the name of Albert Woolley who was also employed in woodcutting. Catford was then standing at the door of an old vacant hut in the creek at the Pandowie Scrub. Woolley spoke to him and found that he was drunk. Nothing further was heard or known of poor Catford until about 3 o'clock p.m. on Thursday, 20th inst., when a little boy about ten years of age casually entered the hut to seek a piece of twine for some childish purpose and saw the deceased lying dead on the floor of the hut, nearly naked and severely burnt. The child communicated the fact to his mother, who lives in a hut on the opposite side of the creek, who in turn alerted the Constable in Pandowie. From the position in which the body was found and from the medical testimony of Dr. Reid, it was clear that the deceased had met his death by

> falling into the fire while in a state of intoxication and the Jury returned a verdict to that effect.

When the boys who'd been in her final year began to die, Anna came home for the funerals, standing head bowed at the graveside—often alone, as if the other kids felt that she'd relinquished all claims to the district and its emotions when she left to live in the city. She came home for those funerals and soon a sense of dread, a paralysis, set in when she was *not* at home. One day she simply walked out on her textbooks and lectures and came back for good. She was waiting, waiting. If only Lockie would write. If only she had not precipitated the break that kept them miles and emotions apart. His two years in the army were almost up; with any luck he'd make it. Anna and Sam buried Michael in a tiny coffin in a tiny hole in the ground. Once or twice at the graveside, Anna had to shake herself covertly, to wake herself up, to fix her drift-dreaming mind on the funeral, but again and again her attention was caught by her father's hands, the way they angled under the casket, the way his fingers were splayed against the varnished black flank, the lopped-off middle finger apparently stuck in a hole. She could see from Sam's face that he wanted to say: You're a controlled one, but he held his tongue. Anna wanted to say: You don't understand. When Sam's father died, Rebecca came up for the funeral, dressed in tailored black trousers. She hooked her arm in Sam's and stayed close to him, at the church, at the graveside, at the house. Anna felt pity for him. The Ascension Church had stepped in and rendered him powerless, an onlooker. His surging grief beat futilely against their implacable busy calm. They made themselves at home in his father's house. He found them in his father's study. They helped themselves to his father's petrol. And to cap it all off, he said, slamming down the phone that evening when he was alone with his wife, daughter and mother again, their chief Bible-basher has the nerve to ring and say his car's just conked out somewhere the other side of Adelaide. I mean, what's he expect *me* to do about it? Lousy so and so. Rebecca snorted, giggled, tried to hold it in. Then Anna, Mrs Jaeger, and finally Sam, all of them laughing, the repressive weight of the dead man evaporating around them. The Committee intends to update the Statue of Remembrance in Redruth Square by carving the names of the war dead of Korea (one) and Vietnam (five) in the marble column. Fine, Anna types, watching her words creep across the monitor, but let's also remember George Catford, who stumbled unrewarded upon the ore body that later returned dividends of eight hundred per cent to investors. Sam says: Why do you always have to twist things, make progress sound as if it's greedy, the old-timers out for all they could get? One year short of the year 2000, Sam will gulp and die. Only fifty-three. One minute he's arguing with the boss, the next minute he's dead. Hard to believe. Arousing outrage in Rebecca's face: Believe it, Mother. Dad's been depressed for years. Couldn't sleep, obsessive, you said so yourself. Ashamed because he was reduced to being a paid manager of his own place. He was a candidate for a heart attack. Couldn't you see that? The cold kitchen will fill with silence around them. Three cups on the sink, tea dregs, the ticking clock. They will walk to the car, three women in black, the baby in her best pintucked white. The silence stretching all the way to the little church, scores of dusty cars angled up and down the nearby streets, people shuffling, looking away, a silence broken by Anna's sudden grief, her helpless, racking tears. Rebecca will touch her arm: Mum, come and stay with us for a while. Gasping: Thanks, I think I will, just till I find a place of my own. In her place by the sea, the phone will ring, another funeral, an old friend, a stroke, a heart attack, cancer. Life entails loss. Toward the end, Anna will find that Lockie is often in her head, and wonder if the lost six weeks had in fact been a lost sixty years. Every month or so she will hear of another death. She will attend some of the funerals—her mother's in Pandowie, Chester Flood's in Victor Harbor—but all of the others will occur in far-off places, places where it's intended that the sun should warm your old bones and keep you young.

Patriarchy

LET ME TELL you about men. Great Aunt Beulah drew Anna to her in an exaggerated pantomime of dread secrets being withheld from ordinary ears: We don't want that old bat listening in. Her outer and inner garments crepitated, the springs moaned in her chair, she drew in a ragged breath: My father was a hard father to us, and a hard husband to our mother. Men were, in those days. It was expected of them. They ruled the roost and watch out if you disagreed with them or disgraced them in any way or disobeyed them. Anna heard a new sound, of ancient bellows huffing into action, and realised that Great Aunt Beulah was laughing: Poor old Father, I did all three. Then she was crying: The one true love of my life and he forbade me to be with him. Anna sought out her mother, who confirmed everything: He was a hard man, all right, your great grandfather. Rarely smiled, apparently. A big, bony fellow, according to the photos we have of him. We always believed he treated my dad badly. Made life a kind of test for him, always setting him obstacles. For example, his will. Enlightened, you might say, leaving it all to his daughters. I'd say pragmatic—he thought my dad wasn't coming back. And I'd say mean—he wanted my dad to have to struggle, as he'd had to struggle. When Grandfather Ison died, leaving everything to Kitchener, Anna's mother sat drained of energy at the kitchen table, twisting a handkerchief in her hands: Just goes to show, if someone does you a mean act it can make you behave meanly to someone else. Hardness breeds hardness, Anna, and don't you forget it. Hardness and the desire to control everything around you. Anna said: Dad's not like that. Her mother smiled: No, he's not. Well, maybe a little. A father can't afford to be too slack when his kids are growing up. So Anna began to look for signs of hardness in her father. She could not see any, but one day Hugo began to go through a peculiar phase. He'd announce: At footy, Dad, at school, and trail off. Yes? And blurt out: I got six kicks. Two more than yesterday. Or he'd say: I haven't cried once since Saturday, and then he'd wait, watching for an acknowledgment, but what he got was always faintly crushing: Try for seven or eight kicks tomorrow, all right? Let's hope months and months go by before you cry again, okay? Anna brought Lockie Kelly home to meet everyone. Afterwards, when he was gone, her father said: The Kellys are Catholics, you know. So? Anna demanded. Her father was harsh suddenly: So he'll put you up the duff and then where will you be? I don't want you seeing him again, you hear me? You can do better than the bog-Irish Kellys, for Christ's sake. He pushed the air at her with his palms: Nope, subject's closed, find yourself someone else. When Lockie received his call-up papers, he drove the length of the Main North Road on a day of hail and sleet to show Anna. She looked Lockie up and down scornfully: It's like the government's some kind of autocratic father and you're a bunch of biddable sons, doing as you're told. Three years into the marriage, Sam said to Anna: I've slaved my guts out for this place, new methods, new equipment, new crop strains, you name it, and the old man still treats me like I'm in short pants. A wage? Christ, pocket money more like it. Having to account for how we spend every penny. Giving you a hard time if you ring your mother, planning our kids' education, wearing us down with all this conspiracy rubbish, totally controlling our lives. What's the bet my mother doesn't even know how to write a cheque? I want to make a go of it on my own. How about it, sweetie, you game? But blood counts for something in the end and patriarchs need sons. Sam and his mother got the lot when the old man died. When Anna thought about it, years later, it occurred to her that Wesley Showalter had breezed on through life after knocking her off the road because for generations the Showalters had been seen as patriarchs of the district, a habit of mind not easily altered. People saw it as a shame that her son had been killed, but not a shame that Wesley Showalter had been negligent and got away with it. Old attitudes linger. Sam has lost all that he invested in the Park's sperm-bank scheme, yet he can't bring himself fully to blame Wesley Showalter. The Showalter name stretches back in time. It means patrician sons and wealth and something solid. Anna has come upon this passage in Mrs Showalter's 1950 history of the Park:

> Young Hugo Ison, of the original Ison brothers, visited the Pandowie headstation on Noltenius Creek, where he noted that a neighbour had 'as ornaments a couple of blackfellows' skulls pegged through the eye sockets to the wall of his hut'. Hugo also recorded that he went hunting with another man (who will remain nameless, out of deference to his descendants) reputed to have shot more Aborigines than anyone else in the district, and who, while discharging his firearm at a mob of kangaroos with young Hugo, boastfully declared that he 'never missed a black who wandered into his sights'.

Anna wonders if that man was a Showalter. Maybe Mrs Showalter wanted the fact to be recorded but could not bring herself to name her husband's forebears. One day Anna will hear Rebecca argue: Patriarchy's talent is for compartmentation, separating intellect from emotion, emotion from action, vision from reality. It sets up disconnections and institutionalises them. Women, on the other hand, connect. We don't fix the boundaries of our egos. We find it difficult to distinguish between our own needs and those of others. And Rebecca will hark back to her father's confusion about the new baby and family notions: Think about it, Mum—when Mikey was killed, Dad was left with me, a daughter, and we all know that daughters don't carry on the family name. Not only that, I ended up living with another woman. Not only that, I presented him with a granddaughter without being the biological mother. And to top it all off, she was conceived as though his half of the race were irrelevant. Remember that lapel button we pinned to her little jumpsuit?—'My family is my mother, my mother and me'. It was ages before he could bring himself to introduce the poor little thing as his granddaughter, or his daughter's child. It was always: This is the child of my daughter's friend. Poor Dad. Anna will retort: That's enough, Becky. He grew to love and accept, that's all that matters.

Waiting

IF ANNA WERE to bend her head into a book or gaze into the distance, she heard things: Pete, I can feel them waiting for Auntie Beulah to go, can't you? It's as if they're biding their time over there, ready to charge in with their things as soon as she's carted out the door. Then: It's indecent. She's barely cold in her grave. Then: I feel just awful. I can feel them waiting for us to hurry up and get out so they can have the whole house. Anna's mother broke off to look at the cool walls, the patterned tin ceiling: I used to love this house. Now it's just a bad taste in my mouth. Waiting for the school bus, waiting for exam results, waiting around for something to happen. Anna's father fastened Kippy to his chain, dropped the flap of mutton between his paws, walked across the patch of moonlight to the back door. He must know we're here, Lockie whispered. He knows, Anna said. Lockie had parked his ute where the pine trees beside the tractor shed cast the blackest shadows. We're asking for trouble doing it here, Lockie said, anxiety edging in. What if he comes out again? But Anna knew that her father would not come out, just as he'd not glanced their way when he crossed the yard. Reserved, respectful, he'd not embarrass her, or Lockie, no matter what else he thought. It was *afterwards* that she worried about. Always a waiting game, kissing Lockie goodnight, going inside, making herself a cup of cocoa, waiting for the explosions that never came: Out with that Mick again? What were you doing out there?—as if I couldn't guess. Do you know what hour it is? Anna heard these things in her head, never in fact. Sometimes she wondered if she actively wanted her father to say something. Bracing her bare feet on the glass of the driver's door—What must *that* look like from the outside, her white soles lit by a stray moonbeam?—Anna lifted her rump, helping Lockie, helping herself. She wanted him as deep as he could go. Her hands brushed automatically up and down his back. She stared into the darkness. Fifteen months later, Lockie was fighting in a foreign war. A numbing silence grew between them. She wrote, begging him to write, and in two years of waiting all she got was a postcard. Then one day he wrote to say that he was coming home, tour of duty over, and a weight lifted from her shoulders. He had survived; her luck had turned. She got out the atlas and tracked his passage home, from Nui Dat to Sydney to Adelaide to Pandowie to the Kellys' rundown house. The hours passed. She snatched up the phone ahead of her mother: Welcome back! Yes, love to see you. Anytime. I mean it, I'd love to see you. Fine. I'll put the kettle on. When he didn't arrive, she wondered if he were being cruel to her, paying her back maybe. She waited stubbornly where she could not see the telephone, knowing that it would weaken her resolve. Then it rang and Anna concentrated all of her senses on her mother's voice, the way her mother breathlessly recited the number, the way she paused, the way the words caught in her throat. Anna walked to the kitchen through a fog: Mum? What is it, what's wrong?—and was crying before she knew why. She knew that her luck hadn't turned after all. According to the *Chronicle*: It is believed that sheep drifted across the road, and, in braking to avoid them, Mr Kelly lost control of his car. The Bitter Wash Road is a deathtrap, claiming six lives since it was widened for the Redex Trial in the 1950s. One might inquire how many more will be lost before our esteemed councillors stir themselves. The advice books, the legions of mothers before her, told Anna that breastfeeding was a time of profound satisfaction for mother and child. So what was Anna doing wrong? How could she make it right? Sure, Michael was born to suck, and she loved the tidal sensations, the rush of milk to her breasts, the ebbing as he filled his little soul with her, but why didn't their times ever coincide? Sometimes he slept for six or eight hours at a stretch, when her drum-tight breasts cried for relief at four. Should she wait for him to awake, and suffer ropy, knotted ducts, or should she cruelly snatch him up from his cot and run her nipple between the damp little bow of his lips? She was heavy, so heavy sometimes she could cry. In the rented schoolhouse on the sunken road, they waited for better times to come. They waited for years. Becky, remember when you were sixteen, seventeen, no one asked you out for months at a time? Waiting weekend after weekend for the phone to ring, stuck at home with us in front of the TV set? It broke our hearts. Coldly: That's not how I remember it. Oh? How do you remember it then? For a start, I wasn't *waiting*. It's not as if I was desperate. Do you think I wanted to get slobbered on in the back seat of someone's car? I had better things to do. Sam looked away from her: Okay, have it your way. No, Dad, you're having it *your* way. You're constructing an image of me that suits *your* needs. Anna saw her father every day at the end. Poor Missy, waiting for your old man to kick the bucket. Dad, don't. You're right, bad taste. But *I'm* waiting, Missy. I've had plenty of waiting in my time. They say that an army marches on its stomach—well, it rests on its hands. We played poker, two-up, you name it. Some of us devoured anything with print on it. We carved things out of shell casings, we washed our socks. Waiting, that's what war is about. Anna thought: Was it like that for Lockie in his war, desperate to see me again? Did Grandfather Ison wait for a lucky wound in the Sunken Road Trench at Pozières? Anna is visiting Chester again. He's watching her carefully, in the lounge where visitors to the prison gather, and finally finds the right moment: I suppose you've been waiting for an explanation? Anna hasn't been—or rather, until now she hasn't been waiting consciously for one. I *did* cheat you out of your twenty thousand, he said. Not deliberately, but when Wes Showalter and your Uncle Kitch talked me into joining their Lloyds underwriting syndicate, I found myself stretched for cash, so I borrowed against my clients' trust accounts. Then when Lloyds got hit by a rash of oilspills and earthquakes, Lloyds Names like us lost everything. I couldn't pay you back. I'm sorry, I should have told you. Anna pats his hand: You're telling me now. My regret is that I didn't buy Becky a cello. Talkback idealogues will wait for society to break down and doomsday cults will wait for Mach-holz 2 to hit the earth. Anna? She'll wait for the Committee to decide upon the fate of her manuscript, wait to see Sam decently into the ground, then move to a house beside the sea, where, with time, her grief and guilt might ease.

Flowers

AROUND THE HOUSE itself the generations of Isons had coaxed a cottage garden into existence. Bore water was banned—too salty—and there was more cow, horse and poultry manure than indigenous red dirt in the flowerbeds. Roses and honeysuckle choked the tank stands, lobelia crept toward the white pebble paths, lilac grew hard against the walls of the house. Pansies, daisies, hollyhocks, poppies, dahlias, foxgloves. Daffodil bulbs lurked forgotten and dormant along the borders of the lawn until the spring. One evening the children swung their wooden swords at all the dead and fading agapanthus heads at the road gate, a beheading frenzy that left them high-coloured and unmanageable at the dinner table. Beulah had also planted a herb garden—not for cooking, foreign muck, but for the idea itself. Rosemary goes well with lamb, Auntie Beulah, Anna's mother said. Rubbish, the old woman replied. Anna liked the odour of the bruised leaves on her fingers. Hugo wheezed and sneezed and rubbed his eyes from September to February. There was nothing to see in the vast blue bowl of the sky but, according to Dr Pirie, the air swam with miniscule particles of dust and pollen. Make sure he doesn't run around in the evenings, no cut flowers in his room, and keep him away when the men are reaping. Anna stood with her mother and the doctor, three heads peering down at Hugo, who gasped on his pillow and tore at his throat as if to open the way for a healing draught of air. The soil on the six-forty acres was very poor, but it always supported a dense blue carpet of Salvation Jane. Anna's father would stare at it with his hands on his hips. What's a man to do? Spray year after year? He took her out into the thick of it and taught her how to pinch-pluck the tiny funnelled flowers and suck the base. A hint of honey on her tongue, and she realised that the air was heavy with bees, slowly, dopily lurching from one flower head to the next. Anna was expected to pin a rosebud to her ball gown or tuck a flower behind one ear but she hated all that fuss, that business. A boy gave her a chunky envelope. She opened it and inside the soppy card was a sachet, essence of rose. Anna thought of Beulah's old-woman smells, 'The Rose of Tralee' grinding out of the pianola, all that soppy business to do with flowers and love. The boy was waiting, a pink, pimpled, mouth-breather, so she tore open a corner of the sachet and rubbed a drop of the fumy oil between her thumb and forefinger. For a moment she thought of a rose thorn catching in the round pad of her thumb, drawing the blood. You like it? he asked. She blinked awake, put her finger to her nostrils. Cheap and nasty. Anna reeled with it. Put some behind your ears if you like, the boy offered. Anna smiled. On the inside of my wrist for now, she said. One day in Berkshire, Anna bought a postcard to send home. A stone house, a thatched roof, a real cottage garden. She thought it would amuse her mother: The seat of the Isons, Mum! It was a favourable sign, buying and sending that postcard, thinking of someone else for a change. She was starting to recover, she'd found her return ticket. When she got home, a year had passed. She made a pilgrimage to the spot where Lockie had been killed. She was not sure of the exact place, and knew it would worry her parents if she asked, so she set out on foot to find it. Somewhere past the schoolhouse ruin, apparently. The road twisted like a snake through cuttings and washaways. Gravel dust accumulated on her toecaps and tiny pebbles flicked into the cuffs of her jeans. It might have happened anywhere. Would there still be scratches on the rockface, oil or blood in the dirt? In the end she found a jam-jar of wildflowers and a flimsy wooden cross no higher than her knees. Anna guessed that Mr Kelly had made the cross, using slats from the broken-backed chairs he used for kindling wood. Mrs Kelly would have provided the wildflowers—there were never any cultivated flowers where the Kellys lived. The wildflowers were dusty, wilting, four days old. One year and four days since the day Lockie died. Anna saved the water in the jar but tossed out the wildflowers. There were plenty more growing on the banks of the sunken road. Those poor people and their grief. Would they have brought Lockie's dog with them? Anna was willing to bet that very few locals came a-visiting the Kellys after it happened. When her father took over the Four Square Store, he seemed to grow into a big, beaming, contented man. He had townspeople around him all day long, the very thing he'd sadly lacked, out there on the six-forty acres. He sold everything and dispensed coffee, tea and biscuits in a small cleared area between the groceries and the hardware, warmed by a potbelly stove. Everything, and that included potplants, creepers and cut flowers in a bucket, trucked up from Adelaide three times a week. He suggested a Flower Show at a council meeting. Mrs Allen won with a hybrid rose cultivated half a century earlier on Showalter Park and perfected by her in the garden behind the manse. All month Sam has been telling Anna that it's cruelly ironic, the bank's new logo. No phone call, no invitation for a chat with the manager, just this letter out of the blue, announcing the foreclosure, one paragraph on recycled paper decorated with the Sturt Pea. As if they fancy themselves as environmentalists, he snorts. When Anna visits Chester Flood he takes her for long walks in the prison compound, pointing out climbing roses, herb gardens, vast fields of carnations ready for harvesting and sale to the city's florists. I've discovered that I've got green fingers, he says. I actually enjoy gardening. Anna will meet the challenge of cramped conditions in her house near the sea. She will enlist Rebecca and Meg to nail lattice walls to the open porch and they will take her to nurseries in the hills behind the city when the weather is fine. Hanging ferns, geraniums in terracotta pots, an African violet on the shelf above the kitchen sink. Flowers on the sideboard, flowers by her bed, flowers in her last grasp.

History

A POTTED HISTORY, Mr Wheelwright said, squealing a chalk line across the blackboard to represent the horizon, then humping the Razorback upon it. In shape, the Razorback suggesting a profit and loss graph, sharp growth followed by a ragged decline past the peak. Finally Mr Wheelwright faced away from the board, clapped one palm against the other, and began a dry washing motion: The plates of the earth rubbed together, creating oceans and forcing landforms like the Razorback to the surface. We're talking millions of years, you understand. Unique plants and animals evolved, isolated from the rest of the world. Between fifty and a hundred thousand years ago, the first humans arrived, island-hopping from the north. Who knows when they would have reached here, where we're standing now, but rest assured they're not here now. All we have are the placenames the Ngadjuri people left us. Right, take up your pens: The richest copper lodes in South Australia were discovered by shepherds. When grass and water were plentiful, and attacks by wild dogs and Aborigines rare, the shepherd had plenty of time on his hands for fossicking. Besides, he would have been on the lookout for the rich colours of oxidised copper, following the accidental discovery of copper at Kapunda in 1843, and the offers of rewards by the mining companies. Who were these men, these shepherds? Many were ex-convicts or men fleeing from trouble in one of the other colonies. Most were old and reclusive, preferring the company of a dog and the comfort of a plug of tobacco to the society of other men. There were few women, you understand. Paid ten shillings per week, what did they have to spend it on but grog the next time they were near a shanty? In July, 1850, came the news of a promising lode on the Pandowie Creek, discovered by one George Catford, shepherd. There were shepherds on the Pandowie Creek as early as 1843. We know this from watercolour sketches of the area, showing shepherds' huts, made by the colony's surveyor, Colonel Frome, who was making the first northern surveys. These sketches are in the Gallery on North Terrace, next time you're in the city. Anna paused, realising that Mr Wheelwright had made an aside. Then she bent over the page again: Of all the shepherds who discovered rich deposits of copper in the colony, none was so meanly rewarded as George Catford. No rent-free cottage, no shares, no allowance, no memorial in the form of a town, street, landmark or building named after him. George Catford was paid just twenty guineas for revealing the lode to the Adelaide syndicate who had ridden up to examine the site, and a further twenty by the South Australian Mining Association, whose shareholders were earning dividends of eight hundred per cent just two years later. And so a fine, long, local tradition of avarice and misanthropy had its beginning here on the northern highlands. A bit of a pinko, is he, your teacher? Uncle Kitch wanted to know. Anna sought out her other grandfather. No, he didn't know the last name of the shepherd whose son had drowned in Ison's Creek. The top face of the gravestone had long since flaked away, but the date was there, 1875, so it was unlikely that George Catford had been the shepherd. Anna's father liked to shock and tease her. She once stood with him in Redruth Square to honour the dead: We grow not old as those that are left grow old. He waggled his tipless finger at her slyly: Here's a part of me that will grow not old as the rest that is left grows old. Anna was studying in the city when Mrs Showalter and Mr Wheelwright formed the Pandowie Historical Society. They had meetings in the Institute, sought contributions of money and artifacts, wrote pamphlets and convinced the council to adopt a preservation policy and a restoration fund. Every time Anna came home there was a new plaque to see, a Cornish miner's cottage restored on Truro Street, another item of lacework in the museum, the miners' dugouts fenced off in Noltenius Creek, a row of ancient almond trees saved from the axe. Successive waves of tourists, film-makers and weekending QCs swept into the mid-north, laying claim to the quaint and the beautiful, leaving only long-abandoned huts and farmhouses for the city poor who came in after them. When Anna lay in Chester Flood's arms she murmured: What was it like, living in the convent? He replied: It used to be a reformatory, did you know that? There's a new plaque inside the front gate now, if you're interested. Let me answer this way—from reformatory to convent was not such a big step. I breathed the same spiritless air in 1960 as breathed by some kid in 1860. When Anna's father-in-law died, leaving the farm to his wife and his son, Sam, fearful that his ageing mother would sign her share over to the Ascension Church, bought her out at seventeen per cent. He did not want the work of the generations of Jaegers before him to go down the gurgler, especially to a bunch of holy rollers—not your well-established holy rollers, mind you, but the Ascensionists, formed just twenty years ago, with no history or tradition behind them. Anna likes to say that she started in the dark ages of print technology, when the *Chronicle* was set by hand, then she passed through the offset period, and now she writes, cuts, pastes and designs on a computer screen. This week's 'One Year Ago Today' column is interesting: Workmen gutting the interior of the historic Showalter Park homestead have found newspapers dating from the nineteenth century concealed under floorboards in the ballroom. Included was a perfectly preserved copy of the *Chronicle* for August 1877, where we learn that owing to the continuous flooding of the mine shafts and the high cost of recovering copper from the ore body, the Pandowie mine has closed, but that the district itself is expected to flourish as a centre for the colony's pastoral industry. Anna's Jubilee history is almost complete. She's had enough of history. She has her memories, and memories are not necessarily history. Many years later, when she is in her eighties, Anna will read that a rare earthquake had hit the mid-north, dislodging a time capsule sealed in a unique stonewall fence used by the early settlers to pen their sheep. According to the Adelaide *Advertiser*, the capsule was inscribed with the words 'Interred in the Year 2000 to Mark the 150th Jubilee of Pandowie and Environs' and as such was considered too recent to be of interest to historians. The wall would be repaired and the capsule resealed in it. Anna will put down the paper and try to recall everything that Sam had collected for the capsule. The Showalter family memoir, a twist of wool, a copper wristband from the Tourist Office, wheat heads, old clippings from the *Chronicle*. Picking up the paper again she will see yet another edgy reference to Mach-holz 2, which may or may not be on a collision course with Earth. The last time a comet hit the planet, the force was sufficient to create the Gulf of Mexico and wipe out the dinosaurs. So why bother with time capsules?

Regret

IF YOU WERE old you were regretful, concealing it like a vice or wearing it like a scar. I think my old man secretly regrets coming here, Anna's father said. Feels he acted too hastily, hadn't thought enough about the isolation, something like that. It's not as if he's been able to forget what happened to my mother, after all. And if he'd stayed in the city he might have met someone else, who knows? It's not something he's ever talked about. It's just a feeling I have about him, the far-off look he has sometimes. You know what I mean, love? Anna's mother nodded. As for me, he went on, I think once you've made your bed you lie in it. I mean, I would like to have been a doctor—don't laugh, I would—but the opportunities were never there, so what was the point in feeling sorry for myself because it didn't happen? Look at Beulah, still eaten up with regret about that fellow her father wouldn't let her marry. Anna listened. She went to Great Aunt Beulah. She leaned restlessly on the arm of the old woman's chair, chattering, chattering: Our smallest lamb died. We're going to Adelaide next week. Mum's running me up a new dress. Auntie Beulah, did you ever see him again, the one you loved? In an instant, Beulah's eyes spilled over, regret for the man she'd lost, regret for not having made a stand against her father. She murmured: If only I had my life over again. One day the children went out with Grandfather Ison. He juddered them along the sunken road in the Land

Rover, occasionally shooting out his left arm to save them from hitting their heads, and as they climbed out of the deadliest bend and reached the high ground, where the stonewall fence marked the border between Isonville and Showalter Park, a sudden shadow drenched the Land Rover and a throttled-back aero engine deafened them. The children turned their heads and saw a silver fuselage side-slip over them, the braced undercarriage touching down in the dirt then coasting toward the windsock. Buyers, Grandfather Ison grunted, flying in from New South Wales to look at the rams. I regret, he told the children, the day my father split Isonville. Think what it could have been. Now all that's left is the homestead and five thousand acres instead of twenty-five thousand. How your uncle Kitch is going to get on, I don't know. He paused: Your mother was friendly with the Showalter boys, you know. No reflection on your father, of course, he added hastily. Long as she's happy. Mum, were you engaged to the Showalter who died in the war or the other one? Heavens above, Anna, what gave you that idea? I married your father and I don't regret it, not for a minute. Ah, Anna, back among us I see, Mr Wheelwright said, when Anna showed up a week late at the high school in the town. He gazed sourly at the desks and chalk dust and doltish minds: Let's hope you don't regret running back here from the city if it means being among this lot again. And so he marked her, set her apart. Think you're better than us? they demanded. I came back here, she pointed out, but logic had nothing to do with the way they saw her. She regretted opening her mouth to Maxine about the Pill. It's to control my *periods*, she shouted, but they were already labelling her and, in the end, she obliged them a little. When Lockie was killed, the words were there relentlessly in her head: He was the only one I loved and yet I said no to him. Too late, we hurt the ones we love, and we hurt ourselves. I shall never love again and I shall never forget, not until the day I die. The words grew melodic in her throat, rising and falling, until she began to sing them in a low, strained voice: For I have loved a boy but one, and he is lost to me/Forsaken love I will lament, lament what might have been. Now you're being absurd, her mother said. Give it time, you'll meet someone else, and Anna sang: Alas there's none for me. It was a lament, she was inconsolable, and for six weeks of her life she floated in the inner dark. Chester Flood stroked her and said: I love your little belly. She watched his hand, thinking: He will give me back my luck. Then his head dipped and when he looked up he said: Salty fuck-taste, I love it. He wriggled his way back up to kiss her lips: Taste it? His eyes clouded: Remember old Wheelwright saying he'd make me regret the day I was born? Remember? Anna didn't and was ashamed. Well, the bastard tried, all right, and he failed, Chester said. I survive, that's what I do. These days Sam is apt to say, over and over: Of course now I regret not making more of an effort to stick it out with the old man. He has another regret: It's tragic. There have been Showalters here from the year dot. They were good to me, giving me work. Now some flaming Saudi Arabian outfit looks like ripping the guts out of the place. Pity old Leonard Showalter wasn't still alive—he wouldn't have let it happen, that's for sure. There are things worth hanging on to. There's history here. That's why this Committee's a good thing, Anna—don't knock it. The letter from the bank is burning a hole in the shallow cane basket on top of the refrigerator: We regret to advise you. Anna doesn't think it's regret. The letter has come from head office, not the local branch, not someone they know. Cruel, bloody cruel, Sam says. Then he cries, and Anna touches his neck to calm him, thinking: I can't do more than this. I've done what I can and I hope he realises it. It's up to him, now. In her solitary walks at the water's edge an old regret will revisit her: I wish I'd known my grandmother, snatched away in the jaws of a shark. Such awful luck. Beautiful, young, gleeful, a risk-taker, someone I could have talked to. I never knew her, yet I miss her. Anna will go to the grave with a few regrets like this one. She will regret Michael, she will regret Lockie. They will not be cancerous regrets; they won't take hold of her and creep through her bones over the years: If only I'd . . . If only I hadn't . . . Regret, she'll say, admonishing her granddaughter, is the cruellest emotion. It paralyses you. There is no point to it. The past is past. Life is a matter of tactics, not grand strategies. Anna will look back squarely on those she has loved and say: I cannot total it all, but I want you to understand this—what else could I have done? I was distracted, ignorant, too proud, too young, blameworthy, faintly absurd, given to anxious love and loving too well. Did you think that I had a key?

Love

OF ALL THE varieties and acts of love on Isonville, there was this: the children's mother clamping their heads between the palms of her hands and saying: I love you, my darlings. Do you believe me? When she leaned forward to touch noses with them, their small, ear-sized hands flew up and smacked damply, ecstatically against the sides of her head. They knew she loved them. She was always saying it. Anna loved her father. He was on the road by breakfast time, and coming back from some far-flung saleyard when it was time for bed, and because she so rarely saw him, each time was a new time. She loves her dad, people said. She loved certain dolls, an invisible friend, Kip with grass seeds in his thumping tail, and, for a short time at primary school, an orphan boy who had jet-black hair and the face of a ravaged angel. Her love for him was a pure, straightforward yearning, as much to look like him as to stand near him. Then the weight of district opinion wore her down: The Floods are poor, shifty, smelly. What she got out of it was an interest in romantic love: Tell me about the man you wanted to elope with. Did he love you? We loved each other through and through, Great Aunt Beulah replied. We were meant for each other but my cruel father drove him off. Aunt Beulah was creased and rouged and talcumed with age, yet she wept like a heart-broken slip of a girl. Anna imagined how her parents might have wooed. She stared her way into old photographs the size of playing cards and watched her parents kiss and canoodle. Her father wore his slouch hat and cigarette at cocky angles, a knowing grin bending the narrow planes of his handsome face. Beside him her mother tipped back her head to laugh, revealing her throat, her hands on her thighs, fighting down the gritty wind on a city street. Who took the photos? Dad's army mate. Anna's love for her friend Maxine lasted until they were both fifteen, when things went unaccountably wrong. Anna would spin around on the spot, saying: I want to be a wild, free, erotic perfect lover for my lover, failing to notice how earnest and chaste her friend had become. They grew further apart and Anna found herself branded slack, a moll. It was an undeserved reputation, but who would listen to her? So she grew into it, becoming flippant, arbitrary, careless, callous, qualities that intensified as the small-school whispers intensified. She was a fixed target in the moral landscape. Then she blinked, saw Lockie Kelly, and at once grew still and restful. She was a lover, now—all the other acts had been acts of grief, greed and hate. She made tender declarations to Lockie and the hateful whispers faded to nothing around her. But if she thought that love and a lover were solutions to life, she was wrong. Life had a way of insinuating itself. First, she left Lockie behind to study in the city, then she began to think about things outside of love. Ideas have consequences, some of them unpleasant. When it was clear that Lockie was going unquestioningly away to war, she took a lover to hurt him. And hurt herself, for the lover was egocentric and manipulative. She longed for him, was ecstatic when she made love to him, frustrated when she couldn't be with him. Yet he was no one to write home about—dry skin, age-lines, a hint of desperation at the passing of the years. He would present himself to Anna as a man with an inner pain, and she would see herself as the solution to his pain, the place where he might come to rest. A day, a fuck later, he would be austere and withholding again. Anna's head spun. She was poised to start her life after her childhood in the bush: surely he would start it for her? Everything in her that was lovely, unknowable, unclaimable and full of drama was waiting to be released. When eventually the ecstasy faded, the pain remained. Then one day she woke up: the boys from home were falling in a foreign war. A few years later, Anna met Sam Jaeger. He was three years older, someone she'd scarcely noticed at school. She scarcely noticed him now, so sunburnt was he, so anxious, so desirous of settling down. But: I'm tired, Anna told herself. He's a decent man and I can rest in him. I won't tell him that I don't love him. Perhaps he senses that anyway. Perhaps love and companionship will grow. Sam seemed to adore her. He adored the kids in a thousand little ways. At bedtime, the CB radio crackled into life on the kitchen wall as he wished Michael, then Rebecca, goodnight, the tractor engine rumbling in the background, the tractor's headlights crawling along the valley floor if the children cared to look for it from their bedroom window. Anna wondered if women sought a woman friend in the men they married. They were unlikely to find it. For example, if Anna wanted commiseration from Maxine, she got commiseration. From Sam she got advice and bolstering and a jollying-along that left her exhausted. She wondered if Michael and Rebecca saw love behind the inflexibility and harsh propriety of their grandparents in the house below. Sometimes they came back up the hill from the Jaegers to their mother, the sinner, full of love for the Saviour. Mum, have you found God? These days Anna tries to make allowances. She doubts that many relationships can withstand very much scrutiny. Old man Jaeger is dead, Mrs Jaeger is dying, and if they were not united by love then at least they were united by faith. Of her own situation, Anna has told herself that you may find ways to resolve the loss of a true love but not the loss of a child. Any love interrupted is devastating, but the lost love of a child is the only one that can't be mended. It tends to blunt and mute you. That's how she sees it now and she hopes that Rebecca understands. Anna will take out her manuscript from time to time and read what a mother in Berkshire had written to her only surviving son, leaseholder of pastoral land near Pandowie, in the colony of South Australia, in the year 1854:

> It wouldst afford us great comfort if thou couldst find it in thy heart or thy day to write to us oftener than heretofore, my dear one, but, if thou art so occupied as to be unable to do so, might thou engage thy good wife to address a few lines in thy stead? All unite in love to thee, from thy affectionate Mother, Rebecca Ison.

Anna will close her eyes and feel affection for the intensity of every one of her younger selves, all that pain and love.

Author's note

ALTHOUGH THIS IS a work of fiction, the setting is an actual region of South Australia called variously the mid-north or the northern highlands, and I found the following sources invaluable for suggesting material that I have reworked for the story:

ADELAIDE OBSERVER, 29 November 1851; Ian Auhl, *Thomas Picket*, National Trust pamphlet, n.d., n.p.; Frankie Hawker and Rob Linn, *Bungaree: Land, Stock and People*, Turnbull Fox Phillips, Adelaide, 1992; Angus McInnes, *Reminiscences of the Ulooloo Gold Diggings*, Angus McInnes, Burra, 1995; Roma Mattey, *Deceptive Lands: a history of Terowie and surrounding hundreds in the mid-north of South Australia*, Country Women's Association (Terowie Branch), 1968; Nancy Robinson, *Change on Change: a history of the northern highlands of South Australia*, Investigator Press, Leabrook, 1971; Nancy Robinson (ed.), *Stagg of Tarcowie: the diaries of a colonial teenager*, Lynton Publications, Adelaide, 1973; *SOUTH AUSTRALIAN REGISTER*, 1842 (various editions).